THE ACCIDENTAL MARRIAGE

ROGER B. THOMAS

The Accidental Marriage

IGNATIUS PRESS   SAN FRANCISCO

Cover art photograph ©iStockPhoto.com

Cover design by John Herreid

© 2014 by Ignatius Press, San Francisco
All rights reserved
ISBN 978-1-58617-908-3
Library of Congress Control Number 2014902191
Printed in the United States of America ∞

Chapter One

Scott was in the house again, the house with the rice-paper walls. He was wandering from room to room, admiring the prints and the delicate branches painted on the walls—branches in bloom with flowers of some sort, blood-red at the center but fading to delicate pink toward the edges of the petals. As always, every room was a model of perfection: every piece of furniture in perfect proportion, utensils and other items arranged in harmonious order. A light rose glow suffused the rooms. He felt completely at peace.

Then, somehow, Scott was outside, but still among flowering branches. These weren't pink flowers painted on walls but real flowers on branches waving in the breeze. He recognized them: they were apple blossoms, just like there had been at the orchard on the farm where they'd lived when he was a boy. They'd rented a dingy old farmhouse from Mr. Martin, who kept his orchard and had let Scott run all over it. Scott had hated the cramped, drafty house, but he'd loved wandering around the orchard, especially when the trees were flowering. He fondly remembered the sound of Mr. Martin's tractor rumbling about the farm.

Why, here came Mr. Martin now! Rounding the end of the row, the old blue Ford turned to come between the trees. Mr. Martin was driving, but—no, this was all wrong. He was towing the sprayer, fogging the trees as he came. This was all wrong. He couldn't spray when the trees were in bloom. He'd kill the bees, and the flowers needed the bees to pollinate, or there'd be no crop. Scott ran down the row waving his arms. This was all wrong.

Mr. Martin saw Scott coming, and waved back, but kept driving and spraying. Scott came alongside the tractor and shouted up to him, but the engine was too loud and Mr. Martin kept leaning over and calling, "Hey? Hey?"

"The bees!" Scott shouted, jumping as he ran alongside the tractor. The sprayer roared behind, misting the branches with poison. "Your spraying will kill all the bees!"

"I got to, son", Mr. Martin called back above the engine's roar. "I got to!"

Scott was running beside the tractor, leaping to get Mr. Martin to pay attention even though the long grass whipped his shins painfully. It was Mr. Martin who'd told him about how important the bees were, and now he was killing them.

"Not now, Mr. Martin!" Scott hollered over the sprayer fan. "Not while they're in blossom! After the fruit forms, when the apples will need protection against scale and bugs!"

"I got to, son", Mr. Martin repeated as he kept driving. "I got to."

"But ... you'll kill all the bees, and there won't be a crop", Scott cried, ceasing his jumping and standing in the grass, tears streaming down his face. Mr. Martin kept driving, and Scott was too distressed to attend to the howling behind him. It finally grew loud enough to demand his attention, and in alarm he turned just in time to see the sprayer almost upon him. He opened his mouth to scream, and—

Woke up. The sheets were twisted all around Scott where he'd thrashed them into knots, so he started to extricate himself. He was accustomed to stressful dreams; at least it hadn't been ... that one.

Scott was alone in the bed, which meant Greg hadn't yet returned from wherever Greg had gone off to. Just as well. Scott padded to the bathroom and then to the kitchen, where he grabbed a pint of ice cream out of the freezer. The microwave clock said 2:35— great. Wolfing spoonfuls of ice cream, he sat down to check his e-mail. Nothing important, and nothing of interest on any sites. He brushed his teeth and headed back to bed, knowing it was probably futile.

It was. He lay there for ten minutes, trying to relax, until it became clear that it was to no purpose—he was awake. He sighed and threw back the covers. He may as well head to the office as lie here staring at the ceiling. He could at least get a few hours' work in before the most recent "helper" whom Brian had assigned showed up and started getting underfoot. By 3:30 he was showered, dressed, and turning the Jetta toward the office.

6

About midday, Scott's phone chimed. It was a text from Megan.

"Lunch?"

Scott smiled, and texted back.

"Sure. Usual, .5 hr?"

"OK", came the response.

Meeting Megan for lunch would be a good break. He'd already put in a full day on little more than energy drinks and candy bars. He saved his work and headed out.

Megan was a great pal. She worked for the assessor's office, just a block or two away from his office. They'd first met at a local bistro one crowded lunch hour when he'd asked if he could sit at an unoccupied seat at her table. They'd hit it off immediately, sharing stories and frustrations about work and home situations.

Megan lived with her partner Diane. They weren't married. They'd planned to marry during the brief period when it had been legal, but then the window had closed. Diane had insisted on going through with the ceremony anyway, with the rings and vows and certificate and all, and Megan wore a wedding ring, but the relationship had no legal standing. Life with Diane was . . . well, complicated, and often a point of stress for Megan.

As it proved today. Scott noticed that Megan was wearing her "haunted" look as she sat down, so he decided to dispense with the pleasantries.

"What's up?" he asked.

"Pardon?" Megan responded.

"Something's bothering you. I can tell by your eyebrows. Spill it", Scott insisted.

Megan sighed. "It's Diane. You'll never guess what she wants now."

Scott grinned. Diane always had a new thing. Her most recent thing had been paleo dieting, and Megan had had to get rid of all her cookware and learn to use cast iron. Before that, it had been feng shui, and life had been nothing but acquiring new furniture and then endlessly rearranging it to make auspicious arrangements.

"Soul food?" Scott gibed.

"Ha, ha", Megan replied, unamused. "She wants a baby."

Scott cocked an eyebrow but checked the urge to make a smart remark. This was clearly distressing Megan, and he didn't want to make it worse.

"Specifically, she wants *me* to give her a baby", Megan continued, her petite face falling further.

Scott had repeatedly been told that he had the social skills of a rhino, but even he could grasp that the situation called for tact.

"Okay", Scott acknowledged. Situations like this were unusual but not unknown, particularly among lesbian couples. "Is there some, ah, problem with her having the baby?"

"She's older, so the risks are higher", Megan explained. "At least that's what she said, and the fertility specialist concurred."

Ah. That answered Scott's next question, which was whether they'd sought medical help. "So that leaves you", Scott said. "Do you want a baby?"

Megan made a wry face. "Well, I think that every woman, deep down, wants a baby at some point."

This was news to Scott. He'd known plenty of women who seemed to have no interest in children. But Megan was continuing.

"The question is whether I want a baby *now*, under these circumstances. But Diane is convinced that she wants a baby, so that settles it. You have no idea how determined she can be when she sets her mind on something."

Actually, Scott did have an idea. Reading between the lines of their lunchtime conversations over the past year, he got the impression that Diane was a manipulative, overbearing woman who viewed Megan as a combination pet, life-sized doll, and housemaid.

"But now", Megan said, her voice catching, "not only does she want me to carry the baby, but she's complaining about the cost of the fertility clinic. I wish she'd thought of that when she was insisting on the granite countertops and inlaid cupboards."

"But", Scott asked, mystified, "doesn't your insurance—"

"Insurance doesn't cover fertility services", Megan interrupted, giving him what he called the "silly boy" look. "It's voluntary medical treatment, so it's all out-of-pocket. In this area a simple consultation runs about three hundred fifty dollars. A full treatment involves several visits, plus testing, AI, and sperm-bank costs, and—oh, excuse me." Megan suddenly stood and dashed down the hall.

Scott knew what that meant. Megan had anxiety problems, and one of the manifestations was irritable bowel syndrome. She would be back shortly, so he munched his sandwich and thought. She'd tossed out some jargon that he didn't understand. To him, "AI" meant "artificial intelligence"—but it would be easy to research. Shoving aside Megan's cranberry and pecan salad, he pulled out his phone and searched on "AI" and "fertility".

"Oh, my—Artificial Insemination?" Scott mumbled under his breath and continued researching.

By the time Megan returned, Scott was more knowledgeable about fertility matters than he had been—or wanted to be, for that matter (he'd never heard of "sperm washing" before). He had some thoughts that he was hesitant to offer, but Megan's distress gave him courage.

"Want some of my sandwich?" Scott offered. "You've got to have something more substantial than rabbit food. A steady diet of that can't be good for your condition."

"No thanks", Megan replied weakly.

"Look here", Scott said, pushing his plate aside and taking her hands. "I've been doing some research on your type of situation. Yes, you can go whole hog with the tests and experts and procedures, but there are simpler, less expensive alternatives. You just need some basic equipment—I've got the links right here—and a donor, who can be whomever you'd like. I'd be willing to be the donor, if you don't have anyone else."

"You?" Megan asked, looking at him wide-eyed.

After a moment's silence, Scott cocked a mischievous eyebrow. "What's the matter? Am I that poor a prospect?"

"No, no, it's not that", protested a flustered Megan. "It's just that ... you ... I wouldn't have dreamed of asking that of you."

"Asking what?" countered Scott. "It's not like donating is, ah, difficult."

"That's not what I meant", Megan replied. "It's more that ... with Diane and me ... and your baby ..."

"That's a question of perspective", Scott said. "So far as I'm concerned, it would be your and Diane's baby. I'd just make my small contribution and walk away."

"I don't know, Scott", Megan said after a moment. "It's very generous of you to offer, but—"

"Look, Megan", Scott said, gripping her hands. "I consider you one of my best friends. Every couple of weeks you and I meet here and listen to each other's problems. That's helpful, but usually we can't do anything more than just listen. I don't know about you, but that sometimes frustrates me. I wish I could do more than just lend a sympathetic ear. This is an opportunity for me to help tangibly at hardly any cost to me. Please, at least seriously consider it."

Megan gave a tremulous smile. "I will. I'll talk it over with Diane."

"Good", Scott replied briskly. Megan squeezed his hands in return.

"And Scott, I really appreciate your concern. It means a lot—not just the offer, but the sympathetic ear."

"Bah", Scott said dismissively, waving his hand in slight embarrassment. "Anything for a friend."

On the way back to the office, Scott looked up a few more things and made a phone call.

Early the next week the expected e-mail came in. Scott scanned the results with satisfaction, and a little relief. He printed it out and tucked it in his pocket. Not having heard back from Megan, he texted her.

"Lunch?"

The response took a while, but came. "Today?"

"Yes. 12:30?"

"Great. See you then."

At the restaurant, Megan was looking a little less strained, but still tentative, when she sat down across from him. Again Scott dispensed with the niceties.

"For you", Scott said, handing her the printout.

"What is it?" Megan asked, unfolding the sheet of codes and numbers.

"Test results", Scott explained. "It occurred to me that one thing that might—and should—affect your consideration of my offer is the question of whether I'm carrying anything communicable. So I hopped down to the corner clinic for the full battery of tests. This"—he tapped the paper she was holding—"certifies that I am free of any pathogens that can be transmitted via bodily fluids."

"Aw, Scott", cooed Megan. "You shouldn't have."

"I know it's not the only factor you're considering, but it's one less unknown. By the way, those are just the unofficial test results that they e-mailed to me. The certified results give the same information, but I have to sign for them, and there's an additional fee."

"I'm sure this will be fine", Megan replied, waving the printout and tucking it in her purse. "Speaking of fees, how much did all that testing cost?"

"Don't worry about it", Scott said, waving his hand. "How's progress? What does Diane think of my offer?"

"We've been talking it over", Megan explained. "And we discussed it with the fertility specialist. The specialist looked over the links you sent me and agreed that that was the proper equipment for at-home AI. She warned me that the results for at-home AI aren't as reliable as professional AI, but if cost is a factor, it is at least worth a try. Oh, she also told us to get you to sign a legal waiver, which she sent to us."

"No problem there", Scott assured her. "What about Diane?"

Megan gave a little grimace. "I'm working on her. She's not averse to the idea, and she definitely likes the lower cost. But she seems to be leery of the fact that I know you."

"What?" Scott asked. "Anonymous sperm is somehow better?"

"I know", giggled Megan. "That's what I was wondering, though I didn't put it to Diane like that. Diane kept asking questions about how I knew you and why I thought you might be offering to do this. I kept insisting that it was because you wanted to help, but she didn't seem to hear that. It was almost like she was jealous."

"Jealous?" Scott was incredulous. "Of what? It's not like I'm even going to be touching you."

"It doesn't make any sense, but Diane can be that way", Megan responded. "I asked her if she knew any guys who'd volunteer, but she didn't. I assured her that you didn't want any payment or favors, I told her you were gay, I told her about you and Greg, I told her that gay guys do this sort of thing all the time as favors to friends. That's true, isn't it?"

"I know that it happens", Scott admitted. "I can't say how common it is."

"Good enough", Megan said. "I think she's softening, and she's the one who wants the baby anyway. This"—she patted her purse where the printout was—"should help."

They spent the rest of lunch chatting about trivialities. Scott was glad to see Megan less stressed. He was also in better spirits—which he knew he would need—as he headed back to his office. Just before leaving he'd gotten an e-mail that Kumar, his helper, had given notice this morning, and that meant another tense meeting with Brian sometime soon.

Later that evening he got a text message from Megan.
"Diane says OK."

Chapter Two

Scott and Megan agreed on a suitable evening for him to come over. As he approached the address that Megan had sent him, he realized that he felt a little odd. He'd met Megan only at restaurants for meals, so this was his first visit to her condo. It felt strange to be coming for such an unusual reason. Also, he'd never met Diane and wasn't sure how that would go.

Meeting Diane turned out not to be an issue. When he knocked at the door, Megan met him wearing an apron with her sleeves rolled up, clearly in the midst of kitchen work.

"Hi! Diane's out shopping, and I'm preparing her a late supper. Hope you don't mind."

"No—not at all", Scott replied.

"Okay, then", Megan said, heading back toward the kitchen. "The kit we ordered is in the bathroom, along with some instructions from the fertility specialist. Let me know if you need anything." Scott could hear sounds of chopping and rinsing.

"Okay", Scott replied, sitting on his desire to make a quip about not needing any help. He looked around at the small but tidy apartment. It was clearly the abode of women—it was a little frilly but had the order and harmony that few men bothered with. Maybe it was the feng shui.

Scott stood by the door for a bit, listening to Megan bustle about the kitchen, and finally figured he was supposed to find his own way to the bathroom. He made his way down the hallway, passing a bedroom that was already done up as a nursery. It had pastel paint with little prints on the walls, a matching dresser and crib, and some stuffed animals lying about. Diane was clearly taking this baby thing very seriously. For some reason that made him feel a little creepy.

The bathroom was across the hall from the main bedroom. There on the vanity was the kit with instructions, most of which had to do with Megan's end of things, and the fertility specialist's letter, which said a lot of the same things. His part was simple and straightforward.

On the way out, Scott stuck his head into the kitchen, where Megan was still busy. "Okay, you're good", he said.

"Thanks", Megan replied. "Oh, there's a form on the dining room table there for you to sign. Our lawyer drew it up. Apparently it's boilerplate language for situations like this."

"Okay", Scott shrugged, locating the document. It was a standard legal form, all laid out in paragraphs and full of language he couldn't understand. Megan had signed and dated the last page, and there was a place for him to sign as well.

"There you go", Scott called. "If that's all, I'm out of here."

"Thanks again!" Megan called from the kitchen.

"Let me know how things turn out", Scott said as he opened the door.

"Will do!" Megan replied.

It was a couple of weeks before Scott heard from Megan again. He was busy at work putting the finishing touches on a maintenance release of his company's storage-virtualization software, but the project had given him lots of ideas for improvement. He wanted to organize his thoughts so he could present a solid case to Brian and Marcus. He was sure that with a concerted push they could pull off a major jump on the competition with an aggressively superior product.

He was pacing the halls, marshaling his thoughts and muttering to himself, when his phone chimed. It was Megan.

"Lunch?"

"Sure. Where?" Scott texted back.

She named one of the local Thai spots. He got there first and ordered her some pad thai, which he knew was her favorite. That proved fortunate, for when Megan arrived she was wearing a down-cast expression.

"So," Scott said, "what news?"

"No luck", Megan said in a weak voice with a little shake of her head.

"This time", Scott added. Megan looked up with a quizzical expression. "Hey, I know how this works. It's an odds game, even done the usual way. I was figuring this would take at least a couple of tries."

"You were?"

"Sure I was", Scott assured her. "I mean, if it had worked right off, that would have been great. But I wasn't so naïve as to assume that would happen."

"And you'd ... be willing to do it again?" Megan asked tentatively.

"I just said I would, didn't I?" Scott replied. "You're behaving like this is a huge deal. It's not like you're asking me to run a marathon. Just tell me when to show up again."

"Really? Oh Scott!"

"Yeah, yeah. Now eat your pad thai."

Scott's next visit was on one of the many clammy evenings that occurred around the Bay Area in high summer. It was dark when he knocked on the door, and he wondered if Diane would be there this time. He guessed not, and he was right. Megan greeted him, her phone in hand, clearly in the middle of a text conversation.

"Hi", she said. "Let me take your jacket."

He shrugged it off and looked about the room, again amazed by the tidiness. This looked like a home; his apartment looked like a locker room.

"So," said Megan, settling back on the couch and returning to her texting, "you, ah ..."

"Know the drill", Scott completed for her.

"Know the drill", Megan echoed. Scott headed back down the hall, disconcerted by something but unable to put his finger on what it might be.

When Scott came out, Megan was still texting away. "Well, there you go", he said clumsily, not knowing what to say.

"Thanks", Megan said, looking up with a smile. "Oh, there's a letter for you to sign."

"Another one?" Scott asked, puzzled. "I thought—"

"The last one was for last time, this is for this time", Megan explained. "Better safe than sorry, the lawyer said, and Diane agreed."

"Oh. All right", Scott said, grumbling something about lawyers. He signed the paper and got his jacket. "Well ... good night."

"Good night. And thanks", Megan said with a wave, not looking up from her phone.

Another few weeks passed by. Work was getting intense. Brian had been excited by the potential of Scott's proposal, so Scott and Marcus had put their heads together to draw up a proof-of-concept project. That kept Scott late at the office most nights, and often when he was home he was buried in his laptop.

Scott hardly saw Greg at all. Sometimes when he got home late there would be debris on the counter indicating that Greg had come and gone again. Once or twice Greg staggered in during the wee hours and collapsed on the bed, too drunk or stoned to do anything. That was just as well—Scott was finding work too demanding to have to worry about relationships.

One day when his stomach was starting to remind him that lunch-time was approaching, he realized how long it had been since he'd met up with Megan. A quick glance at the calendar told him he was overdue for some news, so he texted her.

"Lunch?"

"Today?" came the response.

"Unless you ate?" Scott asked.

"No. Usual in 30m?"

Scott didn't know how he could tell from a text exchange, but he strongly suspected that something was amiss. His suspicion was confirmed when he saw Megan come into the restaurant, head down, shoulders hunched. When she sat down, he saw that her eyes were rimmed with red and there were dark circles under them. Her whole carriage bespoke defeat.

"So ... no soap?" Scott asked. Megan said nothing but shook her head, dropping her eyes to her lap.

"Well ... okay", Scott continued, wondering what to say to cheer his friend up. "Disappointing, certainly, but not the end of things. Strike two, I'd call it. We still have some time at bat."

"Scott, I couldn't ask that of you", said Megan quietly. "You've already—"

"Look, we've already established that this is a trivial exertion for me, and one I'm happy to make", Scott countered. "I think the problem is on your end. Not you personally, but your whole situation. I take it Diane isn't handling this well?"

Again Megan shook her head. "She ... she seems to be blaming me. Oh, she doesn't say it plainly, but she keeps dropping hints about my trying harder, or how she wished she knew someone who loved her enough to give her a baby. I *am* trying, as hard as I can!" She slammed her hand on the table.

"Sure you are", Scott assured her, taking her hand. "What does the fertility expert have to say?"

"She's not certain", Megan said. "She's pretty sure we're timing my cycles correctly, and there doesn't seem to be anything abnormal about them. She suggested a full hormonal battery, but those are expensive."

"For that matter, it could be me", Scott admitted. "I've never had a fertility workup."

Megan shrugged. "If everything's biologically okay, then the specialist suggested that the most likely point of failure is the transfer."

Just then the waitress arrived and they ordered their lunch, which gave Scott time to figure out what "the transfer" meant.

"You mean", Scott asked in a quiet voice when they were alone again, "that there's some kind of problem when you ... put it up inside you?"

"The specialist doesn't know, but that's the first thing she suspects", Megan said. "Other causes get more complicated and expensive to detect."

Everything that Scott could think to say sounded either trite or patronizing, so he kept his mouth shut. Her head was still bowed, and she was quiet, but he saw a few tears drop into her lap.

"And ... and", Megan continued in a stuffy voice, "she's under pressure at her work because contracts are down and she's had to let people go." Diane owned a small catering business. "So she doesn't have the spare cash that she did. But somehow having a baby is supposed to make that all better! She keeps hinting that I could help pay for the testing and professional AI and everything, while I can barely make ends meet as it is!"

"And aren't babies kind of expensive?" Scott asked.

"Of course they are", Megan confirmed. "Any reasonable person knows that, but Diane's being anything but reasonable about this. A baby would brighten our days and make life worthwhile! I'm expected not only to bear the baby but to help pay the costs as well—on my salary!"

Scott could see that Megan was getting more worked up, so he tried to distract her by describing how things were going at his work, and the new ideas he had, and how the company wanted to explore them further. She didn't even understand what storage virtualization was, but she was glad that things seemed to be going well. By the end of lunch she was sounding more like her cheerful self again, so Scott felt safe broaching the idea that had been percolating in the back of his mind. He didn't know how she would take it. He was hoping it wouldn't add more stress to an already-stressful situation, but he didn't want to send her off without at least suggesting something.

When their dishes had been cleared away, Scott again reached over and took Megan's hand. She looked at him, a little startled.

"Look, Megan, I consider you a good friend—one of the best I have", Scott said earnestly. Megan rewarded him with a brilliant smile and gripped his hand in return.

"Thanks, Scott", she answered. "Your support through all this has been tremendous."

"Well, I'd like to keep it up, so hear what I have to say in light of our friendship", Scott continued. "I only want to help you, and I'd never take advantage of you or use you."

"I know you wouldn't, Scott."

"Keep that in mind, because I have a suggestion that could be open to serious misinterpretation. Promise that you trust me?" Scott said.

"I trust you, Scott", Megan replied with a patient smile.

"Okay, then", Scott said. Now that it came right down to the matter, it was more difficult to suggest than he'd anticipated. "One place the problem could be is in the transfer, right?"

"That's the specialist's first suggestion", Megan confirmed.

"Then maybe we could reduce that element of uncertainty by streamlining the process—making it more efficient", Scott explained. Megan's eyes narrowed in puzzlement. "I'm not saying this very well. Maybe, instead of your having to transfer the, ah, goods to where they're needed, I could just put them there in the first place. Direct deposit, so to speak."

Scott's cheeks were burning. He hadn't realized how embarrassing it would be to suggest that. Megan's expression was hard to decipher, but at least she wasn't shocked or sobbing or screaming, and she was still holding his hand.

"You mean", she asked in a near whisper, "we should ... try the insemination without the artificial?"

"Yes, that's what I mean", Scott answered. "I mean ... we could, if you wanted to."

Megan dropped her eyes to her lap, her expression still unreadable, though she still held his hand. After a minute's tense silence, Scott felt he had to say something.

"It's only an idea. If you don't like it, we can just forget it. Please don't think I'm trying to—"

"Scott," Megan interrupted, looking up and squeezing his hand, "I don't think you're trying to do anything but help. Thank you for having the courage to overcome your embarrassment and make the offer."

Well ... Scott hadn't been expecting that.

"Truthfully," Megan continued, "I'd already thought of that. It was the first thing that sprang into my mind when the specialist said where she thought the problem might be. I knew I could never suggest it, because ..." She trailed off.

"Why? Because I'm gay?" Scott asked. "Megan, that's what makes it easier. I am what I am, you are what you are, so there's no risk of anything going further. It doesn't have to mean anything."

"Scott, it's sex", Megan replied. "It always means *something*."

"Well ... maybe." Scott was puzzled by Megan's comment but decided to leave it. "If so, it can mean what we want it to mean, right? The way I look at it, it's just a slight variation on what we're already doing. Think of it as ... as a precisely targeted sperm donation. It might help, or it might not, but it's worth a try. If you want to, that is."

"It's tempting", Megan admitted. "But I don't think Diane ..."

"She doesn't have to know. Nobody has to know! You just tell her that we're going to give it one more try. You won't even be lying, because as far as I'm concerned, that's all I'm doing. You don't have to give her all the details. She doesn't need to know that we'll be a little closer together and doing without some of the paraphernalia. It's not like she's around when I come, anyway."

"That's true", Megan admitted.

"Look, I don't want to sound like I'm trying to talk you into this", Scott said. "It's totally up to you. We could try again the way we've been doing it. We could try what I'm offering. You could drop the whole idea and look into adopting. Whatever you want to do is fine

19

by me. I just want to help as much as I can to try to take some of the pressure off you, because I hate to see you miserable."

This got him another sunny smile and hand squeeze. "Thanks, Scott. I don't know ... it's a lot to consider."

"And there's no reason you have to decide right now", Scott reminded her. "Take your time, think about it, let me know. I'm good with whatever you decide, so don't worry about me."

"Okay, I'll consider it and be back in touch. And—oh heavens, look at the time! I've got to be going!" Megan started fishing in her purse, but Scott waved her off.

"Go, go. I'll settle up."

"Thanks." Megan swept her purse onto her shoulder and stood to go but then stopped behind her chair and looked at him. "Seriously, Scott, thank you for lunch, for being a thoughtful friend—and for the strangest conversation I've ever had."

Scott chuckled all the way back to the office on that. He was glad to see Megan in good spirits again.

A couple of days later Scott's phone rang. He saw it was Megan, which surprised him—she almost always texted. Guessing it would be about the sensitive topic, he stepped from his cube into an empty conference room and closed the door.

"Megan?" he answered.

"Hi", Megan said shyly.

"What news?" Scott asked.

"Well ..." Megan drew a breath. "I've decided to take you up on it. I talked it over with Diane, and she's agreed to let us try one more time. I'm going to be taking my temperature and working with the specialist to time my cycle just right. I'll let you know the right date."

Scott made a mental note to look up what she meant about the temperature. "Okay. You'll want to order another one of those kits. We want to make this look as legit as possible." The AI stuff came in little twin-pack kits that Megan ordered online.

"Right", said Megan. "I'll be back in touch. Got to go!"

That night Scott again found himself in the house with the rice-paper walls. As always, he was wandering through the rooms, appreciating the neatness and order, relishing the delicacy of the images on the walls. But for some reason, the patterns seemed dimmer this time, the colors not as vibrant. From time to time the walls seemed to shiver— not severely, just a light rattle.

Wondering what could be causing this, he wandered outside. In the western sky he could see building a great, dark storm line of the type that used to sweep over his town when he was growing up. In the spring and summer the storms would form over the farmlands to the west and come crashing eastward toward the lake with amazing speed and overwhelming force. They were terrifying and mesmerizing at the same time, and when Scott was young he used to stay outside to watch them come on for as long as his mother would allow. Once he'd even seen a tornado start forming!

Now, in his dream, he was going to get to see it again. He felt the adrenaline rush of excitement and fear, and saw the leaves of the surrounding trees hushing and ruffling in the fitful gusts that preceded the main storm. He watched, enchanted, as the towering line of dark clouds loomed closer overhead. There! He caught a flash of lightning lace up the front of the cloud line. There went another! The low rumble of thunder rippled through the air, and the tall trees all around were waving and bending in earnest as the wind grew to a steady roar. Great raindrops were falling now, swept nearly horizontal, and the lightning was flashing constantly. Somewhere, barely audible above the howling, he heard the sharp crack of some great branch giving way and crashing to the ground before the onslaught. The tempest was still building, and above the booming thunder he heard the crack of another branch.

Scott glanced up to see if he was in any danger from falling limbs. He was in a clear spot, but he saw that the house was overhung with branches—great, low-hanging branches that were rocking and twisting dangerously just above the frail house. There was a loud boom as lightning struck nearby, and now Scott was truly afraid. He wanted to run inside, back to shelter, but the big branches were swaying constantly now, their leaves whipped by the savage wind.

Crack! One branch above the house finally gave way, twisting as it fell in an avalanche of leaves. It barely missed the front of the house, and Scott could see where some of the limbs had clipped the corner, tearing into the paper. His hands flew to his mouth as, with another ripping crack, a huge branch, almost half a tree, tore away from its trunk and dropped onto the back of the house, smashing in the rear half.

"Noooo!" Scott screamed into the raging wind, but his cry was blown away as the branches writhed and slashed in the gale. He watched in horror as one branch that overhung the center of the house began to twist and splinter, swaying dangerously low over the roof. No! Not his beautiful house!

Then another bolt of lightning struck near, and the boom of thunder awakened Scott. He lay staring into the dark, his heart hammering.

Chapter Three

Megan's text came one morning, asking if that evening would work. Scott confirmed that it would, so they set a time. For some unaccountable reason, Scott spent the remainder of the day in a mild state of nerves. His evening appointment with Megan was the only thing he could figure was the cause, but that was silly. He would just be doing what he'd already done twice, with a few minor changes. Nothing to it, his mind assured him. But something in his gut wasn't sure.

Work kept Scott late, but he still made a point of swinging home for a quick shower before heading to Megan's. The sun was setting as he left. He texted Megan.

"On my way. 15m."

Shortly thereafter the response came. "Waiting. Door unlocked. Diane gone."

Scott drove the now-familiar route to Megan's condo. At the door he halted briefly, then stuck his head in. "Hello?" he called.

"Back here!" came Megan's reply from the rear. Scott slipped in and locked the door behind him—and then slipped on the chain. Tentatively he made his way down the hallway, where the only lights in the place were burning in the bedroom.

Scott didn't know what to expect, but he found Megan sitting up in bed reading a pamphlet of some sort and wearing the same exercise outfit she'd had on the last time—at least the top of it, for the covers were pulled up to her waist. She looked at him and gave a shy but friendly smile.

"Hi, Scott", she said, laying the pamphlet down.

"Hi", Scott responded, wondering what to say. Strange as it seemed, given some of the places he'd been and some of the experiences he'd had, he was a little embarrassed. Sure, it was just sex, but this was Megan, for Pete's sake, a good friend. In fact, he considered,

23

she was one of his best friends, and he didn't have many. It felt very
. . . strange.

Scott shook himself, realizing that he'd been staring at Megan for
a good minute without saying anything. She was just looking back,
gently smiling.

"Well, then", Scott stammered. "I suppose we should get on with
things?"

"I suppose we should", Megan echoed quietly.

"Do we, ah, need the lights?" Scott gestured to the overhead.

"No, of course not", Megan answered, reaching for her bedside
lamp. "The switch is right there by the door." Scott flicked the
switch, and the room was plunged into darkness. Gathering his courage, he walked over to sit on the bed and started untying his shoes.

"You're sure you want to go through with this?" Scott asked.

"Sure . . . if you don't mind", Megan assured him.

"Oh, I don't mind", Scott replied. "It's just that . . . well, we're
both adults, and I wanted to ensure we were covered on the 'con-
senting' part."

Megan giggled in the dark. Having removed his shoes and socks,
Scott swung into the bed and pulled the covers up to his waist as well.
He was willing to help in this way, but neither of them seemed to
want to get naked.

"Ready, then?" Scott asked.

"All ready", Megan replied. Scott reached under the covers to
remove his shorts as Megan did something similar.

Scott's body knew what to do, even if Megan was a woman.
Megan didn't respond in any way but just lay there beneath him.
They didn't talk or even look at each other. Scott kept his head
beside hers, though not against it. He noticed her scent, which was
subdued and lightly floral. He tried to keep himself propped up on
his elbows so as not to press down on her.

Scott finished and rolled away to the other side of the bed. After an
uncomfortable silence, he felt he had to say something.

"Well . . . hopefully that will work."

"Hopefully", Megan replied. There was another pause. "Scott . . .
thank you for being willing to do this."

"My pleasure", Scott blurted out instinctively, then realized what
he'd said. "That is, ah, anything for a friend."

That got a genuine laugh.

"You know," Scott continued, "I've heard that if you tip your hips up a little, it can help—"

"Scott," Megan interrupted gently, patting his arm, "I assure you, I'm up on all the fertility tips."

"Oh, ah, yes, I suppose you would be", Scott stammered. They lay beside each other in the dark for a little longer before Scott stirred. "Well, then, I ... guess I'd better be going, then?"

"I guess so", Megan said quietly.

"I'll just have a bit of a wash and head out", Scott said, rolling out of bed and grabbing his shoes.

"Can I ... make you coffee or something?" Megan asked, starting to throw back the covers, but Scott smoothed them back down again.

"Nothing doing. You lie still with your hips up, right? I can see myself out", Scott instructed.

"Yes, sir", Megan acquiesced. "Lunch sometime soon?"

"I'll text you", Scott assured her. "Good night!"

"Good night", Megan replied.

Scott washed up and was back in his car in five minutes. He sat still for a bit, taking deep breaths and rolling his shoulders. He hadn't realized how tense he'd been.

"Well," he muttered, "I'm glad that's over." He started the car and drove away.

A couple of days later he remembered that he had a promise to make good on, so he texted Megan about lunch. She couldn't get away then, but they made plans for the next day. When they met, Scott was glad to see Megan upbeat and cheerful—in fact, more so than she'd been in some time. Megan seemed to be tactfully ignoring any mention of their last meeting, which was fine with Scott, who followed suit. The closest they got to the topic was when Scott asked how things were at home.

"Well ..." Megan shrugged. "Diane's still a little off—not glaringly so, but it shows up in little ways. Something about the atmosphere about the place."

"Any reason why?" Scott asked. "I'd think she'd be happy that her plans are proceeding."

"You'd think, wouldn't you?" Megan said. "But she's funny like that. She's really insecure and prone to jealousy. I could tell you stories, but I won't. She acquiesced to your being the donor, but she's never liked it. If we'd been able to afford it, I'm sure she would have insisted on going to a sperm bank."

"Nice to know I was the cheap option", Scott said with a grin.

"Oh, you!" Megan slapped his arm. "That's not what I meant, and you know it!" The conversation moved on to how his project was coming along. When they parted ways, Scott returned to work grateful that their friendship was back to normal.

Later the following week, Scott was getting ready for work when his phone rang. Wondering who could be calling him so early, he was a little alarmed to see that it was Megan. He couldn't ever remember her contacting him by any manner so early.

"Megan?" he answered.

"Scott, can we meet for lunch? I need to talk to you." Megan sounded tense and anxious.

"Sure", Scott said. "We can meet now, if you like, though I have a meeting at ten. Is something wrong?"

"It's Diane", Megan answered, confirming Scott's suspicions. "She's pretty upset. She said some vicious things and then stormed out of the house."

"What happened?" Scott asked.

Megan sighed. "She found the kit—the AI kit, the second one I ordered. When it came, I tucked it in a drawer and forgot about it. After you'd left the other night, I remembered it and meant to get up and throw one of the sets away. But then I fell asleep, and it went clean out of my mind. Diane found it unopened, containing both sets of material, and put two and two together."

"What did she do?"

"She confronted me, and I made up some song and dance about not being able to find it and making do with some kitchen utensils. It wasn't very convincing, and I don't think she bought it—I wouldn't have."

"So . . . what happens next?" Scott asked, feeling somewhat responsible for Megan's predicament.

"I don't know", Megan replied. "Could we talk over lunch? I've got to get ready for work."

All morning long Scott stewed over the situation, and by the time he met up with Megan, he had a plan figured out.

"Look," said Scott, diving right in once they'd ordered, "Diane is being totally unreasonable about this. She's the one who wants a baby, even though you can't afford a lab fertilization. What difference does it make how the sperm got there?"

"Shh, Scott." Megan patted his arm, glancing at nearby diners. Scott was getting a little loud in his indignation. "You're trying to talk reason, and Diane is being anything but reasonable. It's like I said before—she's never liked the fact that you're a friend of mine. She likes even less the idea that you and I were, ah, intimate, no matter what the motive. I think she sees it as a threat to her control over me."

"Control over you?" Scott asked with narrowed eyes.

"Well, I, ah . . . I don't mean it like that", replied a flustered Megan. "She's just a bit . . . territorial. She really considers us married, regardless of the law."

They paused while their lunches arrived, giving Scott time to think. He didn't like this talk of control, no matter how Megan tried to rephrase it, but had no idea what he could do about it.

"Well," Scott said, "at least getting her wish about a baby should calm her down, you'd think. Speaking of which, do you have any idea yet?"

"No—it's still too early. I'm only just now getting to the stage where any test could tell. I plan to pick up a test on the way home tonight", Megan explained.

"Well, here's hoping—not just for success but for Diane to calm down", Scott replied. His was more than a casual interest. He didn't want to be caught again in the dilemma of how he could best help.

Scott was still at work when Megan's text came.

"Test says yes."

Scott closed his eyes and gave a whispered "Yes!" But he was still unsettled.

"Great. Diane?"

"Not told yet. Test can give false+. Try again AM."

"OK", Scott sent back.

"Also, want symptoms, not just test", Megan continued.

"Good. Congrats to both", Scott responded.

"Thx. Gnite."

Scott put his phone aside and began wrapping up his work. He was getting punchy from fatigue and stress and needed to get home. At least Megan's little drama appeared to be over. Hopefully that meant his life could return to some semblance of normal.

Chapter Four

September flew by in a whirlwind. Scott and Marcus pulled together a proof-of-concept demonstration that they presented to management and then had to present to another group that included Brian and at least two members of the board of directors. Then there was a one-day flight up to Bellevue, to the lab of a major storage manufacturer, where Scott had to sign a nondisclosure agreement before they let him past the lobby. He presented the idea to a bunch of people whom he presumed were engineers. They asked a lot of questions and took a lot of notes but didn't say a word about why they wanted to know. Then there was another trip, this time to Chicago, where he was one part of a longer meeting and gave a compressed version of the POC. That room had been full of strangers, except for one of the guys from his company's board of directors. He didn't know what that was about—a cross-country trip for an hour's presentation—but it required an overnight stay. He loved Chicago and was able to swing dinner at a popular spot, where he stuffed himself with stuffed pizza.

Scott was starting to get very excited about the project. It was innovative and daring and could help the firm steal a march on the whole industry. Storage virtualization was a very specialized market, but demand was only going to increase. Since the dot-com bust over a decade before—about which Scott had only heard—the industry had shied away from small start-ups, preferring established players with big budgets for staff and research and development. Scott saw his idea as a chance to prove that a small, nimble firm could be just as innovative as a big one. He ached for the chance to prove it.

In the midst of the bustle and late hours, Scott had few chances even to think about Megan. She was normally the one who contacted him, but that had dropped off completely. He figured she would be busy, because it was the time of year for preparing and sending out tax notices. But the few times he was at his desk and remembered and sent her a text, he got either no response or a brief reply saying she wasn't in the office. Scott just shrugged and hoped that meant everything was all right.

Scott saw almost nothing of Greg all month, which was a relief. Life was trying enough without the particular strain of high drama that followed Greg around.

"Are you there?" Scott texted Megan one day without much hope.

"Yes. Lunch?" came the response.

".5 hr? Usual?" Scott responded.

"OK."

Scott was already seated when Megan came in, but when he saw her, he stood up in alarm and walked swiftly to her side.

"Megan!" he said, giving her a quick hug and holding her chair for her. "You look like a wreck!"

"It's good to see you too, Scott", Megan replied with a wan smile.

Scott was not to be put off by banter. Megan did look like a wreck, and there was no use pretending otherwise. Her hair was stringy, her eyes were sunken and dark rimmed, her face was thin and pale, and she sat with her shoulders hunched and a defeated look in her eyes. Was this what pregnancy did to women?

"I guess this is what I get for being out of touch for so long", Scott said. "What would you like for lunch? You look like you haven't eaten in a week. Order anything you like—on me today."

"Please, Scott," Megan pleaded, handing him the menu, "order for me. I'll eat whatever they bring, but nothing looks good to me."

Scott ordered them both big meals—his diet of late had been heavy on vending machine fare and late-night takeout.

"Now," Scott said firmly as the waitress headed away, "tell me how you're doing. Is this all due to the pregnancy?"

"In one way or another", Megan replied ambiguously. "I've certainly been off my feed. You read about morning sickness, but until you experience it, you don't know. I wake up, the nausea hits me. I can't keep anything down. Even when I'm able to eat, nothing sounds good. I have to force myself to eat, though I know I have to for the baby's sake.

"Some days I feel so out of it that I have to call in sick. That's happened so much lately! Just in this month, I've used up all the personal days I had, Scott! And when I come in, my work isn't up to par. Nobody says anything, but I know it's true. I'm getting sloppy, missing things, forgetting details.

"As if that weren't bad enough, now I'm falling prey to the sleeps", Megan concluded.

"The sleeps?" Scott asked.

"Yes. It's like I can't get up at all in the morning. The alarm will sound, and I'll barely be able to reach to turn it off. Twice in the past two weeks I've had to call in sick because I couldn't get up. Or I'll come home and essentially pass out on the couch, without even removing my shoes. I'll wake up three or four hours later having not moved a muscle.

"It's worst at work. I drag myself around and am always on the edge of dozing off, no matter how much coffee I drink. It takes me forever to finish things, and a few times I've actually dropped off right there at my desk. One moment I'm trying to focus on a problem, and the next I'm being shaken awake by a coworker. My supervisor's really worried about it, because our desks are visible from the service counter, which means the public can see me."

"How is Diane taking this?" Scott asked.

Megan's already-long face fell even further, and she dropped her eyes to her plate. "She's been ... distant. I don't see much of her, and when I do, it's not pleasant. She's not at all sympathetic. It's like she despises me for being weak."

"Despises you?" Scott asked sharply, incredulous. "Whose idea was this whole baby thing, anyway? How can she pressure you into a huge step like this and then not even sympathize with you?"

"I know, Scott, I know." Megan patted his arm. "I've asked myself the same question. I'm beginning to think that having a baby was another one of Diane's kicks—one that she's gotten over even before the baby has arrived. It's my fault, really."

"*Your* fault?" Scott scoffed. "How on earth do you figure that?"

"Well," Megan replied tentatively, as if trying to convince herself, "maybe if I'd been a little stronger and held out against her pressure, she would have given up on the baby idea and moved on to her next thing."

"Or maybe", countered Scott, "she would have kept increasing the pressure until she got what she wanted." Scott had tried to keep his opinions about Megan's "marriage" to himself, but the picture of Diane that kept emerging did not encourage him.

"Maybe", shrugged Megan. "Whatever the case, she sneers at me when I'm bent over the toilet in the morning and sends me snarky texts throughout the day. What really upsets her is when she comes home and I haven't gotten dinner ready—either because I couldn't think of anything that sounded good or, lately, because I've been stone crashed out."

"Gotten dinner ready?" Scott asked. "Wait a minute—isn't she the cook? Why can't she cook her own dinner, and yours while she's at it?"

"Well, that's always been the thing", sighed Megan. "She says that because she works in a kitchen all day, the last thing she wants to do when she comes home is hang around another kitchen. So I've always cooked dinner for us, until recently, when I haven't been able to. She gets pretty upset about it."

"Wait", Scott spluttered, his indignation rising. "She wants the baby that you agree to carry, then when you can't make her dinner because the pregnancy debilitates you, she gets upset? You ought to ... in fact, I ought to—"

"Scott, Scott," Megan interrupted, grasping his hand, "let it go. It doesn't concern you. We'll work it out."

"The hell it doesn't concern me!" Scott pressed. "That's my ... that is, you're my friend, and I don't like to see my friends pushed around like that!"

"Scott, please, calm down", Megan urged him, tears standing in her eyes. "I hate seeing you this upset. It'll work out, it'll all work out."

Scott tried to calm himself for her sake, but he was still seething at the thought of her being ordered around like a kitchen maid. He tried to think of another topic to get his mind off this one.

"So ... this nausea and sleepiness", Scott said. "This has to be a temporary condition, right? I mean, you see pregnant women out and about—hugely pregnant women sometimes—and they aren't sleeping on benches or puking into trash cans."

Megan gave a weak smile and patted his arm. "Scott, you can be so genteel. The reading I've done indicates that it generally passes, certainly the sleepiness, though some women suffer nausea throughout pregnancy. I hope I'm not one of them." She started fishing in her purse. "I hope the whole thing passes soon. My performance evaluation is coming up, and I'd like to be back in something like form before then."

"You go—I've got this", Scott said with a wave, grabbing the check. "Keep in touch, right? And let me know if I can do anything."

"Thanks! I will!" Megan called as she headed for the door.

"Yeah—sure you will", muttered Scott, more concerned than ever.

Chapter Five

Scott's concern proved well-founded. A couple of weeks later, he received a text from Megan. They hadn't been in touch since that distressing lunch, and Scott was just starting to think that he should contact her when the text came in. He immediately guessed that something was awry, because it was late on a Friday—Megan normally messaged about lunchtime toward the middle of the week.

"Scott?"

"Yes?" Scott texted back.

"Dinner? ASAP? Please?"

Dinner? Megan had never asked to meet in the evening. "Sure. Cantonese Palace?" Scott texted back. He packed up his laptop and headed over, arriving before Megan and getting a table.

When Megan showed up, Scott could see even in the dim lighting that she looked worse than the last time he'd seen her. Her head was bowed, she was clutching a tissue, and she looked totally crushed. Scott sprang to his feet and held her chair.

"Scott, I'm on probation!" Megan blurted out before he even had a chance to ask how she was. "I just had my evaluation. My supervisor sharply criticized my recent performance and ended up putting me on probation!"

"That's a shame", Scott commiserated. "Maybe in a few months, when things stabilize, you can ask for a reevaluation."

"It's much more than a shame", Megan replied sharply. "Being on probation is like being a new hire. I lose all my benefits—health insurance, vacation, personal days, everything. *Everything*, Scott!" She buried her face in her hands and sobbed.

"Wow", Scott said. "That sounds extreme, just for having a few off weeks."

"It is extreme", Megan confirmed through her tears. "That's what I can't figure out. For a regular employee to go straight to probation is almost unheard of. Probation is one step short of suspension. My

34

understanding was that you'd have to show up for work stoned and start throwing things at the public to warrant probation. Normally you'd get two or three warnings first."

Just then Megan's phone chimed, and she pulled it out of her purse. Her brow clouded as she looked at the text.

"It's from Diane", Megan whispered. "She wants to know where I am."

"Well, don't tell her you're with me", Scott cautioned.

"No way", Megan said, shaking her head and thumbing in a response. "I'll just say I'm late at work."

The phone quickly chimed again. Reading the reply, Megan's hand flew to her mouth and her eyes widened in shock.

"What is it?" Scott asked, desperate to know what would elicit such a response. Megan said nothing, simply closing her eyes so that tears streamed from beneath her lashes. She shoved the phone toward him so he could read the text.

"Little liar. How's that pregnancy treating you now?"

"That bitch", Scott grumbled at the insult, but was still mystified. "What's with her comment about your condition?"

Megan shook her head, tears still flowing. "You ... you don't understand. You couldn't understand."

"Understand what?" Scott asked.

Megan took a deep breath and wiped her eyes. "It's a code among women, Scott. When we welcome it, we call it 'the baby'. When we're considering doing away with it, we refer to 'the pregnancy'."

"But ... doing away ... how ..." Scott was still clueless.

"Abortion, Scott", Megan whispered. "Diane is not-so-subtly hinting that the pregnancy is causing more problems than it's worth, especially in light of this probation, and that I should consider ending it."

Scott was stunned. He'd considered this to be a matter between Megan and Diane, but ever in the back of his mind he was aware that he'd had a part in it too. "That's quite a switch", Scott began, then stopped. "Wait a minute—you haven't been home, or Diane wouldn't be texting asking where you are."

"True", Megan confirmed.

"Then how does she know you're on probation? You've only just told me. But that text is clearly a taunt about some new development, which has to be the probation."

"You're right", Megan confirmed with a look of puzzlement that slowly turned to shock. "Oh my God, Scott, I've just remembered something I'd totally forgotten—I got that job with Diane's help. She knew some people in the city offices and steered me in when the opening came up."

Scott pondered this for a bit. "So ... an inside contact might be how she knows about the probation."

"Scott, an inside contact might be how I ended up on probation at all!" Megan snapped, then was instantly contrite. "I'm sorry, I'm sorry", she cried, gripping his hand. "I don't mean to be sharp. You're the only friend I have; I can't be mean to you."

"Only friend?" Scott asked. "I thought you had lots of contacts around here."

Megan shook her head. "Those are all Diane's friends. If she's turning against me, they'll all evaporate as well. Some of my coworkers are already shunning me, and that's only going to get worse as word gets out. Scott, what am I going to do? What am I going to do?" Her voice was literally squeaking with desperation, and her eyes wore a hunted look.

Something within Scott surged in response to Megan's plight. Nobody should have to stand alone, abandoned by friends and facing such troubles—not if he had anything to say about it. He covered both her hands with his and looked her straight in the eyes.

"Here's what's not going to happen ...", he began. Megan continued to cry and look down. "Megan! Listen to me: here's what's not going to happen. I'm not going to leave you alone. You aren't going to face this by yourself—I'm going to stand with you."

"Scott, I appreciate your intent, but what can you *do*?" Megan replied tearfully. "I forgot to tell you another thing about being on probation, probably the most important thing."

"What's that?" Scott asked.

"Probationary employees have no seniority. They're first in line for layoffs. When staff is cut, everyone on probation goes, then they start going up the list in order of seniority. The managers are drawing up next year's budget right now, and there have been strong rumors of cutbacks. I believe them too—few know better than our office just how sharply tax revenues are down. The city is dealing with so many foreclosures and bankruptcies and delinquent payments that I'm spending all my time on the phone these days", Megan explained.

"Okay", Scott said, absorbing this. Megan indeed looked to be in a very tight spot. "Yes, that's bad, but I have a few ideas of my own. Let me do some research."

"But Scott, what can you *do*?" Megan cried again.

"I'm not going to leave you, Megan", Scott assured her. "Whatever you face, I will be with you, I promise. I only ask one thing."

"What's that?" Megan asked weakly.

"As you value our friendship, don't make any final decisions without talking to me first. No matter how much pressure Diane puts on you, no matter how desperate things seem, please talk to me before you take any action. Okay?"

"All right", Megan answered quietly.

"The first thing I want to do is get you on my health insurance plan", Scott explained.

Megan's eyes widened. "Oh Scott, I couldn't ask that of you."

"You're not. I'm offering, and the way I see it, you haven't much choice—unless you want to try to purchase an individual policy."

"But . . . isn't Greg on your policy?"

"He is", grumbled Scott. "And he's in my refrigerator eating my groceries, and he's stashing his junk at my apartment, and he's sleeping in my bed, and he's basically living off me and anyone else he can find."

"But I thought you and he lived together", Megan said.

"So did I", Scott admitted, surprised at his own bitterness. "But I've learned over the past six months that Greg doesn't really live anywhere—he flits and perches where he chooses. When we started out, he talked a good line about setting up a home and sharing our lives and all that. The reality has been very different. I've barely seen him in six weeks. I have no idea where he's spent the last five nights. Something has to change, and this is as good an opportunity as any to make that happen."

"I . . . I don't know, Scott", Megan said hesitantly.

"I do", Scott said confidently. "Now, you get going home. Pacify Diane. Try to focus on the present, not what dire things might happen. You still have a job. This may still blow over. Trust me. And please remember your promise—don't make any irreversible decisions until you've talked to me. Okay?"

"Okay", Megan agreed, then gripped his arm. "Scott, you're such a good friend. It means so much that you're willing to help me."

"I haven't done anything yet", Scott replied.

Even in her distress, Megan managed the ghost of a sly smile. "Oh, I don't know about that", she said.

It had been a long time since Scott had blushed.

Scott had much to ponder as he drove home. What he was considering was a big step, and part of him was second-guessing what he'd said. Maybe he should have played the health insurance business closer to his chest for now, taking a bit more time to research and ponder. But when he remembered how distressed and desperate Megan had been, he knew that he'd had to reassure her. He couldn't just leave her without any help.

Also, Scott had been thinking about his situation with Greg for a while and was wondering if it was time for a change. Scott would have to be the instigator, since there was no chance that Greg would voluntarily leave such a cushy arrangement. Well, if Megan's crisis served to precipitate overdue changes in Scott's relationship with Greg, so be it. Now the challenge lay in locating Greg.

That part turned out to be simpler than Scott had anticipated. As soon as he entered the apartment, he knew something was different—more debris on the kitchen counter was the big clue. A glance in the bedroom confirmed his suspicions: there lay Greg, sprawled fully clad across the bed, hard out.

Scott rolled his eyes as he closed the bedroom door. A crashed Greg this early in the evening meant he was drunk or stoned or both. He would wake up later and want to be fed and then start agitating for them to run up to the city to spend the night hitting clubs. Greg wasn't going to want to talk seriously, and Scott toyed with the idea of putting off the discussion. He decided to play it by ear and see how things looked when Greg finally slept it off. Hopefully Greg wouldn't puke all over the bed.

Figuring he was in for a long night no matter how things unfolded, Scott decided to stretch out on the sofa to get what sleep he could. He dropped off quickly.

Scott was back in the dream again, and a small part of him knew he was back in the dream, but it didn't matter. It had to play out, as it always played out.

Scott was five again, back in his little bedroom, the one with the wallpaper that had the cowboys and horses on it. But he was running out of the room, down the short hall, toward the kitchen, toward where the yelling was.

There they were, in the kitchen, under the overhead light that had a bulb like a circle and always flickered. Mom was sitting at the table while Dad was standing by the door, in front of the refrigerator. Baby Lisa was in her little bouncy seat on the floor by Mom's feet.

Mom was crying and crying and pleading. Dad was yelling things at Mom, pointing at her and waving his arms. Lisa was squalling in panic at all the noise, squalling and squalling, but nobody was attending to her.

Scott wanted to cry too, but he couldn't—he had to stop Mom and Dad from yelling. "Please stop crying, Mom", Scott pleaded, patting her arm, but it was like he wasn't there. She kept on sobbing and pleading and reaching out toward Dad.

"Dad, Dad!" Scott turned toward his father, who was still yelling. "Please don't yell, Dad. You're upsetting the baby. Please don't yell, Dad. The baby's crying!" But Dad paid him no attention.

Scott dashed over and knelt beside Lisa, precious little Lisa, to whom he loved to sing. Tears streamed down his face because she was so distressed. "Don't cry, baby, don't cry", he said, trying to soothe her. "It'll be all right. Here's your pacifier. Please don't cry." He found her pacifier amid her blankets and tried to put it in her mouth to calm her, but she refused to take it and just cried the more.

Mom and Dad were still yelling, louder and louder. "Please stop!" cried Scott. "Please stop. You're making the baby cry. Please stop!" But they didn't stop, and Lisa still cried, no matter how he tried to comfort her.

Then Dad's voice thundered, as it always did. "I'm outta here!" The door slammed. Mom's crying rose to a wail, and poor Lisa shrieked in terror.

"Dad!" Scott called, running to the door and throwing it open. "Don't go, Dad! Don't go! Come back! Come back!" But all he could see was Dad's broad back as he stomped down the walk to the road, where he got into his red car and drove away. "Come back, Dad!" Scott called futilely after the car.

Scott longed to run down the walk, to run after Dad and catch him and bring him back. But Mom was still sobbing and Lisa was howling and he had to do what he could for them. He ran back to the table, where Mom had buried her head in her arms and was sobbing her heart out.

"Don't cry, Mom", Scott said, trying to soothe her. He stroked her hair as she liked him to. "Please don't cry, Mom", he pleaded. "You're making the baby cry." But Mom kept crying, and Scott didn't know what to do. He knelt by Lisa, who was now red faced with wailing, and patted her tummy while he fished for her pacifier again.

"There, there", Scott said, just like Mom did, though he never understood what that meant. "Don't cry, baby; I'm right here." Again he tried to give her the pacifier, but she still wouldn't take it— her little mouth was wide open in constant crying. "I'd pick you up and rock you, but Mom doesn't want me to", he explained. He kept patting her tummy with one hand while he rocked the chair with the other, but he couldn't make the chair rock smoothly like Mom could do with her foot. His attempts were bumpy and jerky and did nothing to calm Lisa. He was crying himself, the tears salty on his lips, but still he tried to quiet her.

"It's not helping, Mom", Scott sobbed. "I can't make her stop crying. Can you help, Mom?" He turned to see his mom still weeping uncontrollably, her head on her arms on the table.

"Don't cry, Mom", Scott said, more distressed than ever. "Here, let me get you some orange juice. How'd that be? A nice glass of orange juice?" That was what Mom gave him when he was upset. It had to help. He ran to the refrigerator, hoping there'd be a pitcher of juice.

There was, and Scott carried it to the table. Still Mom cried and the baby cried while he fetched a cup. A cup of orange juice for Mom—that would surely help. That would stop her crying. He put the cup on the table and started pouring, but the pitcher was heavy and unwieldy.

Oh no! The pitcher slipped and knocked the cup over, spilling juice everywhere. Now the juice was spreading across the table and dripping on the floor. Scott was in a panic. "I'll get it, Mom! Don't worry, I'll get it!" he cried. He ran to get paper towels, but there weren't any—only the bare brown tube on the holder. The dishrag! "I'm coming, Mom!" he called, jumping up to grab the rag from where it hung over the sink. "Don't worry! I'll wipe it up! I'll wipe it all up!" He tried to wipe up the orange juice with the rag, but the rag was too dry—the juice just spread around. The rag needed to be damp to wipe up the orange juice, but he couldn't reach the sink without the step stool, and Mom needed to set that up.

"I'll clean it up, Mom, I promise. I'm sorry I was careless, but I'll clean it up, I promise, I promise", Scott assured her as he wiped frantically. But nothing helped—the orange juice was still spreading and the rag wouldn't wipe it up and the baby wouldn't stop crying and Mom wouldn't stop sobbing and Dad wouldn't come back. If he could just get the orange juice wiped up, everything would be all right. Mom would stop crying and she'd comfort Lisa, and Dad would come back and they'd play soccer in the yard again. But the rag wouldn't work, and the orange juice wouldn't wipe up. It kept spreading and spreading . . .

"Hey!" Someone was calling, and kicking his foot. "Hey!" A couple more kicks.

"Cut it out", Scott complained groggily, coming up through the fog of sleep and trying to pull his foot out of range. Looking up from where he lay on the couch, Scott saw Greg standing at the end of it, his foot poised for another kick.

"Oh, it's you", Scott grumbled, groping for his phone. Quarter to eleven—great.

"Who were you expecting?" Greg asked. "Yeah, it's me. You got anything to eat around here?"

"Sure", Scott groaned, throwing his arm over his eyes. "Eggs and bread in the fridge, butter on a plate on the counter. I think there's some juice, but any milk is probably bad."

"C'mon", Greg said, giving Scott's foot another kick. "What the hell am I supposed to do with that?"

"What the hell am *I* supposed to do with it?" Scott snarled back. His distress at having that dream again was aggravated by having been awakened so rudely, so he was in no mood for Greg's foolishness.

"What? Aren't you the one with all the culinary skills?" Greg asked.

"All right, all right", Scott groused, throwing himself off the couch and heading for the kitchen. Tonight was going to be difficult enough; there was no need to die on this hill.

"You know how much I love your omelets", Greg said in a wheedling voice, as if flattery would compensate for his lack of consideration. Scott said nothing but started pulling ingredients out of the refrigerator. He was a little hungry but dismissed the idea of making himself something. There was no way he was sitting down to eat with Greg.

"So," Greg said, grabbing a beer and sitting down at the bar, "what have you been doing lately?"

"Working", Scott replied shortly. "At my job. The one with the paycheck."

"Ooh, somebody's out of sorts." Greg took a swig from his beer. Again Scott said nothing—he wasn't going to rise to that. "Aren't you going to ask me what I've been doing?"

"No", Scott replied, pouring the eggs into the pan and putting some toast down.

"Why not?" Greg goaded.

"Because I already know the answer."

"Shows what you know, bitch", Greg said. "As it happens, I've made several new contacts and anticipate coordinating many shipments in the near future."

Greg was a freelance import-export broker, though Scott had never grasped how such a party earned money. Greg was vague about it, though he spoke often of prospects and connections and leads. Scott had idly wondered if this was euphemistic talk for something illegal but decided that deliberate, planned crime would be too hard for Greg. Incidental lawbreaking, certainly, but systematically staying ahead of the law would be too much like work.

"Well, that's great", Scott said.

"Sure as hell is", Greg affirmed. "In celebration of which, I was thinking we could go up to the city tonight to catch a show or something."

Here it came. "Your credit card or mine?" Scott asked tartly.

"Oh man, don't start that", Greg whined. "I just told you that I'm *anticipating* the jobs—they're not in yet."

"Then maybe we should *anticipate* the celebration until they do come in", Scott suggested, putting the omelet and toast on the table.

"You got any hot sauce?" Greg asked, tucking into the food. Scott rolled his eyes, fetched the sauce from the cupboard, and slammed it on the table. "So, I take it that's a no?"

"Damn it, Greg, I've been working like a dog on a new project, and I've had . . . other concerns as well. I'm just a little wrung out", Scott replied, starting to clean up.

"Y'know, man, I remember you when you used to be fun", Greg said through a generous mouthful of eggs.

"I remember you when you used to be around", Scott snapped. "In fact, I remember when you promised to help pay for this place."

"Why is it always about the money with you?" Greg snarled back. "You're the one with the regular job. You have no idea how hard it is to freelance."

Scott could think of several retorts to this but decided that this evening wasn't going to get any easier, so he may as well deliver the news now. A hollow feeling filled his gut—he hated conflict, especially with people like Greg. But he thought of Megan's desperate situation and steeled himself.

"Well, I'm glad to hear of your impending commercial success, because you're going to need it", Scott said firmly.

"What's that supposed to mean?" Greg asked suspiciously.

"I'm going to have to drop you from my medical insurance", Scott announced.

"Bitch!" Greg erupted. "Why? What am I going to do for coverage?"

"Maybe buy it like everybody else", Scott suggested. "Or get a job with benefits."

"But . . . do you have any idea how much that *costs*?" Greg ranted. "I can't afford that! You cheap bastard! Why are you doing this to me?"

Things went downhill from there, with shouting and cursing and stamping. Scott had known that Greg could be vile and vindictive, but he'd never seen him this bad. For his part, Scott took a dark pleasure in unloading over half a year's frustration and resentment over Greg's treatment of him. What remained of their relationship was shredded in a frenzy of screaming and door slamming, to the point that the downstairs neighbors hammered on the ceiling with a broom handle.

Finally Greg stormed out, having stuffed what he could carry in a duffel, swearing to return for the rest of his gear and threatening dire consequences if anything happened to it. Scott closed the door with relief, his pulse hammering and his insides trembling. At least that was over.

Scott went into the bedroom to find the sheets twisted and pulled out by Greg's thrashing about. Well, he wouldn't have to put up with that anymore. He would have to strip the bed and wash the sheets, and he wasn't up to that tonight. Not that it mattered. With the adrenaline pumping through his system, he wouldn't be getting any sleep for hours. Wearily he dragged out his laptop and fired it up. May as well get some work done.

Chapter Six

"All right, then. Thank you. And you'll send me the link to those rate charts? Great—thanks again." Scott hung up and furrowed his brow. That certainly complicated matters. He'd have to figure out how to break this to Megan, but first he'd have to come up with options to offer when he did.

The lady at the human resources firm had been quite helpful. Scott never liked calling 800 numbers if he could help it, but the firm's website didn't have the details he needed. Also, every plan had its own peculiarities, so he needed to talk to a person who could interpret the contract. Dropping Greg from his coverage had been simple enough, but adding Megan was a bit more complex, for a couple of reasons. The easier part was the maternity rider. He hadn't even known that maternity coverage cost extra, and the rep had hinted that it was a lot extra. As for the more difficult part . . .

His e-mail chimed. There was the message with the link to the rate schedules. He clicked through and gave a whistle—the cost was substantial. Even without Greg dragging on his finances, it was going to be a feat to cover it. But first he had to figure a way around the other obstacle.

At lunchtime, Scott called Megan to check in. He was calling more than texting recently because he liked to get a read on her voice. Megan's moods were swinging all over these days. Some days she seemed convinced the world was going to end; other days she was as cheery as ever. Scott knew that stress played a part in this, but his research told him that pregnancy brought fierce hormonal swings as well.

"Hey", Scott said when she picked up. "How are you doing?"

"Great!" Megan answered. Apparently this was one of the better days. "I feel very productive today."

"Feeling better, then? Less nauseated?" Scott asked.

"I found a suggestion online for a mixture of a B vitamin and an over-the-counter sleep aid that really helps. I still feel queasy, but I can function", Megan explained. "The sleepiness has tapered off a little too. But I'm still in the bathroom every twenty minutes."

"Sleep aid?" Scott asked. "Is that safe? Aren't you supposed to be careful with drugs during pregnancy?"

"This is safe", Megan assured him. "It's a very mild drug, and you only take half a pill at a time."

"Ah." Scott let the matter drop. "How are things at home?"

Megan's voice dropped to a whisper. "Not too bad. Not good, but not horrible. Diane still drops the occasional hint and is away a lot more, but she's not being as hostile as she was for a few days there. It's like she's on a slow simmer now. Maybe she's just waiting for me to come around."

Scott grimaced. Of all the factors in this complex situation, Diane's passive-aggressive treatment of Megan concerned him the most. He could tell that Megan was concerned too, which was why she and Scott weren't meeting for lunches anymore. She didn't know which of her coworkers might be in contact with Diane, so she didn't want to risk being seen with Scott anywhere near her workplace.

"Also," Megan whispered, "we're not, ah, sleeping together anymore."

"Um—okay," Scott fumbled not knowing what to say about that. "Listen, I've been doing some investigating about the benefits. I've dropped Greg from the policy, but the change will take a pay cycle to take effect, so that's another week or so."

"Oh Scott", Megan replied. "That's sweet of you, but I'm hoping that won't be necessary."

"Really? How so?" Scott asked.

"I'm hoping all this will just blow over. I seem to be back on my feet these days. People are put on probation all the time. There's an automatic reevaluation after ninety days. I'm hoping I'll be back in the swing by then and be reinstated with full benefits."

"That'd be great", Scott admitted. "But what about the possible layoffs?"

"Oh, you know workplaces, Scott", Megan replied. "There are always rumors of layoffs floating about, and most of the time they're false."

46

"Well ... okay", Scott said. He didn't know how much of this outlook reflected actual reality, how much was Megan's current mood, and how much was Megan trying to convince herself. "I hope you're right. But just in case, I've checked into adding you to the policy. It shouldn't be a problem, provided we address a few details and formalities."

"Thanks so much, Scott", Megan said. "Let's see how things play out here before you put any more work into it. Hopefully none of this will prove necessary. If it does, we can deal with the details and formalities then. Oops—got to go!"

"Bye!" Scott hung up, wondering how she would react when she heard what some of those details and formalities were.

A few weeks passed, with the new project at work soaking up most of his attention. Management seemed close to approving it but kept asking for last-minute details and minor changes. Scott kept in touch with Megan every few days, which was helpful for learning about Megan's emotional state on a given day (which, of course, varied widely) but nearly useless for getting solid information on the actual state of affairs at home. The only thing he could glean was that Diane was getting sharper and more distant. Megan pretended this meant nothing. Scott wasn't so sure.

The state of uncertainty ended dramatically at the close of the month. The last workday was a Friday. Scott got a text from Megan midmorning.

"Lunch? 11?"

This startled Scott. A text? About a lunch date? So early? He was tempted to call her right then but decided against it. If she'd texted, there must be some reason she didn't want to talk. He texted back to confirm and name the restaurant.

Unusually, Megan was already there when Scott arrived. He sat down across from her and almost gasped. She was pale, and her eyes were sharp with panic. She grasped his hand as if it were a lifeline.

"Scott", she nearly cried.

"Megan, what's wrong?"

She said nothing but reached into her purse and withdrew two items, which she laid on the table. One was a slip of paper that looked official, and the other was a plastic bag that contained what looked like little scraps of paper.

Scott picked up the slip of paper, looked it over, and nodded grimly. It was a layoff notice, effective the end of the year.

"So, it happened after all?" Scott asked.

Megan nodded. "They have to give us sixty days' notice, so there it is. Lots of us got them."

"And what's this?" Scott picked up the bag and opened it. It did contain scraps of paper, though there was something heavy toward the bottom. Megan gave a small, choked cry.

"It's ... it's our wedding certificate. When I got up this morning, Diane was already gone—but she'd left the certificate on the kitchen table, torn to shreds, with ... with her ring."

Scott pulled the gold band out of the bag and examined it while he pondered these developments. "So ... she's repudiated you."

"She's what?"

"Repudiated. It was how divorce was handled in some ancient cultures, and still is in some places in the world. The husband would divorce the wife by simply telling her they're no longer married. He'd sometimes do it in a public place like a town square, so there'd be witnesses."

"So," Megan asked, as if wanting confirmation of something she'd already suspected, "this is a divorce?"

"I don't know how else to interpret it", Scott acknowledged. "Megan, I'm sorry. Maybe you could talk to her—"

"No!" Megan interrupted sharply. "I don't want to talk to her. I don't want to be near her. Scott, the last few days have been terrifying. Diane has been strange, glaring at me and muttering. I've tried to keep out of her sight. Of course, if she's been planning this, that explains some of it, but—"

"That bitch", Scott interrupted. He'd been only half listening to Megan as he stared off into space and pondered.

"Pardon?" Megan asked.

"That cruel, scheming bitch", Scott continued. "Megan, it's no coincidence, these two events happening on the same day." He patted the slip and the bag. "She knew the layoffs were coming, and timed her repudiation to coincide with them."

Megan's hand flew to her mouth. "I hadn't even thought of that. I was in such shock when I got to work that I thought it was just a piece of bad luck."

"I'm guessing she was going for maximum effect, to force you into something", Scott said.

Megan looked around with panicked eyes. "I only know one thing she's trying to force me into ... but Scott, what can I do? Where can I go?"

"Well," Scott said, gesturing at the items on the table, "you've just lost your two big ties to the area. Do you have any reason to stick around? Is there anywhere you could go, any family to return to?"

Megan shook her head. "There's only my mother, down in Phoenix. She ... threw me out when I told her what I was. Told me never to come back."

"No siblings? Aunts or uncles? Grandparents?"

"None that I know of", Megan answered, looking aside and sniffing. "I never knew my grandparents. They'd thrown my mom out in her time. All I know of them is that they live somewhere in New England."

Well ... that certainly limited the alternatives. Had circumstances been otherwise, Scott would have suggested Megan make a completely clean start—move to a new city, get a new job, essentially reboot herself. But she could hardly do that while expecting a baby.

With a chill Scott realized that Diane's repudiation had removed the biggest reason for Megan's pregnancy. The baby had always been Diane's idea. He was sure that the same point had occurred to Megan—or had it? If he was going to help Megan evaluate options, shouldn't he point that out?

Scott looked at Megan, who was trembling with the trauma of the day. She was white as a sheet, and her eyes were darting every which way. He couldn't abandon her. He couldn't just walk away. Suggesting that she pack off to a strange city to rebuild her life from scratch was hardly better. Hell, she'd probably fall into the clutches of another Diane. No, he couldn't forsake her in her need. Abruptly he made a decision. Pulling out his phone, he started typing up a message to the office.

"Here's what's going to happen", Scott said with brisk authority. "I'm not going back to work this afternoon."

"You're not?"

"No—and neither are you", Scott replied firmly.

49

"Scott, I have projects I'm in the middle of", Megan began, but Scott interrupted her.

"What are they going to do—fire you? Megan, I'd bet that half the people who got notices this morning won't be coming back from lunch today. They have important arrangements to make—as do you."

"I do?" Megan asked.

"Yes", Scott answered, taking her hands and holding them tightly. "We're going to go to your condo, get your gear, and move you in with me."

Megan's mouth flew open. "Scott, I couldn't ask that of you!"

"You keep saying that", Scott said with a smile. "You're not asking. I'm offering. In fact, I'm insisting. And besides, my dear Megan, my good friend—what else are you going to do? Go back and spend the night with Diane? Go to a hotel? Move onto the street?" He hated to put the screws to her like that, but she needed to see reason.

"But Scott," Megan stammered, "I . . . I just can't. You . . . I mean . . . it wouldn't be—"

"Wouldn't be what? Proper?" Scott asked, rather enjoying this part. "What are you worried about? What the neighbors might think? My intentions toward you? That I might get you pregnant?" This last was said in a whisper as he leaned forward and grinned wickedly.

"That's not it", Megan protested weakly, a little pink coloring her cheeks.

"The way I see it, it's simple", Scott pressed. "You're a roommate. I've had lots of roommates over the years and have by no means shared a bed with them all. You're in immediate need of a place to live; I have a spare room. What's the problem?"

"I . . . it's so . . ." Megan protested weakly, trailing off into muttering about presuming on generosity.

"If you'd like to help with household expenses, you're more than welcome to", Scott assured her. "In fact, it would be a pleasant change. Besides, this would be a temporary arrangement, right? Just until you get back on your feet."

That seemed to mollify Megan, and they started working through their lunches discussing practical details. Scott was quietly glad this was working out—having Megan nearby would give him time to work on her, to soften her up for the big surprise he was going to have to spring. Not today, certainly, and probably not this week, but soon. Ironically, Diane's cruel stunt had made his job easier.

"Well, then", Scott said as they wrapped up lunch. He'd established that Megan had very few possessions to move, so no special arrangements were needed. He'd been willing to rent whatever resources they needed to move Megan, but she'd repeatedly assured him that the trunk of the Jetta would suffice. Scott wondered how anyone could own so little. "Is now a good time? If we can, we want to do this when Diane's not there. Is midday suitable?"

"I think so", Megan said hesitantly. "She's sometimes home early or leaves later in the morning, but I think she's usually at the kitchen about this time. Of course, I'm so rarely home in the middle of the day that she might come home for lunch regularly and I wouldn't know it."

"Let's do it right now", Scott said, seeing that Megan would dither all afternoon if allowed.

As they drove to the condo, Scott could see Megan grow increasingly apprehensive. She was gripping the armrest so tightly that her knuckles were white. Her breath was coming in ragged gasps, and she stared straight ahead as if dreading what awaited her.

"There ... there it is", Megan said, pointing out her building, quite unnecessarily, since Scott had already been there a few times. "Now, if only Diane is gone."

When they poked their heads through the door, all was quiet. "Whew!" Megan sighed in relief. "Seems she's out. Let's move quickly."

"Megan, aren't you overdoing things a bit?" Scott asked. "What are you so afraid of? It's only Diane, and I'm sure she's upset, but I'm here with you. Surely—"

"Hush", Megan said, laying her hand on his arm and looking about nervously, as if his words were unlucky. "You don't know Diane; you haven't seen her moods. If she were to come back now—*especially* if she were to come back and find you here with me—oh, which reminds me ..." Without a word of explanation, Megan dashed off to the kitchen, leaving Scott standing there. Mystified, he wandered across the living room and started down the hallway while Megan banged and clanked at something. He poked his head into the first room.

51

Scott was stunned. The room that had been set up as a tidy little nursery had been totally redone. Gone were the crib and the dresser and anything like baby furniture. Even the prints had been taken down—violently, it seemed in a couple of instances, to judge from the damaged paint. The pastel walls remained, but the room was now being used for storage, with stuff piled all over and things leaning against the walls without regard for the finish. In one corner was a pile of blankets with a pillow beside it. This mystified Scott, but as he stared and pondered, comprehension began to dawn. His jaw dropped and his eyes widened and his blood began to hammer in rage.

Just then Megan rejoined him. Scott pointed at the blanket pile. "Is that ... have you been sleeping *there*? Why, that bitch!"

"Leave it, Scott, leave it", Megan said, tugging at his arm. "Let's just get finished and get out of here." Grumbling in indignation, Scott let himself be led away.

Back in the bedroom, Megan threw a suitcase on the bed and handed Scott a garbage bag. "Please, everything in those bottom three drawers, in the bag." She began picking through the clothes in the closet, occasionally pulling an outfit from a hanger and throwing it into the suitcase. Scott did as he was told, piling handfuls of socks and underwear and exercise wear into the black bag. He tied the top shut and put it on the bed—pausing to wryly reflect that it had been a ten-minute encounter on that very bed that had engendered all this uproar. He was beginning to suspect that, when all was said and done, that brief interlude would cause even greater disturbance.

"Aren't all these clothes yours?" Scott asked, waving his hand at the bar still hung with numerous outfits. Megan was taking only about every eighth one.

Megan wrinkled her nose. "Technically, yes, but I hate them all. They're outfits Diane got for me. She'd spot them in stores as she passed, or online, and buy them because she thought I'd look good in them. She'd make me put them on when we went out or when she had friends over. I was like a life-sized doll she played dress-up with." Megan pitched another outfit into the suitcase and kept flicking through the hangers. "I hated it."

Within five minutes Megan had selected all the outfits she was taking. Scott stuffed them into the suitcase while Megan swept the bathroom for toiletries. Ten minutes later they were out the door, carrying all Megan's worldly goods in a medium-sized suitcase, a garbage bag, and a toiletries kit.

"Let's go, let's go", Megan urged as they pitched the luggage into the Jetta. Scott still wondered if perhaps she wasn't overdramatizing, but then he remembered the stripped nursery with the blanket pile in the corner.

Megan visibly relaxed as they drove out of the parking lot. "At least she didn't come home while we were there", she muttered to herself. "She'll be furious, of course, but we're—oh damn, I forgot to get them back out. Oh well, she'll find them. I didn't hide them that carefully."

"You hid something?" Scott asked.

"The knives", Megan said, nodding.

Scott turned slowly and stared at her in shock.

Back at his apartment, Scott was a little self-conscious ushering Megan into what was for him a normal living state but for a guest had to look like an untidy dorm room. Megan was polite enough about it, but she was clearly still reeling from the day's events. She sat numbly on the couch while Scott cleared junk out of the office.

"This is mostly Greg's stuff, which he'll be back for", Scott explained as he lugged a snowboard and a duffel of climbing gear to a corner of the living room. "Some of it's mine, though. I'm afraid I tended to use the office as a bit of a dumping ground. I'll have it cleaned right out, though. It'll be small, but it'll make a nice bedroom."

"I'm sure it'll be fine, Scott", Megan mumbled. Just then her phone chimed. Jumping with surprise, she pulled it out and glanced at the screen. "It's from Diane", she said in dismay.

Scott plucked the phone from her hand and shut it down without reading the message. "Whatever she's got to say, you don't need to hear. Action item for tomorrow: we both get new phone numbers."

The weekend was spent doing that and many other household errands, including a trip to the grocery store, where they rang up a bill five times Scott's usual amount. When he expressed amazement, Megan coolly informed him that the cart contained what she

53

considered the bare minimum stock for a properly equipped kitchen. Some quick online checking turned up several items of used furniture available at local addresses, so on Saturday afternoon Scott rented a small truck to pick up a bed, a dresser, and a mirror. At the end of the day Megan had a tidy little room.

Scott got his first taste of how different it was having Megan around when he was showering the next morning. There was something unusual that he couldn't quite put his finger on, so he looked carefully until he figured it out.

"Hey!" Scott called when he stepped out of the bathroom. "Did you clean in here?"

"Yup", Megan replied from the kitchen. "While you were out fetching furniture yesterday afternoon."

"Megan," Scott admonished, "you didn't have to clean my bathroom."

"Yes, I did", Megan shot back. "I'm going to be using it as much as you are—in fact, as a pregnant woman, rather more—and that place was gross. Have you ever cleaned in there?"

"I, ah ..." Scott stammered. Now that he considered it, he couldn't remember ever cleaning the bathroom.

"Thought so", Megan said. "No matter. Come on, breakfast is ready."

"Do I have time to get dressed?" Scott asked.

"Not if you want your breakfast hot", Megan replied. In the dining room was a properly set table, with a small vase of flowers and all manner of dishes set about.

"Megan," Scott said reprovingly, "I certainly don't expect you to make me meals while you live here."

"Good", Megan answered. "Because at this stage of pregnancy, half the time I can't stand the sight of food. I have to force myself to eat it and can't even think of preparing it. Those times you're on your own. But this was a good morning, so I got a little extravagant."

"Oh ... well, that's great", Scott replied. "What have we here?"

"Cheese strata made with chorizo sausage, cranberry muffins, cantaloupe, orange-papaya juice, and Kona coffee. *Bon appétit!*"

Scott almost swooned.

It was not only the best breakfast but the best meal of any kind he'd had since he could remember. He and Megan laughed and chatted lightly, enjoying the brief reprieve from their trials. As they conversed, Scott found himself increasingly impressed with Megan's resilience. To his thinking, anyone who'd been hammered with the kind of traumas she'd endured over the past weeks had every right to curl up in a corner and whimper. Yet here she was, cooking breakfast, helping tidy up the house, cleaning the bathroom, and chatting gaily as if she hadn't a concern in the world.

Of course, Megan's eyes betrayed her. Scott could see that they were shadowed with fear and uncertainty. That was understandable—her future had very few options, and far more questions than answers. Well, this morning looked like a good time for dealing with some of those questions. It would call for finesse and tact—not so much in explaining the problem as in getting her on board with the solution he was going to suggest. Unfortunately, finesse and tact had never been his strong suits.

"Well," Scott said, standing up, "how about this: I clean up and then get some clothes on while you relax in the living room. Then I'll come in with more of this fantastic coffee, and we can tie down a few details we need to cover."

"A few details?" Megan asked, instantly wary. "What kind of details? Should I be worried?"

"Of course you should", Scott said, winking at her as he started clearing the table. "Anytime I start my scheming, you should start worrying."

"Ooh", Megan said, grinning and raising her eyebrows in mock fear, but Scott could see that she was still apprehensive.

Presently Scott was joining her with his laptop case, from which he pulled a manila folder. He extricated some printouts and handed them to Megan, being careful to leave behind the ones with the rate charts. It wouldn't do to let her see those.

"Now, about this coverage", Scott began, gesturing to his set of printouts. "I talked to our human resources people—"

"HR people?" Megan asked. "Isn't your firm a bit small to have an HR department?"

"We are—we contract with one of those HR services firms", Scott explained. "But they have a help desk, and I got a good rep who explained it all to me. It turns out that I can enroll you under my policy, but only under certain circumstances."

"What circumstances?" Megan asked. "I thought you could just designate whomever—you did with Greg."

"I thought so too, and that's the strange part", Scott replied. "Greg was covered under the same-sex partner benefits provision, which is on page five. I can add any man to the policy, or you could add any woman. But in my case, because you're a woman—or if you wished to add a man—then these conditions apply."

Megan looked puzzled. "But ... that's stupid", she protested. "If you can add someone, why can't you add anyone you like?"

"Well, that's what I think", Scott said. "And the HR rep agrees, but she doesn't make the policy, she just explains it."

"Okay", Megan conceded, her face falling. "What are these conditions? I suppose they'll mean I can't be covered."

"No, they don't", Scott encouraged her. "I can add any woman so long as she's an immediate blood relative. So I could add my mother. If the baby you're carrying is a girl, I could add her. I could add my sister—"

"You have a sister? I didn't know that", Megan interrupted. "What's her name?"

"Lisa", Scott answered. "She's about your age, maybe a little younger."

"Sweet! Do you talk to her often? If I had a sister, I'd talk to her every day."

Scott was taken aback by the change of subject. "No, I ... I don't talk to her at all." His throat was suddenly constricting, and he looked aside to blink. "I don't have ... her number. I think she's living somewhere in Louisiana these days."

An awkward silence fell for a minute. "I'm sorry, Scott", Megan said with just the right amount of sympathy. There was a little more silence while Scott blinked a bit more. Then he cleared his throat and continued.

"So ... about these benefits", Scott went on. "There's absolutely no problem adding you to the policy if you're an immediate blood relative."

"Which I'm not", Megan said with resignation.

"But you could become one", Scott ventured tentatively, looking sideways at Megan.

"And how could I—" Megan began, looking sharply at him. Catching his eyes, she furrowed her brows. Then her eyes widened as realization dawned. "Oh no, Scott ... don't tell me."

"I'm afraid so", Scott said with a shrug. "If we were married, coverage wouldn't be a problem. In fact, it would be automatic unless I specifically chose otherwise."

"But ... but ..." Megan stammered. "*Scott!*"

"I understand this is a big step to consider—" Scott began.

"Big step?" Megan interrupted, incredulous. "Scott, this is *marriage* we're talking about!"

"Please, Megan, calm down and listen to me", Scott reassured her. "I'm not suggesting we do anything but go through a formality to satisfy some policy requirements. Other than that, it doesn't have to mean anything."

"Scott, it's marriage", Megan replied. "It always means *something*."

"I know," Scott said, "but can't it mean what we want it to mean? I know who you are and I respect that, as you know who I am and respect me. We could get married for the sake of getting you under my coverage, both of us understanding that it means nothing beyond that: no personal bonds, no changes of lives and identities, nothing beyond a legal formality."

"I don't know, Scott", Megan replied, shaking her head. But Scott could see that she was wavering. He'd have to tread cautiously, making his points subtly.

"I understand your hesitance, believe me", Scott continued. "And please don't think I'm trying to talk you into this. I'm just laying out the options and making clear what I'm willing to do to get you covered.

"The way I see it, we're already doing most of it. We're living in the same place, we're going to be sharing financial obligations—hell, we even have a baby on the way. None of that has changed the fact that we're gay, nor will it. We're both doing this voluntarily and are equally free to walk out the door at any time. We could do this marriage thing in the same spirit. Nothing would change, except the barrier to your coverage would be removed. I certainly wouldn't be expecting any 'marital privileges'. Nobody would even have to know!"

"Except that marriage records are public", Megan pointed out.

"Actually, I checked that out", Scott replied somewhat smugly. "We can get a confidential license for a minor additional fee. Besides, when was the last time that anyone you knew wandered down to the courthouse to peruse the marriage licenses?"

"There is that", Megan acknowledged. She glanced down at the printout in her hand and was quiet for a minute. "I understand what you're saying, Scott, and it makes a lot of sense. But you have to admit, it's a big step."

"I do admit that, freely", Scott replied. "Though it's not as big a step as it once was. We can get married understanding that the minute either of us wants out for any reason, we just hit the legal documents website, download the divorce papers, sign 'em, and walk away."

"That sounds kind of callous", Megan said.

"Who cares?" Scott said with a shrug. "There's nothing romantic about this. We're talking about a rational decision by two adults in response to an administrative policy. If the policy were different, we wouldn't be having this discussion. We could try contesting the policy and agitating for change, but that would take a long time and would drag a lot of things into the open that we might want kept quiet. Or we could get married to accommodate the policy, with a mutual understanding from the outset of what we mean by 'being married'. I'd even put it in writing, if that would make you more comfortable."

"No!" Megan said with surprising sharpness. "I'm tired of having such personal matters tied up in legal terms and threats of court action. I trust you, Scott, whatever we end up doing, and I trust that you will keep your word and deal with me with integrity."

"I, um ... thanks", Scott stumbled. "Again, please don't feel like I'm trying to pressure you into this. I'm willing to do it, under any conditions you're comfortable with, but the choice is entirely yours. My only interest is in getting you covered, and this is the only path that I can see right now. You think it over and decide what's best for you. Whatever that turns out to be, I'm here to help."

"I know you are, Scott", Megan said. Suddenly she leaned over and kissed him on the cheek, then burst into tears and buried her face in her hands. "I'm sorry, I'm sorry", she sobbed to a mystified Scott.

"Please know how much I appreciate all you've done for me ... for us. It's been a difficult few days, and this all is just ... a lot."

"I understand", Scott said consolingly, putting an arm around her shoulders and giving her a hug. "You take all the time you need to think it over. Then let me know what you decide."

"Okay", Megan said, and sniffed quietly. Scott picked up his stuff and eased out of the room.

It was a subdued day for both of them. Scott tried to keep out of Megan's way, giving her plenty of space to think. He even took a long walk so she could have the apartment to herself. For her part, Megan took a few naps and spent a lot of time sitting in the corner of the living room, sipping tea and thinking.

Scott picked up some Chinese food for dinner. After a subdued meal of chicken subgum and fried rice, Megan set her plate aside and looked squarely at him.

"Well, Scott, I've made my decision", she announced.

"We don't need to decide this today", Scott countered. "There's plenty—"

"I know, but I've thought it over as much as I need to", Megan interjected. "I know myself, and I could go round and round the topic for weeks and keep coming back to the same place. Let's do it, as you've described it. A marriage in form only. What would you call it?"

"A 'technical marriage' suits me just fine. No change in our personal relationship or living arrangements—just a piece of paper that gets you onto my policy", Scott replied. "Again, I'd be happy to put something in writing."

"Thanks, but no, Scott", Megan said. "I trust you to be as good as your word, and if we need to clarify anything, I trust you to talk it over in good faith. You're a good friend, Scott." She extended her hand across the table.

"Thanks", Scott replied, taking her hand warmly. "You're a good friend yourself—about the best one I have right now."

"You're the only one *I* have right now", Megan admitted.

Chapter Seven

The county clerk's website made it easy to get a marriage license, even allowing them to dispatch some of the preliminaries online. They took a long lunch on Tuesday to drive to the county offices. As they waited their turn, Megan looked over their application.

"Hey", she said. "It says here your first name is Joseph."

"It is", Scott replied. "Scott is my middle name. I go by J. Scott Kyle."

"Hmm", Megan mused. Then again after a minute, "Hmm."

"What?" Scott asked.

"Just thinking how strange it is that I'm carrying your baby and am about to marry you, and I've only just learned your first name."

"You had no cause to learn it—" Scott began, but just then they were called in. The clerk's assistant, who would perform the ceremony, asked if they had brought any witnesses. They hadn't, but one of the office workers was happy to serve.

"And have you the rings?" the assistant asked.

Scott and Megan looked at each other—they hadn't even thought of rings. Megan responded quickly.

"We're having them sized", she said. "The jeweler fell behind, and they weren't quite ready", she added in response to the assistant's puzzled look. Shrugging, the woman moved on with the ceremony— apparently missing rings were a relatively minor misstep in this business. Scott didn't listen much to the words being said—he was mostly looking at Megan and not knowing whether to be glad that she was such a quick thinker or disturbed that she was such a smooth liar.

"Do you, Joseph Scott Kyle, take this woman . . ." Scott's attention focused—his turn was coming up.

"I do", he said when expected.

"And do you, Megan Sarah Wilson, take this man . . ."

"I do", Megan said in her turn.

60

There was a bit more ceremonial reading, which concluded with, "I now pronounce you husband and wife. You may kiss one another."

Scott and Megan looked at each other—this was something else they should have anticipated.

"If . . . you wish", the assistant added tentatively.

Scott and Megan stepped close and gave each other a stage kiss. Then there were handshakes and smiles all around, and documents to be signed and witnessed and notarized. They were on their way within ten minutes, fresh marriage certificate in hand. As they walked to the car, Megan giggled.

"What?" Scott asked.

"That had to be the stiffest kiss that clerk has seen in her career", Megan said.

Scott grinned. "Maybe, but I get the impression she's seen a lot of odd things. Smooth work on handling the bit about the rings, by the way—I'd totally forgotten about that."

"Not that we want rings anyway, if we're keeping this quiet", Megan replied.

"Right", Scott said. "Rings aren't important. I took care of the important thing."

"Which was?"

"Having a copy of the marriage certificate sent to the HR firm. Once they have it, your coverage will start with the next pay cycle", Scott answered.

It took a while for Scott to adapt to having a regular roommate again, especially one of the opposite sex, but Megan tried to make it easy. He had to get accustomed to wearing at least his bathrobe whenever he left his bedroom, and closing the bathroom door. But most of the adjustments were pleasant ones, like getting used to the tidier state of the apartment, or the fact that the dishes got washed after every meal. Scott had never objected to doing such things, but Megan's presence encouraged him to do them more often. Having her around slowly transformed the apartment from a place that resembled a locker room to something more like a home.

Megan insisted on giving him funds to help with the household expenses, which Scott gladly accepted and then effectively turned right back over to her to purchase what she called "basics". Scott had never kept more than a few items in the kitchen—enough to make sandwiches or eggs or maybe a burger. Megan knew how to stock a kitchen properly, and Scott was now seeing flour and sugar and soups and all manner of staples on his shelves. This in turn meant that there was food to wake up and come home to, which meant Scott was doing fewer coffee-shop breakfasts and delivery dinners. He also ate better, since there were fresh fruits and vegetables about.

Scott's work was intensifying. Approval of the project hinged on some out-of-sight management machinations that Scott was left out of, but he and Marcus kept getting requests for niggling details or estimates of project times. Scott handled anything to do with engineering, while Marcus covered the project-management side. The demands were relentless and often kept Scott late at the office.

Megan headed off to her work every morning, though Scott sensed that she was dreading it more each day. Given the condition of California's economy, anyone who worked in property taxation and valuation was having a very stressful time. And it couldn't be easy to go to work knowing you would be out of a job in a couple of months. He didn't discover that there were other factors until nearly the end of the month.

It was the Wednesday before Thanksgiving, so there was no working late—in fact, most of Scott's coworkers had already bolted by the time he packed up and headed home. He came in the door to find the dinner ingredients laid out on the counter and a pan of water boiling furiously, but no Megan in the kitchen. Mystified, he turned off the stove and went looking.

"Megan?" Scott called. The bathroom door was open, and a quick glance established that Megan wasn't in her room. He found her in the living room, sitting hunched over at the end of the couch.

"Megan?" Scott asked again, but she seemed oblivious. As he drew closer, he could see that she was rocking slightly and striking herself on the arms and torso, all the while muttering. It wasn't until he was right beside her that he could discern what she was saying.

"Worthless. Useless. Meaningless. Insignificant", Megan was reciting in a sharp whisper, with each word striking herself another blow.

"Megan!" Scott said sharply, kneeling before her and grabbing her wrists. "Megan, look at me! Are you all right?"

Only then did Megan look up and notice him. "Scott?" she asked, like someone coming out of a stupor. "Scott? I ... I'm sorry. I was starting dinner and it all just came down on me, all around me."

"What came down, Megan?" Scott asked, releasing her wrists but taking her hands firmly. "Why were you hitting yourself?"

At Scott's prompting, the whole ugly business came tumbling out. Megan's past few weeks at work had been hell. Certain coworkers had been making snide comments, leaving rude notes, and generally making her life miserable. As Megan quietly told of the incidents, Scott fumed, wanting to go down to her office and knock some heads.

"I try to ignore it, I really do", Megan pleaded. "I try to keep my head down, mind my own business, and focus on my work. But you have no idea how petty and vindictive some women can be when they choose."

"This has to be Diane's influence", Scott said.

"That's what I figure too, but what can I do?" Megan cried. "And I've another month to go! I'm beginning to wonder if this pregnancy is worth it."

Scott inhaled carefully, not wanting to show his alarm. He had to move delicately. He put one hand on her shoulder and pushed gently until she lifted her head.

"One thing is certain", Scott assured her, fixing her eyes with his. "I'm not going to let you, or the baby, go through this alone. I promised to stay with you, and I will."

Megan gripped his hand and looked at him quizzically. "But why, Scott? Why would you?" she asked.

Scott was puzzled in his turn. "But ... because you're my friend. Friends stick by each other."

"They do?" Megan asked. "Then I guess I haven't had many friends."

"Well, you have one now", Scott answered firmly.

"But what can you *do*, Scott? You can't come to my office and stand beside me all day", Megan said.

"Probably a good thing too", Scott replied darkly. "Or I might be tempted to start knocking heads. Give me a little time—I'll think of something. Come on, I'll cook you dinner and we'll consider this situation."

"Oh, let me cook", Megan asked, hopping up from the couch. "I've already begun, and it helps me to have something to do."

Megan cooked and chatted with deceptive cheerfulness. Scott helped her and set the table, but mostly he was thinking furiously about how to help with her dilemma. He detested the idea of her heading off to a hostile environment every day but had to admit that he had no means of shielding her at her workplace. The solution he decided to propose was radical but the only one that came to mind. He'd have to finesse his proposal carefully to get her to consider it.

After dinner, Scott reached for his tablet and tapped up the calendar. "So," he said, "including next Monday, you've got what—four and a half workweeks to go?" He showed her the calendar.

"Pretty much", Megan confirmed, her face falling. "We work half a day on Christmas Eve and have Christmas off, but otherwise it's every workday between now and the end of the year."

"It's not that much time, really", Scott pointed out.

"It is when every day feels like an eternity", Megan said glumly.

"So ... why not quit?" Scott asked.

"Quit?" Megan looked at him, puzzled. "But ... I'm—"

"Getting laid off at the end of the month, I know", Scott interrupted. "I mean quit next Monday, when go you back. Hand in your notice, clean out your desk, and leave."

Megan looked shocked. "But ... I couldn't do that!"

"Why not?" Scott asked.

"Why ... what would I do for a living? I have expenses, and—"

"Do you?" Scott countered. "You live here. I've maintained this place without help since I moved in. It's nice to have you help with rent, but if you can't for one month, it's no problem—I'm no further behind than I was before."

"But ... Scott!" Megan exclaimed in dismay. "That's ... I couldn't ask that of you!"

"You're not asking", Scott again replied. "I'm offering. And I'm not suggesting that you loaf around. You were planning to start looking for another job, right?"

"Well, yes", Megan said.

"This would just get you started a month earlier", Scott reasoned. "You were already looking at an indefinite period of job hunting, weren't you? If I don't mind your starting a few weeks early, you certainly shouldn't."

"But … *Scott!*" Megan wailed. "I've got to contribute *something*. I mean … what about food? I've got to be able to help with that!"

Scott laughed. "My dear Megan, I greatly appreciate your desire to pull your own financial weight, especially in light of my recent experiences with other roommates. But with regard to your food-related expenses, be advised that your presence is saving me money."

"*Saving* you money?" Megan asked. "I've felt like I've been buying out the grocery store!"

"That's been mostly the money you've contributed", Scott said. "And though I haven't run the exact numbers, I do know that I'm spending substantially less to feed both of us than I was spending to feed just myself—and I'm eating better and healthier."

"How is that?" Megan asked.

"Because of you", Scott explained, sweeping his hand toward the full cupboards. "Your skill and diligence keeps good, fresh food on hand, so I can come home to proper meals. Hence, I spend less on eating out. Your help is saving me money."

Megan looked dazed—she hadn't thought of this. Scott pressed his point. "Your just being here and doing what you do anyway is contributing something. It isn't just a token contribution, either, but a tangible financial addtion."

"Really?" Megan looked skeptical.

"Trust me", Scott assured her. "As roommates, we make a great team. I do what I do best, you do what you do best, and we're both better off for it. Given that, there's no reason you have to go work in hell just to squeeze out a few more weeks of paltry pay."

"Really?" Megan asked again, incredulous.

"Really", Scott assured her. "Megan, you're my dear friend. Whatever upsets you upsets me. I can't tell you what to do, and I don't want to pressure you. But I can ask—please don't go back to that snake pit. Quit Monday, and we'll work out the details together."

Megan dropped her head and cuffed her eyes, but not quickly enough. Scott could see tears drip onto the table. "I … I'll think about it", she whispered.

"Fair enough", Scott said, standing and starting to clear the table. "No, no", he scolded as Megan started to rise. "You cooked; I'll clean up."

The next day they worked together to prepare a Thanksgiving feast that involved a chicken ("Even a small turkey would have been excessive", Megan explained), mashed potatoes, green beans, and a sweet-potato casserole that Scott swore he wouldn't touch because he hated sweet-potatoes (he ended up eating most of it). Afterward he ducked into his room for a bit while Megan busied herself with cleanup. He emerged a while later, a bit subdued.

"Just calling my mom", Scott explained in response to Megan's inquiring glance. "I try to touch base with her on major holidays."

"Ah", Megan replied. "Did you let her know about your latest acquisition?" Scott looked at her in complete befuddlement. "That technically she now has a daughter-in-law?"

"Oh, that", Scott said. "No, I try not to distract her with trivialities." He started putting away some of the clean dishes.

"So, how's she doing?" Megan asked casually.

"Who?" Scott replied.

"Your mother, of course", Megan responded.

"Oh. She's fine, she's fine. Always glad to hear from me. Say, how about tomorrow we take a drive up to Napa? It's a bit of a spin, but we could make a day trip of it. I don't want to go anywhere near a mall."

"Okay, but no wineries, at least for me", Megan replied. At Scott's puzzled look, she patted her stomach.

"Ah, yes", Scott replied. "Not good for the little one. Well, it's pretty country anyway."

All that weekend Scott tried to come up with activities to keep Megan distracted and engaged. He didn't want her to think too much about work and sink back into one of those fits. Megan didn't give any indication of what she was thinking or had decided and was cheerful company. But Monday morning came eventually. They both headed to their respective jobs, and though Scott tried to focus on his work, he was on edge all day. He resisted the temptation to text Megan and offer to meet for lunch, and she didn't contact him, so even as he headed home he had no idea how things had turned out.

Scott found out when he entered the apartment and found a box full of desk accoutrements sitting on the table. He grinned as he looked over the collection of mugs and paperweights, guessing what their presence meant.

"So?" he asked Megan as she came out of her room.

"I did it!" Megan said with a triumphant grin.

"Terrific!" Scott cried, sweeping her into a twirling hug. "I was so scared that you wouldn't believe me."

"I almost didn't", Megan admitted. "I went in this morning nearly convinced that I'd been exaggerating things, and they couldn't really be that bad. Well, they were worse than ever. Just before lunch I went in to my manager and told her I was leaving. She professed to be upset and said they needed me for the busy season, but I was firm. I didn't even tell anyone at closing time, when I just packed up my desk and walked out."

"Good for you!" Scott said, grinning. "Now, with that burden gone, we can get you set up for some serious job searching."

They spent the evening polishing Megan's résumé and posting it on websites. She was upbeat and excited and seemed convinced that it would be only a few weeks before she found other work. Scott, who was a bit more aware of the employment climate, wasn't so certain but didn't want to dampen her excitement. It was enough for them that she was out from under the cloud that had been over her for so long.

At Scott's office, shortly into December the long-awaited word came: the new project had been green-lighted. This was cause for an afternoon's raucous celebration followed by a week of sheer panic. The scope of the project was broad, but the timetable was almost hopelessly aggressive—a fully market-ready product, tested and documented, in nine months. A terribly tall order, given that they had to fully support their installed base, continue to sell the products they had, and hold the line on hiring (though Brian had once again assigned Scott another "assistant", who hopefully would be better than the last two).

Thus, between caring for Megan and her employment situation and the frantic pace of his own work, Scott was only dimly aware of the fact that his own social life had become nonexistent. Of course, part of that was financial. Even though he'd known it was coming, he'd winced when the payroll deductions for the maternity coverage kicked in. There went any spontaneous drives to LA for the weekend or the spur-of-the-moment trips to Tahoe. Even when he considered running up to the city, he found himself mentally estimating the cost, which was something he'd never done before.

Besides, the rhythm of Scott's life was changing. After an intense day of work, the prospect of spending the night cruising for action wasn't nearly as appealing as relaxing around the apartment with Megan, catching a movie or just reading. She was a homebody too, and though she would have said nothing about anything he'd chosen to do, he didn't like the thought of leaving her alone. It wasn't that he considered himself to be no longer gay; it was just that he'd found a contented place and saw no reason to leave.

It never occurred to Scott that anyone else would view things differently, or even think about him at all, until one day toward the end of December. There was a project-kickoff meeting at which Scott was going to make a very technical presentation. He spent a week of long days preparing, and on the morning of the meeting he dumped the finalized file to the public share, where it would be accessible from the conference-room workstation. He sent the handouts to the printer and headed to Marcus' office to go over a few final details.

When the meeting time came, Scott saw that well over half the company was there. As he sent his handouts around, he noticed that there seemed to be an inordinate amount of chatter and laughter from the rear of the conference room. The noise seemed to center around Jason, who was surrounded by a gang of his pals. Jason worked in quality assurance, and was queer as well. Scott had bumped into Jason a few times while out with Greg, and they got along cordially, but Scott didn't have much to do with him. Partly this was due to a decision Scott had made not to get involved with anyone from work, but mostly it was due to Jason's abrasive personality. He was a loud guy with a braying laugh and a frat-boy sense of humor that delighted in practical jokes and laughing at the embarrassment of others.

That trait was in full display as the meeting got rolling, with Jason and his cadre toning down, but not ceasing, the whispering and nudging. Scott thought that he had to be imagining that Jason kept shooting surreptitious glances in his direction. When Scott's time came, he saw that his file had already been loaded, so he clicked up the first slide and started explaining.

Scott was deep in the technical details and about five slides into the presentation when he advanced to the next slide. But when he gestured toward the screen to emphasize his point, he saw not the slide he'd been expecting but some sort of strange schematic diagram. Taken completely aback, he stared at this unknown graphic while Jason's strident voice called from the back of the room.

"Look, guys, it's a *breeder* reactor!"

About half the room dissolved into guffaws while the other half looked around in bewilderment. Scott glanced at Marcus, who wasn't laughing but looked a little sheepish. Scott clicked the remote again and saw the slide he'd prepared, and he tried to pick up again as if nothing had happened.

Not ten minutes later it happened again, except this time the strange slide seemed to involve horses. The room, particularly the rear half, erupted into peals of laughter while Scott stared at the slide, trying to figure out what it was about. It seemed to be a screen capture of a website page for a horse farm somewhere. Then he spotted it: right in the middle of the screen, right below the farm's logo and sandwiched between "Boarding" and "Training", was "Stud Services".

A chill gripped Scott's insides, and without thinking he glanced to the back of the room. Jason was staring right at him and grinning wickedly.

"All right, boys, let's keep it professional!" Brian hollered, and gestured for Scott to advance the slide. Scott fumbled and stammered, trying to recapture his train of thought, but his mind was racing. This hadn't been a slipup on his part—someone had gotten to the file and altered the slides.

Scott's temper was rising as he chewed on that problem, but he tried to refocus on his presentation, which was important to the business. Rattled though he was, he got back into the swing and was making good progress until, toward the end, another rogue slide popped up. This one was bluntly obvious—a screenshot of the Babies "R" Us website home page, complete with prominent logo. Being ready for something like this, Scott quickly clicked past the slide while the usual suspects roared with laughter. Brian scowled around the room while Scott tried to continue without breaking his stride. Scott could understand how confused Brian, and probably several others, must have been. To them it looked like nothing more than a few prank slides dropped in to break up a monotonous business meeting. They had no way of knowing that the slides were a coded message, an "outing" of a very different type.

Scott concluded the presentation quickly, almost on autopilot, his mind racing. Without asking for questions, he sat down while Brian prefaced Marcus' presentation with a few words about the workplace balance between fun and professionalism. Scott didn't even listen, instead staring at the ground and fuming. Shortly after Marcus began his presentation, Scott slipped out as unobtrusively as he could. He couldn't help glancing in Jason's direction as he left, and saw that Jason was watching him leave, still wearing that malicious smirk.

They knew. Despite his best efforts at secrecy, not only did they know that Megan was living with him, but they knew about her condition—and how she'd gotten that way. Essentially, they knew everything, and anything that Jason knew was by definition common knowledge. Scott sat at his desk, his heart sinking through the floor. The community down here on the peninsula was smaller than it was up in the city, so it was more close-knit. Everybody knew everybody else's business, and in this case, that meant that Scott and Megan's intimate concerns were the subject of gossip and the butt of jokes in bars and bedrooms all over the area. Scott strongly suspected Greg's involvement in this, but he couldn't discount that it was the work of Diane, who seemed to be at least as vindictive.

Those bastards! What business had they . . . ? Cold fear gripped Scott as he pondered the implications of this development. He realized that socially he was finished in the area. He wouldn't be able to show up at any clubs or other gay venues without being ridiculed mercilessly. He'd seen it happen to others—hell, he'd even participated in it from time to time. He vividly recalled instances when he'd joined in the general mockery of some poor schlep who'd transgressed a social protocol—sometimes in the person's presence. With dismay he realized that he'd never stopped to consider what it would be like to be the target of that kind of derision. Well, he was finding out now. He realized that today's events were certainly just a foretaste of what he could expect. Then he remembered that he'd gotten this job with Greg's assistance, so it was likely Greg had several contacts here.

Scott busied himself with trivial tasks until his team returned to their cubicles, the meeting over. Their demeanor was just a little too nonchalant to be convincing. They understood that he'd been publicly humiliated. Despite his workload, Scott packed up and headed home as soon as he could. On the drive, he pondered how far the effects of his actions had spread already and wondered how far they could ultimately go.

Chapter Eight

Despite his lingering distress over the incident at work, for Scott coming home was like entering an oasis of peace. Megan had spent the month adding homey and holiday touches to the apartment, even to a little Christmas tree in the corner. She almost always had something baking or simmering when he came home, and today was no exception.

"How was work?" Megan inquired, which was something she hardly ever asked. She seemed to sense that something was amiss.

"Please—don't get me started", Scott said. "What's that I smell?"

"Apple crisp", Megan said with a grin. "Trying a new recipe."

They had a subdued dinner, with Scott trying to keep the conversation on superficial topics and Megan figuring that was what he was doing, and trying not to pry. It was hard for Scott, since he was longing to express his frustration but didn't want to burden her.

Megan's December had been trying, though she'd tried to mask it with busyness and sunny optimism. Her initial euphoria of being free of her old job had faded in the face of the harsh realities of job prospecting. Her qualifications were scant, her restrictions (such as being dependent on public transportation) were severe, and almost nobody was hiring. She searched websites and posted her résumé and tried to tell herself that nobody hired just before the holidays anyway. But she could read the news as well as Scott could, and knew the economic prospects didn't look any better for the new year. So she pecked away at the job hunting and filled her spare hours with turning the bachelor apartment into a home—which, fortunately, Scott didn't mind.

Christmas Day itself was quiet and, for Scott, surprisingly enjoyable. Megan's culinary flair was in full display, the apartment was tastefully decorated, and the two of them were enjoyable company for each other. Scott couldn't help but compare the pleasant dinner he and Megan shared to the profane "holiday" parties that Greg had dragged him to the year before. After cleanup Scott again ducked into his bedroom with his phone, and came out a while later.

"Mom again", Scott explained.

"Ah", Megan said. "How is she?"

"Good, good", Scott replied. "A little sad—she was hoping to hear from Lisa today. She made light of it, but I could tell she was disappointed."

"Ah", Megan said again as Scott walked past her into the living room. She wanted to say more but judged that it wasn't a good time.

The next day they took a long drive out to Monterey and beyond, gas prices be hanged.

January came in a little drearier than usual, which may have had to do with Megan packing away the Christmas decorations. Scott was working with his head down—doing his job, attending meetings, exchanging e-mails—but not chumming around as he once had. He knew that he was being talked about, that his humiliation at the presentation was becoming an office legend. He could remember times he'd gleefully gossiped when such things had happened to others; now he knew that kind of gossip was circulating about him. He tried not to descend into paranoia. He tried not to think that every time some coworkers saw him coming and abruptly broke up their conversation, they had been talking about him. But there was no denying that his coworkers didn't seek him out for social engagements anymore, be it beers after work or weekend get-togethers. Those who spoke to him were brisk and professional, not familiar and friendly.

But Scott had worries beyond the workplace. One day he came home to find a dejected Megan lying sideways on the couch, staring blankly into nothing. Literature from a plastic tote bag lay scattered across the coffee table.

"Hey!" Scott said in greeting, but got no response. Stashing his gear and sitting down beside her, he grabbed some of the literature and asked, "Hey, what's all this?"

"Oh", Megan said, startled out of her lethargy. "Hi, Scott. I didn't hear you come in."

"Clearly", Scott replied. "What's this stuff?"

"Oh, literature. From the clinic. I had another prenatal appointment today, and they gave me a sackful", Megan explained.

"Was everything all right?" Scott asked, seized by an unexpected chill.

"Oh, everything was fine, health wise—baby's growing fine, I'm gaining the right amount of weight", Megan answered in a flat voice, still lying on the couch.

"Then ... what's going on?" Scott persisted.

Megan sighed. "It's just . . ." she started, then stopped and sat up, burying her face in her hands. Scott waited, toying with a pamphlet—she seemed to be trying to gather her thoughts.

"I've been wondering lately", Megan began again. "What's the purpose of this baby?"

"The purpose of the baby?" Scott asked, mystified.

"I mean ..." Megan said, struggling to articulate her thoughts. "Nothing against the baby, or you, but . . . this never was my idea, you know. It was Diane who wanted the baby. Insisted on it, in fact. Then she didn't want the baby; then she didn't want me. Almost everything in my life has changed, but this baby is still coming. So I've been wondering—to what purpose?"

Scott could see Megan's point but was still puzzled by the question. "Megan," he blurted out, "babies don't have a purpose—babies are the purpose."

Megan looked up at him with sharp annoyance. "What the hell does that mean?"

"I ..." Now it was Scott's turn to struggle to express himself. "I mean ... it's ... you never had any siblings, did you?"

"No", Megan replied. "What does that have to do with anything?"

"When I was growing up," Scott explained, "we were poor as dirt. My dad had left us and my mom had to work in town at some minimum-wage job. She'd leave me with my little sister, probably breaking lots of laws in the process. One summer, when I was about seven and my sister was about two, I watched her for whole days at a time. I had to—Mom's job couldn't afford even basic food, much less a babysitter.

"We were renting an old house on a farm, not much more than a shack. We'd get so tired of those four walls that I'd take my sister rambling. I'd make peanut-butter sandwiches and wrap them in newspapers and mix up Kool-Aid and pour it into empty Faygo bottles—"

"Faygo?" Megan interrupted.

"A cheap local pop", Scott said. "Anyway, I'd pack everything into old grocery bags, and we'd go wandering across the meadows or through the orchard. I'd tell Lisa the drainage ditches were rivers to China and the cornfields were African jungles. We'd find a patch of grass and sit in the sun and eat our sandwiches and drink our Kool-Aid and talk about wonderful things. I'd catch grasshoppers for her, and she'd stare in wonder and then jump with surprise when they'd leap away. I'd make a whistle out of two blades of grass between my thumbs, and she'd squeal with delight at the noise. Or she might fall asleep, and I'd lay her in the shade so she wouldn't burn.

"Anyway, the point of all this was that even back then, when I'd see her sitting on a rock clapping her hands and laughing at an Indian dance I was doing for her, with her mouth all stained with Kool-Aid—even back then, I remember thinking that it was all for her. It's hard to explain, but I remember it like it happened yesterday. It seemed my vision would shift, and I'd see the world differently. It was like ... it was like she was at the center of the world, this little kid in a dirty dress with golden curls and dancing eyes. It was like the whole world was made just for her, and all the mountains and oceans and clouds and deserts were made so she could laugh on that rock or sleep under that bush.

"Except that it wasn't just for Lisa. It was for all babies—it seemed that the world was made for them, that they were at the center and everything revolved around them. I'm not saying this very well ..."

"I don't know", Megan said quietly. "You seem to be saying it just fine."

"So ... I guess that's what I meant when I said that they are the purpose. Of course, that's just my opinion. I'm not saying you ..." Scott trailed off. There was a minute of silence while he thumbed the pamphlet.

"Scott," Megan asked gently, "what happened with Lisa?"

"What ... happened?" Scott blinked, taken aback.

"Yes", Megan said, laying her hand on his arm. "She clearly means a lot to you, but you're estranged. I don't want to pry, so if you'd rather not talk about it—"

"No, no, it's not ... it's fine", Scott said, waving his hands, his throat tightening. "I don't mind. Yes, we were close—very close.

But when I went on to college, and she was in junior high and high school, she started hanging out with ... trash. That's what they were, nothing but trash. She was far too good for them, but she ran with them anyway—pierced punks speeding through town in their junk cars. Her grades started to suffer, and she and Mom were yelling at each other all the time. I tried to tell her, I tried to talk sense to her, but she wasn't listening. I yelled at her, trying to get her to see, but she yelled back, and said ... cruel things." His throat was constricted tight now, and the tears were seeping out despite his best efforts. "Then one day, Mom ... Mom called me at college, asking if Lisa had come there. She hadn't. She'd just left home without any word or note or anything. Just ... gone."

"Have you heard from her at all?" Megan asked.

"Just a handful of calls—on Mom's birthday once, a few other times. Never any specifics, always from a pay phone. Always to Mom, never ... never to me. Looking back, maybe she was right. Maybe I got too caught up with my friends in high school and left her alone. But I never *meant* to leave her ..."

Scott was now kneeling on the floor, his head on the table, sobbing with the ache of the void left by Lisa's absence. Megan was kneeling beside him, stroking his back and holding him, her head on his shoulder, tears seeping through her long lashes. "I'm sorry, Scott, I'm sorry", she was saying.

"It's ... it's hardly your fault", Scott gasped.

"No, but I'm sorry it happened", Megan replied. "It must be terrible to lose someone you love like that."

"Yeah", snuffled Scott. "Well, maybe someday, eh?" He sat back in the chair, shaking his head and wiping his eyes, a little embarrassed but grateful for Megan's sympathy. Groping for a distraction, he glanced at the pamphlet he was holding. "What's this?"

"Oh, that?" Megan said. "That's for the childbirth classes the clinic offers. It's to help you get ready to have the baby as naturally as possible—special breathing, few drugs, minimal intervention, that sort of thing."

"Ah", Scott said. "So, were you planning on going?"

"Well, you really have to have a partner", Megan explained. "Someone who'll not only go to the classes with you but see you through labor."

"So," Scott asked, "what about me?"

"You?" Megan asked in shock. "Why would you ..."

"I do have an interest in this baby, you know", Scott reminded her. "Besides, I want to support you."

"But I ..." Megan stammered. "I never thought ..."

"Hey, I'm a gay guy, remember?" Scott teased her. "I'm supposed to be good at all this sensitive, emotional stuff. Count me in! Look, they've got a series starting up on Wednesday nights—where do we sign up?"

Megan offered some token resistance, but Scott could see she was interested and was glad to have someone to go with her. They busied themselves with the online registration and scheduling details. They were both glad to have something to focus on that took them outside their respective struggles.

So it was that Wednesday nights became class nights, with Scott and Megan sitting with other couples in a circle on the floor while the instructor spoke on fetal development and nutrition and stages of labor and breathing and a host of other things Scott knew nothing about. He learned why tennis balls could be useful during labor, what he could expect during "transition", and all manner of intimate things about women's reproductive systems that would have been quite embarrassing if the instructor had not spoken of them so clinically.

All this helped Scott understand that he had been thinking of the pregnancy as a medical condition that Megan had, as if it were diabetes, or her irritable bowel syndrome. But rubbing Megan's shoulders and kneading her back and getting in her face to practice breathing through a contraction and feeling her abdomen helped him grasp that there was another little person between them, and it wouldn't be long before that little person would enter their lives more dramatically. This excited him, sobered him, and frightened him a little. Life in their apartment would change in a few short months.

Megan too seemed to be grasping this more clearly, but still she seemed unsettled. She was enthusiastic enough about the lessons, and willingly took part in the exercises, but during unguarded moments Scott could see that she was distressed. It was something in her eyes, or the set of her brow, but she seemed to be haunted. Scott attributed it to her growing realization of the magnitude of what they were facing. He still remembered her distress about the "purpose" of the baby and wondered if that still troubled her. Also, she was beginning to show, and made occasional quips about how clumsy and gross she was. The instructor frequently reminded them that hormonal swings could contribute to moodiness and emotional instability during this stage of pregnancy. Scott was sure that this was part of what Megan was going through but wondered if there was more to it. As it turned out, there was—which he learned very shortly.

One day Scott was going through a typical day at work when a lunchtime mishap dumped most of a large cup of coffee all over him. After trying valiantly to mop himself up with paper towels, he concluded that a change of clothes was required, and zipped home. Dashing through the door, his shirt already half removed, he nearly tripped over a full suitcase sitting right in the hallway.

"Hey!" he said angrily, recovering his balance. "What's this doing here?"

"Oh!" exclaimed Megan, dashing out of her room in the commotion and catching sight of him. Scott was shocked at her appearance. There was nothing of the sunny, perky girl who had seen him out the door that morning. Her eyes were red and puffy, her hair was clumsily tied up, and she'd changed into bedraggled old sweats. She seemed dismayed to see him and turned her back quickly as if to hide her appearance.

"Megan?" Scott asked. He glanced at the suitcase. "Is this yours? What's going on?"

"I . . . I'm sorry, Scott", Megan nearly whispered. "I wasn't expecting you home. I was going to leave you a note."

The heat of Scott's irritation was suddenly displaced by a chill radiating from the cold, empty spot that had appeared in his middle. "Leave me a note?" he asked, trying to keep the quaver from his voice. "What do you mean? Why not call or text me?"

"I couldn't face . . . it was too . . ." Megan sniffed, then seemed to pull herself together. Taking a deep breath, she turned to face him, wearing a look of grief and determination that nearly broke his heart. "Scott, I'm leaving."

"Leaving?" Scott whispered, the chill now filling his torso. "Whatever for?"

"B-because I have to", Megan forced out. Then, pointing at his clothes, she said, "You have coffee all down your front."

"I know. That's why I'm home", Scott replied absently. "What do you mean, you have to?"

"Why don't you go change, and then I'll explain?" Megan suggested.

"Because I'm not moving from in front of this door until you promise you won't go through it until we've had a chance to talk about all this."

"Okay", Megan said, nodding tearfully. "I promise."

Scott, not totally trusting the distressed Megan to keep her word, dashed into his room and stripped to the skin. Wrapping himself in a bathrobe, he came back out to find her seated at the dining room table, gripping a handful of tissues.

"So," Scott asked, sitting down across from her, "what is all this? Does this have something to do with your interviews this morning?"

"In a way", Megan began. "Particularly the second one. The interviewer was pleasant, and I was hopeful that I'd be a good fit for the job. I was encouraged when she asked me if I'd like to go for coffee after the interview."

"'She' being the interviewer?" Scott interrupted.

"Right", Megan confirmed. "She was very kind, like a big sister. Over coffee she told me the bad news. She explained that it was obvious that I was pregnant and that no employer was going to hire me in that state. She said that nobody would consider someone who would be applying for paid family leave within a few months."

"I'm surprised she was so frank", Scott said.

"That's why she asked me to coffee", Megan explained. "She said it wasn't a topic she could broach in any connection with the interview, and knew that she was still taking a risk, but she thought I didn't seem like the type to file a hiring-discrimination lawsuit. And she was right.

"She hated to give me such news but wanted to save me a lot of wasted effort and disappointment. I appreciated that part, though it was hard to hear that I wouldn't be getting a job anytime soon."

"Is that what's wrong?" Scott asked.

"Well ... that was the first blow", Megan confirmed. "So I came back here, pretty upset. I've been mooching off you long enough and ... and started to think of what options I might have."

"Megan, you're not—" began Scott, but Megan waved him to silence. Whatever she wanted to say next was clearly taking an effort. Gripping her tissues and staring at the table, she continued.

"So I started thinking about Medicaid, and looked up what kind of pregnancy benefits they had, and ... and went looking for that folder you had with the paperwork about your plan's benefits, and ..."

Scott needed to hear no more. He could guess what came next.

"*Scott*," Megan nearly cried, "I had *no idea* you were paying so much extra to have me on your plan! Why didn't you ever tell me?"

"I ... because ... because it didn't matter", Scott stammered. He'd guessed she would be alarmed if she ever learned; he'd never thought she'd react this emphatically.

"Didn't matter?" Megan repeated incredulously. "Scott, that monthly fee is more than a quarter of one of my paychecks from my old job!"

"Well, health insurance costs are going up", Scott offered lamely. His heart was pounding and his mind was racing.

"Scott, that's too much. It's just too much. I thought my being on your plan was just an option selection. I had no idea you were shelling out that much."

Scott floundered, trying to marshal his arguments. His brain didn't seem to be working properly. The possibility of Megan walking out that door and out of his life loomed too ominously, scrambling his thinking. The money! The stupid money! How could he convey that he'd pay twice that—three times that!—just to have her around, brightening his mornings with her cheerful smile and lame jokes? How could he tell her how much it meant to have her there when he came home, to have her ready to listen and sympathize, smoothing the rough edges of his life with her quiet presence? Damn the money! She was the only friend he had in the world—he couldn't lose her!

"Listen, Megan", Scott finally stammered. "I know the cost of the coverage is more than either of us expected, but I can handle it, at least for a while. I'd been meaning to talk to you about it once you got back on your feet with a job, and—"

"Well, that isn't going to happen now, is it?" Megan interrupted bitterly. "Not for several months at least, probably a year."

"That doesn't matter, it really doesn't", Scott said, trying to reassure her.

"Scott, it's too much, it's just too much", Megan repeated. "I can't ask that of you, I just can't."

Scott resisted the temptation to remind her that she wasn't asking; he was offering. Instead he tried to keep her talking while he scrambled for a solution. "Where would you go? What would you do?"

"Well ..." Megan replied hesitantly. "There are women's shelters, and I imagine I could apply for public assistance ..."

Scott had to curb the urge to heap scorn on these lame ideas. Why would she give up a good home just because she was too proud to accept a gift?

"It's too much ... maybe find some low-end job ... can't ask that", Megan was mumbling now. She was so hung up about the money. Scott didn't understand. He was happy to give it to her. Delighted to give it to her. It wasn't like he was asking anything in return—

Then the glimmer of an idea hit him. If Megan wouldn't take his help as a gift, then maybe ...

"Megan, listen", Scott urged her. "I have a proposal for you."

"What kind of proposal?" Megan asked dully.

"A job proposal", Scott answered, trying to think fast.

"A job proposal?" Megan scoffed. "What kind of job?"

"Admittedly not much, but you just said you'd be willing to settle for a low-end job, so I thought I'd jump in", Scott explained, the idea firming up in his mind.

"All right, hit me", Megan persisted. "What kind of job?"

"I'd like to hire you as my, ah, household manager."

"Household manager?" Megan asked skeptically.

"Yeah, household manager", Scott replied, recalling bits of an article he'd read some time back. "It's the newest status symbol. They're all the rage up in Marin. People hire household managers to ... well, manage their households. They clean, buy food, pay bills, plan menus, whatever."

"Sounds kind of like a maid", Megan suggested.

"We could negotiate the terms of employment", Scott continued. "But I'd like to have one, and you seem like a ready candidate."

"For what pay?" Megan asked.

"Ah, room, meals, health insurance coverage", Scott listed. "I'm sure we can negotiate some spending funds in there."

"That's all?"

"Look, Megan, you can't have it both ways", Scott replied. "If the medical insurance coverage is worth too much to accept as a gift, then it can't be worth too little to serve as compensation."

"You have a point there", Megan admitted.

"And like I said, we can negotiate terms", Scott pressed gently. "You could take over food purchasing, so you'd have a budget there, and ... well, we'd work things out." He was struggling to play it coy. He felt like blurting out that she could name her terms, which was true, but that might scare her off. For now, he was happy to keep her thinking and talking, anything to keep her from grabbing that suitcase and walking out the door.

"I ... hadn't thought ... maybe ..." Megan mumbled, wringing her tissues.

"Look at it this way", Scott said. "You know how much it costs to rent this place. You know how much we spend on food. Now you know your health insurance costs. Halve the food and rent, for the sake of argument. Add all that up, and you'd have to find a job or an assistance package that provided at least that much, and probably much more. Weigh that against your living situation here."

"I don't know", Megan dithered. "Maybe it's worth considering."

Scott clenched his teeth and sat back in his chair. He wanted to shake Megan, to shout at her, to plead with her, to force her to see reason. He *couldn't* lose her, not now. He could sense how precarious things were. He had no idea what dynamics were churning inside her head, but he sensed that if he pushed too hard, she'd bolt. Mustering every ounce of his will, he stood.

"Megan, I don't want to pressure you", Scott lied. "We've always gotten along as friends, respecting each other's decisions. I'll accept whatever you choose to do. I'll even print up divorce papers for us to sign before you go, if that's what you want. I just ask you to consider my offer carefully and objectively. I'm dead serious about it. You know better than anyone that I need someone to manage my household. And ... I don't want to lose you." He stopped, wondering whether he should have said that last part, but it sort of slipped out. He didn't say anything more because he was already struggling to keep his voice steady. Megan was staring at the table but nodded a little.

"I'm going to get dressed and go back to work", Scott continued. "Take as long as you like to think things over. Make your decision

based on what matters to you. I ask only that you talk to me before
... doing anything."

"Okay", Megan whispered.

Back at work, Scott couldn't concentrate on anything. Disturbing
images flicked through his mind: Megan walking alone down a sidewalk bustling with strangers, pulling her suitcase behind her; Megan
sitting on the corner of a hard bed in some bleak shelter, muttering self-imprecations and striking herself; Megan being humiliated by
a supercilious bureaucrat at some government office; Megan being
slighted and abused by coworkers at some menial job. Half a dozen
times he grabbed his phone to call or send her a text with one more
argument or encouragement. But he always laid the phone back
down. It made no sense for her to leave, but she was feeling pressure
that he didn't understand. Matters balanced on a razor's edge, and
ham-handed attempts at persuasion could push her the wrong way.
Gut-wrenching though it was, he was helpless. He had to await her
decision, and every minute was agony.

Also weighing on Scott as the interminable afternoon ground on
was his own self-pity. Now, under the shadow of loss, he realized
what he'd gained since Megan had moved in: a home. He and Megan
had made a living home out of his bachelor's apartment, and she was
the very soul of it. If she left, it would die. He groaned in grief at
the thought of walking back through the door to find her gone. The
apartment would be like a tomb—the walls would echo with her
absence. He couldn't bear the thought. He'd move, that's what he'd
do. If she left, he'd give notice and move out. She couldn't leave,
could she? If she did, he couldn't go on living there alone. But, she
hadn't contacted him yet, had she? That had to be good, because it
meant she'd not yet decided, right?

"Scott, are you listening to a word I'm saying?" Marcus was sitting
in Scott's cube going over some notes on progress with some of the
modules. Scott had been attempting to focus, but to no avail.

"Sorry, sorry", Scott muttered, picking up the papers. "Just a little
distracted today."

"Obviously", Marcus said with a frown. "Anyway, like I was
saying—"

Just then Scott's phone chimed, and he grabbed it hastily. There
was one message, ended with a smiley face: "I'll take the job."

Scott gasped, covering his eyes while a tear escaped. He felt like iron bands had been cut from his chest.

"Scott?" Marcus asked anxiously. "Scott, are you okay, man?"

The phone chimed again with another message from Megan.

"We can talk terms when you get home."

Scott grinned, then drew his fingers across his eyes and turned to Marcus. "Yeah, I'm okay. In fact, I'm fantastic. This"—he waved his phone—"was really good news. Damn good news. Sorry I've been out of it this afternoon, but now ... damn good news."

"Well, I'm happy for you, whatever it is", Marcus said, grinning back. "Hey, if you need to take care of stuff, this can wait."

"No, no, let's tackle it", Scott answered. "I'll probably head out soon, but I've got time for this—especially now that I can focus on it."

They wrestled the problems to resolution in half an hour or so, after which Scott headed out. He was useless for the rest of the day anyway, and he wanted to get home before Megan had a chance to change her mind.

Dashing up the steps and through the door, Scott saw that he needn't have worried. Megan was in the middle of prepping something for dinner, and the air was rich with the aroma.

"Megan!" Scott called, dropping his laptop by the door and rushing into the kitchen. She turned to him with one of her brilliant smiles, and unable to restrain himself, he caught her up in a great bear hug.

"I'm so glad you stayed", Scott murmured into her hair.

"So am I", whispered Megan, hugging him tightly in return. They stood like that for a minute, then Scott reluctantly let her go.

"This is hardly a professional way to treat my household manager", Scott fumbled.

"Maybe not", Megan smiled, patting his cheek. "But it's a fine way to treat a friend. However, since you bring up the matter, I've a few terms to discuss with you." She laid down her cooking spoon and led the way into the dining room, where they sat down and she picked up a piece of paper that lay on the table.

"In response to your generous offer of room, board, and health insurance coverage, I accept the post of household manager, with attendant responsibilities", Megan began somewhat formally. "However, I have a few conditions, as well as things I need from you."

"Those being?" Scott asked.

"I will take over responsibility for all cleaning and laundry, some kitchen duties, and finances if you wish."

"That sounds great", Scott replied. Laundry hadn't even occurred to him.

"Well, hear my conditions first", Megan cautioned. "With respect to finances, I'll need access to your accounts if you want me to pay bills."

"Done", Scott said. "I'll have you added tomorrow."

"With respect to laundry, I'll do all our clothes, plus sheets and towels, but I'm going to do them at a Laundromat", Megan went on. Their apartment complex had pitifully inadequate laundry facilities, and more than once they'd taken everything to a Laundromat to wash, dry, and fold it all in a couple of hours. Megan always preferred that. "So I'll need a small allowance for that—maybe twenty dollars a week."

"No problem there", Scott assured her.

"I'll be putting three baskets in your room, and I expect you to use them. I'll wash your laundry, but I won't sort it."

"It'll be tough, but I'll try", Scott said with a grin.

"And speaking of allowances, I'd like a small one of my own for incidentals—maybe twenty-five dollars a week?" For the first time Megan sounded tentative.

"At least", Scott acceded easily.

"With respect to kitchen duties, I'll be happy to do all the shopping but not all the cooking. The cooking and kitchen cleanup we continue as we've been doing things", Megan continued.

"Wouldn't have it any other way", Scott confirmed.

"With all this, especially the laundry and shopping"—here again Megan sounded hesitant—"I could use the car for at least one day a week, possibly two."

Scott pondered this for a minute. "You know how to drive a stick?" he asked.

"Not yet", Megan said, smiling. "But I know someone who'll happily teach me."

"You're right. I don't see any problem—you could drop me off and pick me up. You may have to be flexible about particular days. Usually I know in advance when I'm going to have to leave the office during the day, but which days can vary."

"Sounds good", Megan said with a smile, then put down the paper and looked soberly at Scott. "With respect to cleaning, I'm happy to continue doing what I've been doing, but I have one condition."

"What's that?" Scott asked.

"Aim better."

Chapter Nine

Scott and Megan swiftly settled into their new routine, which wasn't very different from their old routine except that there was a bit more structure behind the arrangements. Megan learned how to drive the Jetta with less than the expected amount of gear grinding. They went on an exhaustive tour of several stores wherein Megan grilled Scott about his preferences and dislikes on everything from food to toothpaste, even to the point of taking notes. When Scott ventured to suggest that perhaps she was taking her household manager duties a bit too seriously, she dismissed him breezily. She'd been engaged for a task and had every intention of discharging her responsibilities completely.

Just how completely, Scott found out a few days later when he was heading to work. As usual, Megan was up (she was an atrociously early riser) and had cooked them both breakfast. As he was heading out the door she called to him from the kitchen.

"Don't forget this", she said, tapping on a small cooler sitting on the counter.

"What is it?" Scott asked. He couldn't remember seeing the cooler before.

"Your lunch", Megan explained. "And an afternoon snack."

"My lunch?" Scott walked over to the counter and opened the cooler.

"Yup", Megan confirmed. "You've often complained about how poorly you eat at the office. Looking over the accounts, I see that you spend an awful lot doing it. I'm trying to address both problems."

Scott lifted a can of vegetable juice from the cooler. He hadn't even known it came in cans.

"You said you like that, didn't you?" Megan asked.

"I do", Scott confirmed. "I just don't think of it very often."

"Well, there it is. Better for you than a pop or an energy drink."

Scott was a bit skeptical. He hadn't taken lunches anywhere since junior high, and still remembered them as bland bologna sandwiches accompanied by squishy, warm pickles. But when lunchtime rolled around, he was pleasantly surprised by what Megan had packed. It was a delicious wrap of some type with a side of crunchy vegetables and dip, with a little bag of dates for dessert. The snack was some sesame-covered pretzel bits with a little bottle of tea drink. He didn't feel the need to hit the vending machine all day and didn't get drowsy midafternoon. He was smiling in satisfaction as he headed home. If this was what he could expect, then having Megan manage his household was going to work out very nicely.

It proved well that things were coming together at home, for life was beginning to unravel at work. Unanticipated complexities were forcing last-minute design changes, and that was having a ripple effect on module integration. Deadlines were starting to slip, and meetings were getting heated. The rollout date, which had once seemed a comfortable distance in the future, now loomed larger on the calendar, especially in light of everything that needed to come together by then.

Scott needed to stay atop all the complexity, moving from team to team to review each team's code and try to pinpoint problems. Somewhere in there he lost his "assistant", who didn't quit like the others had but transferred to another department. That was fine with Scott. He had enough trouble staying on top of his own work without trying to keep someone else busy.

By contrast, Scott and Megan settled into a pleasant rhythm. With clear responsibilities and the resources to discharge them, Megan seemed happier. Scott didn't have to worry about running out of either clean clothes or food in the refrigerator, or even about having meals ready. If the pace of work meant that Scott wasn't quite pulling his weight on dinner prep, Megan didn't seem to mind. The apartment was clean and orderly, and even well decorated for the first time since Scott had lived there.

As February rolled around, Megan again began to feel more of the effects of the pregnancy. Now she suffered the dual curse of nearly incessant hunger combined with fierce heartburn. Her joints and back ached from the weight of the baby and the effect that had on her posture. She was constantly in the bathroom, and joked about the baby tap-dancing on her ribs. Once she called Scott over to put his hand on her swollen abdomen. He was amazed to find it rock hard, and she explained that it was a Braxton-Hicks contraction—a warm-up for the main event. Scott remembered the term from the classes but had never felt one.

The focus of their home was increasingly on the imminent new resident. The small desk in Megan's room was removed to make room for a crib. They found space in the corner of the dining room for a changing table, which was stocked with diapers and wipes. Scott began to think that he should trade rooms with Megan, so she and the baby could have the larger master bedroom. He knew he'd have to approach that diplomatically, because she was certain to resist. He thought maybe he'd give her a few weeks with the baby in the small second bedroom before making the offer. Her due date was late April, but even if she went over a little, he guessed she'd welcome the offer of a bigger room by June.

Spring brought one unexpected and pleasant surprise: when Scott filed their taxes, he received a larger-than-usual refund because of his new filing status. He used some of it to book a weekend at a local hotel that had an indoor swimming pool. There Megan spent almost every waking hour in the water, which took the constant load of the growing baby off her back and joints.

The due date came with much anticipation but passed with no action. They were on weekly visits to the clinic now, where the practitioner assured them that the baby was well positioned and had "dropped", whatever that meant. (For Megan it meant almost living in the bathroom.) She was completely convinced that the pregnancy would never end. Scott kept his phone constantly at his elbow, but no calls or texts came.

One day he came home to find Megan balanced precariously on a step stool, reaching to clean the top cupboard shelves.

"I've been wanting to clean these for months, and I just couldn't stand it any longer!" she complained when Scott insisted she get down. But Scott recalled a comment made by the instructor of their birth-preparation class, and later did a search on "pregnancy" and "nesting". The next morning Megan wondered why he asked her to keep her phone with her at all times. When Scott got to work, he put out the word that he might be taking a few personal days.

When Scott arrived home that afternoon, he found Megan sprawled on the couch, dead asleep, with the vacuum cleaner spread out all over the floor. Smiling fondly, he laid a blanket over her, called in a pizza, and set up his laptop to wait.

A couple of hours later Megan stirred with a cry. Scott was by her side quickly.

"Hey, hey, take it easy", Scott said gently as she struggled to sit up. "No need to get up."

"I'm sorry ... didn't get the vacuuming done ... and it's my night for dinner", Megan mumbled.

"Don't worry about the vacuuming", Scott assured her. "Or dinner."

"Hey, you don't know my boss", Megan said with a sleepy smile. "He's a real slave driver."

"Yeah, well, your boss is giving you the night off", Scott replied. "Want some pizza? It's cold now, but I could warm it up."

"Sounds good", Megan said. "I could eat a horse. But first ... the bathroom." She threw back the blanket and tried to sit up, when suddenly her eyes widened and her face froze.

"What is it?" Scott asked in alarm.

"Just ... a rather strong one", Megan said with a grimace.

"Well, breathe. Just like we practiced, remember?" Scott encouraged her.

"That's for ... real labor", Megan gasped. "This is just a Braxton–Hicks."

"You sure about that?" Scott asked.

"Ah ... no", Megan replied with a surprised look. "I think my water just broke."

Scott looked down. Sure enough, her sweatpants were dark with spreading wetness.

Later, the only thing Scott could remember about the hours that followed was that there were periods of frantic activity punctuated by intervals of relative tranquillity. He drove Megan to the hospital, where the labor staff set them up in a room, pronouncing that Megan was "coming along nicely". The contractions were regular, just like he and Megan had learned in class, and were growing stronger and closer together. Scott helped Megan breathe through them and rubbed her back and kneaded her calves (of all things), reassuring and encouraging her. Then things seemed to slow down, which concerned Scott, but the midwife assured them that this was perfectly normal and encouraged Megan to sleep as she was able, which she did.

A short nap was all Megan managed before being awakened by a series of sharp, strong contractions. Now things began to proceed rapidly. Additional women arrived to assist the midwife, checking this and prepping that. To Scott's consternation, any semblance of modesty went right out the window. Sheets were cast aside, gowns were pushed up, legs were spread wide, and the most intimate details were called across the room. The attendants took Scott's presence for granted; they had no way of knowing that this was the most he'd ever seen of Megan. He supposed that if she didn't mind, he had no cause to, but all the same he stayed by Megan's head and made an effort not to look at anything ... private.

That was fine by Megan, who clung to his hand and pleaded for neck rubs and appreciated Scott helping her with the breathing. Then suddenly she wanted to push, but something wasn't quite ready, so the midwife told Scott to help her pant. He remembered that part and coached Megan, though she desperately wanted to push. She was wide-eyed and sweating and muttering how she couldn't do this. He wiped her brow and stared into her eyes and assured her over and over that she could do this. She wrung his hand and panted and believed him, muttering that she could do this.

Then whatever was delaying things got resolved, and the midwife said it was all right to push, and Megan was red faced with straining, and the attendants were encouraging her, and somebody said, "Crowning!" and Scott remembered what that meant. Then there was another push or so and the midwife was lifting a little pink thing up in the air, and Megan was grinning and sobbing and everyone else was nearly cheering. They laid the baby on Megan's bare stomach, and Scott was surprised at how scrawny and wrinkled the baby was.

"Don't they cry when they're just born?" Scott asked.

"Some do", the midwife answered. "Many don't, especially with a quick and easy delivery like this. This one, she's breathing just fine, so we aren't worried. Would you like to cut the cord?"

Scott shook his head and turned back to Megan. Her hair was stringy and her cheeks were flushed and tear stained, but her face was illuminated by a smile like he had never seen her wear. Her eyes were fixed on the little person gasping and stirring on her abdomen. Then one of the attendants had to take the baby away for something, and Megan turned the smile, undimmed, on him and seized his hand.

"Scott," she whispered, "she's perfect."

Then there were a few more details that needed attending to, and Megan had to push a bit more and endure another exam, but after that, things were clearly over and people began cleaning up and (at last!) covering Megan back up. One of the attendants brought the baby back, all cleaned up and nicely wrapped.

"Apgar eight and nine, twenty and a half inches, seven pounds, six ounces. Very healthy little girl", the attendant announced, settling the baby in Megan's arms. "Do we have a name?"

"Grace", Megan replied, beaming at the little bundle. "Grace Marie Kyle."

Startled, Scott looked down at Megan, but the attendant was showing Megan how to set the baby nursing, so he decided he'd seen enough for now. He wandered out of the room in search of a restroom and a cola.

When Scott returned, Megan was all cleaned up and ready to be wheeled to the room where she and the baby would get some sleep. To his surprise, a nurse handed him the baby to carry. He expected she'd be sleeping, but she was looking around with big eyes and opening and closing her tiny mouth.

"Hey, little one", Scott murmured, and she looked in his direction for a moment. "Good to meet you at last. You have no idea how much you've complicated things in your short life."

By the time they reached the hospital room, Megan's adrenaline was starting to wear off and she was nodding where she sat. Scott helped her into the bed while the nurse tucked Grace into her crib and rolled it over next to the bed.

"Good job, Mom", Scott said, smiling down at Megan where she was drowsing. She reached up and pulled him down for a hug.

"Likewise, Dad", she whispered in his ear. "I couldn't have done it without you."

"So true, at so many levels", Scott teased in response.

Ensuring that Megan's phone was in her reach, Scott headed out to get some sleep of his own.

Scott took the remainder of the week off, so when Megan and Grace were released from the hospital, he had five days to get Megan rested. The midwife had warned Scott that even an uneventful birth was still incredibly taxing, and Megan would need all the rest she could get for the next week no matter how chipper she felt. So when they returned to the apartment, Scott settled Megan in over her mild protests and started working on lunch.

To Scott's surprise, having a baby around the house wasn't as big a change as he'd anticipated. Granted, they'd had several months to ramp up for the occasion, but even then Scott had expected the difference to be more noticeable. Grace was a contented little baby, happy to lie and sleep. She fussed only when she had some basic need that needed attending to, and once that was taken care of she would rest quietly in her bouncy chair and look around. Being a good mother seemed to come naturally to Megan, who was relaxed and happy with her baby. It seemed incongruous to Scott that just a year before this had been a gay guy's apartment, but now it was a home, complete with mother and baby. He wondered what things might look like in another year. Sadly, that hinged on what Megan would decide to do. Perhaps she would have moved on by then, taking little Grace with her. No purpose worrying about that now. For the time being they were here together, and things looked to be staying that way for a while.

Chapter Ten

By the time Scott returned to work the following week, he and Megan had adjusted to the new arrival. Megan and Grace had been doing a lot of napping, and Megan was starting to feel caught up on sleep and was ready to be moving around. Nonetheless, Scott felt hesitant about leaving her home for the day and insisted she keep her phone in her pocket at all times.

Settling back into the rhythm of work, Scott quickly found that his domestic affairs were a very open secret. He started finding items like pacifiers and disposable diapers left around his cube. He imagined that these were taunts from the likes of Jason. But he also got smiles and handshakes, though not without some befuddlement, for his orientation was well-known around the office. One day a coworker he barely knew, Jake from over in sales, stuck his head into Scott's cube.

"I understand congratulations are in order", Jake said with a grin.

Scott decided there was no point in being coy. "You understand correctly, though how everyone knows is beyond me."

"Office grapevine", Jake replied. "Faster than gigabit switches. So … son or daughter?"

"Little girl, Grace Marie. Mom and baby are doing fine. Don't ask me the specs, because I keep forgetting them."

"So do I", Jake admitted. "Women live by them, though. First thing they want to know is how long and what weight. My wife started writing them down on a card that I could keep in my wallet."

"How many do you have?" Scott asked.

"Four—three boys and a little girl", Jake said, beaming. "She's my darling. Say, if you could use any help, let me know. My wife told me to ask—we're happy to bring in a dinner or drop by to do some cleaning or whatever. My wife does that for all the mothers of newborns that she knows."

"Thanks, Jake", Scott said sincerely. "I'll run that by Megan and let you know."

As it turned out, they were set for dinners, but Megan was touched by the gesture.

With Megan back on her feet, Scott could refocus more on work. This proved fortuitous, for the project was picking up speed, and a lot needed to happen if they were going to make the release deadline. They'd gotten past a set of initial hurdles, and the modules were coming together into the package, but the problems now were subtler and more stubborn. Scott began to suspect that quality assurance was dragging its feet at giving him timely and accurate feedback via the official channels. But he had a friend over there named Sandy who slipped him what he needed to know informally.

Spring rolled into summer, and summer was quickly passing. The urgency of hitting the deadlines was dominating Scott's life. They released a beta to select customers in early August, two weeks behind schedule, but Scott was still confident that they could make the target release date for the full product.

Megan and Grace were an oasis of sanity amid the pressure cooker of work life. Regardless of how late he got home, Megan would make an effort to be up to greet him, usually with a snack of some sort. Little Grace, who seemed to have spent the first couple of months of life sleeping, was getting more alert and interactive. She liked to be held upright so she could look about and squawk. As Scott played with her, he found long-dormant instincts awakening. He knew how to handle babies—knew what made them smile, how to tell when they were approaching dissatisfied, and how to soothe them to sleep. Grace was a calm, contented little baby, and holding her quieted Scott after long and clamorous days.

Though weekends were usually only one day long, which Scott felt like sleeping right through, he made an effort to take the girls out so they wouldn't go stir crazy from being cooped up in the apartment. Jaunts up to the city or down the coast or across the bay were about all they could manage, but they were enough.

One night in late summer Scott had one of his dreams. He knew it wasn't an ordinary dream because of its vividness and detail and how he remembered every minute of it, but it wasn't one he'd ever had before.

In the dream, Scott was walking east along a narrow dirt road through the country. He recognized the landscape—it looked like the farmlands around the small town in which he'd grown up. He could tell he was walking east because he could see the lake on the horizon, glimmering blue above the tops of the trees along the shore. It was sunny but cold, with only a few puffy white clouds dotting the broad blue sky and the wind coming from the northeast across the lake. From that, and from the land around, Scott guessed it to be early spring. The fields were dun brown, plowed but not yet planted, damp with snowmelt. The meadows were drab tan and dusty green, and the deciduous trees in the windbreaks were still bare of leaves, nodding and swaying in the cold wind. It all looked and felt very familiar to Scott as he walked along shivering.

It was familiar at least to his right, south of the road. To his left, particularly over his left shoulder, it was a different story. There a deep black darkness was encroaching on the bright blue sky. It wasn't like a layer of gray clouds, or like a storm line that was darkened by its own shadow, but blackness like black paint spreading across the sky—almost as if some celestial giant had spilled ink on the dome of the heavens. All the land that was overshadowed by the black canopy was quickly shrouded in total darkness. What most alarmed Scott was not just that the blackness seemed to be spreading so quickly but that there seemed to be something like rain that was falling from its underside, staining and coating the landscape. Toward the nearer edge of this dark rain he could see woods and houses and hills still retaining their shapes though coated in black; beyond them everything merged into a deep and uniform darkness. And though Scott tried not to look back at the blackness, there was something mesmerizing about it. Terrifying though it was to watch, it was at the same time vaguely familiar.

In the dream, Scott tried to hurry his pace, to run or even walk more quickly, but found that for some reason he couldn't. He considered turning south, away from the spreading blackness, but there was no crossroad for him to take, and the fields and ditches presented so many obstacles that he didn't want to risk getting bogged down or trapped with that ominous blackness coming on. So he pushed his walking to the quickest pace he could, focusing down the road. For some reason he thought that if he could just reach the lake, the water would protect him. He tried not to look over his shoulder, because it just panicked him and made him more frustrated with the fact that he couldn't go any faster. But he couldn't help glancing back from time to time.

Scott tried to concentrate on the road and hurry his leaden feet along, focusing on the sunshine drenching the fields and the reeds in the ditches bowing in the breeze, trying not to think about the darkness coming behind him. He peered ahead, hoping for some indication that he was making progress toward the water and, he was sure, certain safety. He began to notice a sound that rose above the gentle whisper of the breeze—a dry rushing that reminded him of the time that he watched a truck slowly dump a load of soybeans into a hopper. Glancing back, he saw that the blackness now covered nearly a third of the sky, and he could clearly see dark drops falling—just a sporadic few toward the edge of the darkness, but a steady and thick flow further back. The rain of black seemed to be the source of the rushing sound, and it was getting louder as the darkness came closer.

Nearly screaming in frustration at his inability to hurry, Scott glared down the road for anything that would help—a crossroad, even some woods that came to the edge of the road where he could shelter under trees. Then he noticed something peculiar: the road went in the direction of the distant lake, but it didn't seem to go down to the lakeshore road. Instead it ran to the mouth of a cave.

A cave? There were no caves in this country; Scott knew that well. But there it was—the road ran down to a small hill, in the side of which was a stone arch opening to a cave. The cave mouth was large enough for him to enter, though he'd probably have to stoop to do it. The cave walls were brown stone leading back to what seemed to be a faint, flickering light toward the rear of the cave. To Scott, the cave seemed full of warm, comforting dimness wherein he could hide. It seemed to welcome visitors, unlike the stark blackness overhead that was threatening to blot out the sun. Somehow he knew that if he could just make it into that cave, he'd be safe.

Now the rushing sound was filling Scott's ears. He stared at the cave mouth, as if just by willing he could draw it closer. Out of the corner of his eye he saw what he had been dreading: a great black drop falling on the road. To his surprise it did not splash or run off like a liquid but simply sent up a small puff of dark dust. Scott wondered if the dust had come from the road surface or from the falling blackness when he saw another drop hit a fence post and send up a similar puff. Soon drops were falling all about, and wherever they struck they threw black dust into the air that stained the land. Scott grimly wondered what would happen when one of the drops struck him.

He found out soon enough as one of the falling drops grazed his arm. It wasn't wet but was bitter cold, stripping away both sleeve and skin and leaving a burn or a welt. To Scott's alarm, the welt didn't bleed but exposed dry blackness beneath. He looked at the wound in horror as another drop struck his leg. His leg stung with the impact and fierce cold, but the impact point didn't bleed; instead it flaked off some of the dry black powder.

With shock Scott realized, as one does in dreams, that the falling blackness wasn't staining him—it was stripping him. What lay beneath his skin wasn't flesh and blood but dusty darkness, akin to the falling drops. Everything on his exterior was only a wrapper, a shell surrounding a core of blackness. Each drop cut or punctured that shell, releasing the darkness inside to reunite with the darkness falling all around. The drops were coming more quickly, and Scott knew that if he didn't get out from beneath them, the exterior that was Scott would be shredded and disintegrate. He looked and saw that the cave entrance was only about a couple of hundred yards distant, but the drops were falling steadily around him now. One grazed his face, and when he put his fingers up to feel where it had hit, they probed emptiness and came away smudged.

He pushed and strained to make his feet move faster, trying to reach the cave while icy black drops struck him on the back, the arms, the hands, the head. If he didn't make it, he would be unmade. The black rain was falling more quickly, the rushing cascade filling his ears, and he had horrid visions of being pounded to the ground in a dusty black pile mere yards from the safety of the cave—

He awoke, sweaty and panting, tangled in the sheets from his thrashing.

It wasn't until after Labor Day that Scott began to notice minor oddi-
ties at work. He was so buried in technical problems that it took him
a while to realize how little he was seeing of Marcus. Toward the
beginning of summer they'd met several times daily to discuss how
the development effort was tracking with the project plan. Now,
Scott realized, he might see Marcus every other day, usually in passing. Marcus answered Scott's e-mails and texts promptly, so Scott had
no cause to complain. He didn't want to text Marcus to ask what was
going on, but it seemed strange, at this critical point in the product
rollout, that Marcus would make himself so scarce. For that matter,
Brian's office had often been dark of late.

Once Scott started noticing these anomalies, he began to pick up
on other irregularities. Of course, Scott knew that he was something
of a workplace pariah, at least to certain parties, and tried to down-
play perceived slights lest he descend into total paranoia. Still and all,
he saw things that he simply couldn't explain. One such thing happened toward the end of September when he was walking past one of
the conference rooms that had a glass wall looking onto the hallway.
There was a presentation going on in the conference room, with a
rather large number of attendees. Scott recognized Brian, Julie the
controller, and Marcus, as well as several people from their accounting firm. That was about half the people in the room; the remainder
were strangers. Marcus was doing the presenting, and when Scott
caught a glimpse of the slide on the screen, he saw that it was a fairly
technical summary of an aspect of the project. That wasn't totally
unthinkable—Marcus was tech savvy enough to handle something
like that—but Scott wondered why he himself or one of the other
senior engineers hadn't been asked to explain that sort of thing rather
than a project manager.

For that matter, what was this presentation about? Who were these
people? Scott didn't expect to be included in everything that went on
around the company, but it was a small enough operation that usually
everyone would know that a presentation that size was taking place,
as well as the topic and who the audience would be.

Scott was wondering all these things while standing in the hallway, staring through the glass wall at the slide on the screen. Marcus
noticed him and gave a half smile and a little nod before continuing

his talk. Not wanting to look as inquisitive as he felt, Scott turned and walked away. But when he reached the corner, he glanced back to see that someone had drawn the blinds within the conference room, completely occluding the glass wall.

With the release date less than a month away, Scott had little time to devote to worrying about such things. The results from the beta release were coming back, and they were proving immensely helpful in tightening up the modules. Scott began to be somewhat optimistic that they would be ready to release the product no later than two weeks past the original target date, which would be nothing short of astounding.

One evening Scott came home too late for dinner but in time to play with Grace a bit before Megan took her away to put her down for the night. Scott tried to relax, but his mind kept returning to work problems. He didn't hear Megan slip out of her room, so he was surprised when she showed up beside him with two glasses of wine. She handed him one with a smile and sat down beside him.

"What's the occasion?" Scott asked.

"Guess what today was?" Megan replied with a grin.

"Umm ... Guy Fawkes Day?" Scott answered, pretty certain he was wrong.

"Not sure about that", Megan admitted with a shrug. "But I do know this—it's our anniversary."

"Really, now?" Scott said, a bit surprised. It didn't feel like it had been that long. "Completely slipped my mind."

"Mine too", Megan admitted. "I had to look at our documents to be certain. I was thinking about how old Grace was, and that got me thinking about the birth, and that got me thinking about that ceremony, so I got curious. I pulled out the file, and sure enough—it was one year ago today that we drove down to the county offices and got ourselves hitched."

"Well, how about that?" Scott said.

"So," Megan continued, raising her glass, "here's to our first year!"

"Cheers!" Scott answered, not knowing what to say.

"A very eventful year", Megan went on after they had taken their sips.

"To say the least", Scott concurred, forcing a smile and settling himself in to listen. His mind kept slipping back to code optimization, but Megan clearly wanted some intimate conversation.

"But it's a good opportunity to say thanks", Megan said. "Our marriage may be a mere formality, but you've been a terrific friend and very supportive."

"Oh", Scott replied, a little surprised. "Why, sure. Glad to. I think it's worked out well all around. I get a great household manager and a delightful little playmate in the bargain."

"Well, then," Megan said with a smile, raising her glass again, "here's to mutually beneficial arrangements."

"Long may they last", Scott answered, raising his glass in turn.

Chapter Eleven

From the moment Scott walked into the office the following morning, he knew something was amiss. Rather than the usual hum of activity, there was an ominous silence. Cubes were empty, and people were clustered in break rooms or around printing stations, talking quietly but urgently. Scott wondered what was going on but figured he'd check his e-mail before talking to anyone. Plugging his laptop into the station, he let it power up while he settled in.

"Rats", he muttered as his network login failed. Retyping his password more carefully, he was mystified when he got another failure message. He double-checked his user ID and was two-fingering his password when he was interrupted by an annoying voice.

"Hey!"

Scott turned to see Jason smirking at him by his cube entrance. "What do you want?" Scott asked sourly, finishing his typing only to get another log-in failure. "Damn!"

"Brian wants to see you in his office", Jason sneered.

"Does he, now?" Scott snapped, checking his caps lock and carefully retyping his password. "I'll be there as soon as I check—what is *wrong* with this thing?"

"He says now", Jason said with obvious satisfaction at Scott's frustration.

Biting back a sharp retort, Scott grabbed his cell phone and stormed away to see Brian with Jason laughing at his back.

Brian's office door was closed and all the blinds were drawn, so Scott couldn't even see whether he was in. Scott knocked, and Brian's voice bid him enter.

"Ah, Scott", Brian greeted him, rising from behind his desk. "Good to see you. Have a seat."

Scott eyed Brian warily. There was something about Brian's demeanor that indicated that the greeting wasn't quite true. Scott sat down in one of the conference chairs. "Jason said you wanted to see me."

"Yes", Brian affirmed. "Yes, I did. I ... I wanted to discuss some matters with you before you heard about them—that is, I'd rather you hear them from me than through the office grapevine."

Scott said nothing, but his guts were starting to tighten. This hesitant, stammering Brian was someone he'd never seen before, and he suspected that what was forthcoming was not good news.

"There's been some interest in the project—high-level interest from major names", Brian explained. This made Scott even warier—this was starting out like good news, but Brian's tone and manner did not telegraph enthusiasm. "We've been talking to several parties about our plans, and those plans have been well received."

"Well," Scott offered, "that's good, isn't it? Especially with the rollout date imminent?"

"Yes, yes, it is good", Brian acknowledged. "We've gotten particular attention from VXN Group, who is very interested in our technology."

Scott raised his eyebrows. "VXN Group—they're big." This was an understatement. They were one of the market leaders, and Scott had made sure to test the project thoroughly against their product line.

"Yes, yes, they are", Brian said. "Turns out they'd been doing some internal work along similar lines but liked our design and implementation better."

As lead system architect, Scott couldn't help but feel a little proud about this. That had been part of the reason he'd signed on with the company in the first place—he embraced Brian's vision that small, nimble companies could innovate as well as those with large, well-funded research departments.

"We've been having some in-depth meetings with them, and they're very interested in what we've been doing—very interested", Brian continued as if he was dancing around some point.

"Well, that's good, isn't it?" Scott repeated. "Some contracts with VXN would be lucrative, and also good publicity."

"That's true", Brian admitted. "But ... we haven't been discussing contracts. We've been discussing a buyout."

Scott's eyes narrowed—so that was it. His mind whirred, but there were too many things he didn't know. "A buyout? But ... how would that work? Aren't we privately held or something?"

"After a fashion", Brian explained. "It's really the VCs—"

"VCs?" Scott interrupted sharply. "Since when have we been getting funding from venture capitalists?"

"Since about a year ago", Brian snapped. "How do you think I've been paying all of you during this development push? Product sales? Haven't you been following what's been going on with the economy? Sales are off 70 percent so far this year."

"But ... VCs? Why haven't we heard about this?" Scott asked.

"What do you think that jaunt you took to Chicago was about?" Brian countered. "You were presenting to the VCs. Of course, we didn't want to make a big noise about it, for several reasons. But we needed them to stay afloat."

"So," Scott said, his anger growing, "after all the idealistic talk and high-sounding principles, the minute a big enough offer comes along, you sell out—"

"I have no choice!" Brian barked, slamming his desk. "The VCs want their return, and they figure this is the best they're going to do. The open market is iffy, while this is a sure thing. They're driving the sale."

"And because they've got the gold, they make the rules, is that it?" Scott said bitterly.

"I haven't noticed your objecting to their gold on paydays", Brian replied with a dark look.

Scott sat in dismal silence for a moment, pondering the implications of all this. "So," he said at last, "all those stock options we've been promised?"

"We aren't taking our stock public", Brian confirmed with resignation. "The market has no stomach for new offerings right now, especially tech firms."

"So where does that leave us?" Scott cried. "I've poured myself into this company! The entire project was my idea! I've worked like a dog to engineer and coordinate this project, pretty much solo, and—"

"Look here, mister", Brian interrupted fiercely. "You aren't the only one who works here. A lot of people work just as hard as you. Sales, accounting, customer service—customer service, which has been waiting for documentation you promised months ago and have yet to deliver. And don't get started with the working-all-alone BS. Three employees—three good employees—I've assigned to assist and learn from you. After a few months of trying to work with you, two of them quit outright and the third was ready to. The only way we could persuade him to stay was to transfer him to another division and promise him he'd never have to deal with you again. So don't come crying to me about how hard you're working all by yourself. If you want people to help you work, be easier to work with!"

Scott was stunned. He'd never seen things in that light. But he was still shocked and disappointed, and pushed back in his anger.

"But you have to admit that this project was my innovation—mine! Yes, others have helped build it—and worked very hard, I freely admit that—but the original idea was mine. What are we going to get for that? What am I going to get for that?"

"If you read the employment contract you signed," Brian shot back, "you will see that it contains a clause stipulating that all inventions, innovations, and initiatives you come up with while under employment are the property of the company."

Just then there was a quiet knock on the door. Brian looked up as Jason let himself in, walked over to the desk, and lay upon it a flash drive. He walked out without saying a word but didn't miss the chance to leer at Scott as he passed.

Scott's mind worked furiously. What was that all about? Then it began to dawn on him. "Wait a minute", he said. "That's why the network wasn't working this morning, wasn't it? I'm shut out, aren't I? We all are!"

"The sale was executed at midnight", Brian said in a defeated voice, looking discouraged. "The company no longer exists."

"And our jobs?"

Brian just shook his head. "VXN is willing to interview applicants but warned us that they have a staff surplus. Their people will get the first pick of any positions. There"—he pointed to the flash drive—"are the contents of the documents folder on your laptop. Hopefully you didn't have any personal files on any servers, not just because of company policy but because you won't be able to get to them now. You'll be escorted back to your desk to gather your belongings and then to the door. It's standard security."

Scott reached over and took the drive. Most of his personal files were on his tablet, but he'd had a few photos and such on his laptop. Of course, that meant that Jason now had a copy of them as well, but that didn't matter. A hard silence fell on the room as Scott struggled to control his shock and anger while Brian just sat as his desk looking miserable.

"I ... I'm sorry, Scott", Brian said at last. "I'm sorry it had to end this way, especially after all our hopes and plans. I would have warned you, but they swore me to secrecy and were watching me like a hawk. If I'd stepped out of line, they would have canned me and brought in some stranger to execute the transition."

"Yeah, well, that would have been tough, being out of a job", Scott answered bitterly.

"That's not what I meant—" Brian began, but Scott interrupted him.

"So, this is it? The pink slip and the door? No transition period, no severance, nothing?"

Brian picked up an envelope and fingered it nervously. "The, ah, board agreed that any residual value of the company after settling obligations should be distributed among the employees in recognition of their contributions. Here is your portion of that distribution."

Scott took the envelope, deeply suspicious. Brian wasn't even looking at him, which made Scott suspect that he wasn't going to like what he saw. Peeking at the amount, his suspicions were confirmed: it was for just over fourteen thousand dollars.

"That's it?" Scott bellowed. "That's *it*? After all I poured into this place, after all the value I've added, after all the promises of ultimate payout—this is all that's left? No stock options, no job ... the VCs plunder the place and leave us *this*?"

"That's what everyone got, including me", Brian snapped back.

"My point exactly!" Scott barked, waving the check. "We've all put out for this company on the hopes of getting some equity when we succeed, and all we get is this? Except you, who still have a job, am I right?"

Brian said nothing and looked away.

"This ... this is an insult!" Scott yelled, hammering Brian's desk. "To hell with it, and to hell with you!" In blind fury he ripped the envelope with the check to shreds and threw the pieces at Brian, then stormed for the door.

"Scott, don't be a fool!" Brian called after him, but Scott was too enraged to stop. "*Scott!*" Brian nearly shouted as Scott laid his hand on the knob. Despite Scott's fury, there was something in Brian's tone that made Scott pause briefly.

"What?" Scott asked through tightly clenched teeth.

"A suggestion—don't try looking for work in the Bay Area. I'm told that ... word is out about you", Brian said.

Scott said nothing in reply to that but pulled open the door. Outside stood Jason, wearing his usual self-satisfied smirk. Apparently Jason was his security escort. Scott glared at him, then stalked away to his cubicle with Jason following.

Back at his cube, Scott pulled out a filing box and started throwing into it what few personal effects he kept around. Jason leaned against the cube entrance, watching him and grinning. Scott was still reeling, and so angry that he didn't trust himself to say anything. He strongly suspected that Jason already had a job secured.

"Don't forget to leave your ID badge", Jason taunted. Scott rounded on him furiously, his fist half cocked.

"Here's what you can do with your ID badge", Scott growled, but Jason was not intimidated. He stepped closer and shoved his face right into Scott's.

"Go ahead, family guy, give me an excuse", Jason whispered fiercely. "I'll pound you into the carpet, then sue your ass for assault. I've got three witnesses to swear you threw the first punch."

Scott glanced around and saw nobody near, but he didn't doubt that Jason could produce his "witnesses" if the need arose. He didn't doubt the first part of the threat either, given that Jason was half a head taller and clearly spent more time at the gym than Scott. Snarling, Scott turned to put his last items into the box. Then he pulled off his lanyard and threw his ID badge at Jason.

"Ooh", Jason mocked. "Temper, temper!"

"Go to hell", Scott snapped, grabbing the box and pushing past Jason.

"You know, I'm going to miss you around here", Jason sneered as he followed Scott. "Seeing you always makes me think of the pitter-patter of little feet and the sweet sounds of rattles ..."

Scott said nothing and focused on the front door. About the only good side to this mess was that he wouldn't have to deal with this jackass anymore. He pushed out the door and headed for his car, noticing several other people scattered about the parking lot.

"Ta-ta, stud!" Jason hollered loudly at Scott's back. "Best of luck finding another job!"

Muttering furiously, Scott threw open the trunk and stuffed the box in beside some random baby gear. He was still so furious that he could barely see straight but was already starting to wonder if he hadn't been too hasty about shredding that check. But that made him think about Brian, and that got him going again. He slammed the trunk and turned to see someone walking over toward him. Great—he didn't want to deal with anyone right now. But then he saw it was Jake. Jake was all right, and he may as well say good-bye.

"Hey, Scott", Jake said as he approached.

"Hey, Jake", Scott answered. He didn't mind Jake, but he didn't feel like conversing. He just wanted to get out of there.

"Bad business, this", Jake said.

"Yeah", Scott acknowledged, not trusting himself to say more.

"Listen, I wanted to give you my home phone, in case ... in case we can do anything to help." Jake pulled out a card.

"Thanks", Scott said, tucking the card in his pocket. Then, deciding he couldn't be a total churl, he held his hand out. "It's been good working with you, Jake. I'm sorry it had to end this way. Best of luck with ... with your future."

"Thanks", Jake replied, taking his hand. "Same here."

"Thanks", Scott said. "Well, got to be going." Jake nodded in understanding and stepped aside as Scott drove away.

Scott didn't know where he was going. Away from there, certainly, and definitely not home yet. His eyes stung as he drove. The reality was still hitting him. Suddenly, without warning, he was out of a job. Now it all began to make sense—all the odd happenings, the hints and rumors. Of course! That's why he'd seen so little of Marcus recently. Marcus had known—Marcus had known for sure, the bastard. Which probably meant he'd been avoiding Scott for fear of letting something slip.

Damn! Scott slammed his fist on the wheel in rage. He was beginning to get frightened now—what was he going to do? He turned toward the bay. There was a stretch of empty dock behind a warehouse where he sometimes went when he wanted to be alone to think, and he needed to think now.

Scott found the warehouse and parked behind it, overlooking the water. He was still being battered by rage and fear and indignation and humiliation, but what now overwhelmed him was bleak desolation. He felt like he was the only human on the face of the earth, utterly alone in his distress. He put his head on the wheel and sobbed.

After a while Scott had to stop because he couldn't breathe anymore through his clogged nose. After attending to that, he stepped out of the Jetta and paced along the edge of the pier, listening to the waves slap the seawall and looking out across the bay with red-rimmed eyes. What was he going to do? How was he ever going to find a job in this economy? He could follow the news as well as the next guy. The market was saturated with unemployed tech workers, especially in the Bay Area. He'd heard that many were giving up and leaving the state.

On top of that, there was Brian's guarded but unambiguous final warning, effectively echoed by that bastard Jason. Word was out about him. Scott kicked a bollard savagely. He knew exactly what that meant. The network, the boys, the gay Mafia—whatever you wanted to call it. The informal network that nobody openly acknowledged but that everyone knew existed and was happy to use when it was advantageous. He'd used it himself to get the job he'd just lost as well as other things. Hell, it had been through connections with the Nashville GM that he'd gotten here to the West Coast in the first place.

The problem was that the network cut two ways. When you were in, doors were opened and introductions made. But when you were out, the doors were closed and locked. And Scott was most definitely out, and had been for over a year now. Bitter as it was to admit, Brian's warning was probably right—it was futile to waste effort trying to find a job in the area, with all these factors stacked against him.

What could he do, then? A reckless mood seized him, and crazy thoughts fired in his brain. Southern California was no better than here, but what if he went north? The Seattle area was always a tech haven, even in these times. Somebody had to be hiring. He could leave tonight—right now!—and head north. He could live out of his car until he found something. He could make a quick stop at the apartment for a few things, be on the road by afternoon, and—

And do to Megan and Grace what his own father had done to his mother, Lisa, and him.

Not an option.

The reckless mood evaporated like mist, and Scott sat down on the pier, pressing his fists into his forehead. The girls! What could he do about them? Maybe Megan could find something, but whatever it was, they wouldn't be able to afford to stay where they were. Scott's heart sank even further. Everything was gone—the income, the benefits, everything. Megan had been on the verge of leaving when he'd bribed her with that pretense of a job. Now that he couldn't afford that, she was sure to leave and take Grace with her. For that matter, Megan and he were married only to give her access to his benefits, so the marriage was probably out the window as well. He couldn't blame her. He couldn't provide for her, and he couldn't ask her to endure what was sure to be a lengthy and frustrating job search.

Scott gazed out over the water, tears of self-pity dripping down his cheeks. Megan would leave—she was certain to leave—and she'd take Grace with her, and he'd never see them again. Images shot through his mind: Grace sleeping across his knees while Megan grabbed a quick shower; Grace crowing with glee as he played eat-your-tummy with her little stuffed lion; Grace sitting in her bouncy chair, gazing about the room while making little gasps and sighs, her tiny fists clenching and unclenching.

Scott gritted his teeth until his jaws ached. He had to be strong. He couldn't be selfish. He had to tell Megan immediately, so she could make the best decision for herself and the baby. He couldn't pressure her; he had to steel himself. But then the thought of never seeing them again came crashing in and demolished the structure of resolve he kept trying to build.

The day passed in a blur for Scott. He drove about aimlessly. When he tired of the pier, he drove to a park, and when he tired of the park, he drove to a shopping mall. Sometimes he cried until his throat ached and he couldn't breathe. Other times he just drove in silence, full of a dull numbness. At one point he found himself parked on some dirt road, looking through a chain-link fence at a huge rail yard that he hadn't even known was there. Gazing across the vast space, spotted here and there with forsaken cars, he felt a corresponding emptiness. His life felt like a vacant wasteland, devoid of direction or purpose. Not that he wasn't buffeted by storms of emotion. He'd be furious with rage, then shattered by disappointment, then shocked by betrayal, then stricken by grief—the waves washed over him with such force that he felt he must be crushed. He now bitterly regretted his rashness in tearing up that check. He would need that—or at least Megan and Grace would—but he'd be damned if he'd go crawling back to Brian and beg.

Scott had totally lost track of time, and the sun was already well below the mountains, when his phone chimed. It was a text from Megan.

"Working late?"

This was it. Scott would have to run and hide, or try to defer matters, or simply face it. It wasn't going to get any easier for him, but he'd try not to make it harder on them.

"Home soon", he texted back. Then he sighed, got into the Jetta, and turned homeward.

Scott arrived home feeling empty and exhausted. He had no idea how he was going to broach this topic with Megan, who was clattering about in the kitchen.

"Hey!" Megan called when she heard him by the door. "How was work today?"

"I wasn't at work today", Scott answered dully, walking into the kitchen.

"You weren't? Then where have—" Megan began, but stopped short when she saw his crestfallen appearance. "Scott, what's wrong?"

"I lost my job today", Scott replied, leaning against the cupboard. "There was a buyout and we got pink-slipped—at least most of us did. Some may have gotten jobs with the new company, but I wasn't among them."

"Oh Scott", Megan whispered, wide-eyed. "What are we going to do?"

"I suppose . . ." Scott began, hesitating. Then he thought he might as well get it over with, since this wasn't going to get any easier. "I suppose you'll want to look for a new situation, since I can't afford to pay you any longer. The sooner the better, I'm thinking."

Megan's eyes grew wider yet. She gave a little cry and abruptly fled the kitchen. Scott's heart sank as he heard her door shut sharply. He'd known it would hit her hard; but he hadn't imagined it would shock her that badly. Another wave of loneliness and desolation swept over him. He realized he'd been hoping for Megan's company to help him sort out this mess. No chance of that now, and he couldn't blame her. She had to decide what was best for her and Grace. He wasn't the only one who'd lost a job today.

Grimly Scott set about tidying up. Megan had been preparing dinner for him—there was a place set, and some sort of stew warming on the stove and rice to go with it. It smelled great, but he had no appetite, so he turned off the heat and moved it all off the stove. He was exhausted. The thought of watching some noisy television program revolted him. Early though it was, he'd turn in and bring this disastrous day to a close. Perhaps things would look better tomorrow, though he couldn't imagine how. He stopped outside Megan's door on the way to his room and thought he heard quiet sobbing, but he couldn't be sure. He went on to his bedroom, his heart crushed.

Sleep did not come easily. Despite being bone tired, Scott couldn't settle down. His imagination was tormented by images from the day and fears for the future. He tossed and turned, going over and over in his mind the things he should have said to Brian, or to that jerk Jason. He kicked himself again and again for ripping up that check. He thought of calls he could make or e-mails he could send to appeal some part of what had happened but then dismissed the ideas as futile.

Scott spent most of the time anguishing over losing Megan and Grace. Just a wall separated them, and a couple of times he heard Grace wake and fuss, to be quieted by Megan's ministrations. He definitely heard Megan get up several times to visit the bathroom—poor girl. A couple of times he thought he heard sobbing. The prospect of living without them, of enduring the void their absence would leave, was Scott's greatest torment that night. A couple of times he almost threw off the covers to rush into Megan's room and plead with her not to go, not to take little Grace away. But he forced himself to stay put—it would be selfish of him to put that kind of pressure on her on top of everything else.

When morning finally started to lighten the blinds, Scott gave up and plodded out to the kitchen to start some coffee. It felt strange not firing up his laptop to check e-mail—he didn't even have a laptop anymore.

A door opened behind Scott, and he turned to see Megan walk into the kitchen. He was almost shocked at her appearance—he'd known she'd had a rough night, as had he, but he'd never seen her this distraught. Her eyes were red and swollen, her hair was in total disarray, and her posture radiated defeat. Grace was asleep in her arms. She avoided looking at him, instead staring at the floor. She gave him no chance to speak but began in a flat, dull voice:

"I have no idea what your plans are, but I hope that wherever you go, you'll take Grace with you. I . . . I can wean her off breast milk and have her on formula in about a week, and I'm sure that . . . whatever happens . . . you'll be able to find care for her . . ." Still without looking up, she held the sleeping baby out toward Scott.

Scott was stunned. Of all the things he'd imagined might happen, he'd never anticipated this. He stepped back, holding up his hands and shaking his head. "Megan, what are you saying? I'd never separate you from Grace!"

Megan stepped forward, still holding out Grace. "Scott Kyle, don't make this harder for me than it already is", she implored. "You're already throwing me out on the street! Don't throw her out as well! You don't know what it's like—I do! You'll be able to get another job somewhere. You'll find another partner, and you can raise her in a proper home, while all I can give her is . . ." Megan broke down into sobs.

Scott was reeling and braced himself against the cupboards. What did she . . . did she really think . . . "Megan," he gasped, "what do you mean? I don't . . . I'm not throwing you out on the street! I don't want you to go anywhere!"

Megan looked up sharply, a wary look in her eyes. "What do you mean? I thought you said I'd have to look for another living situation, the sooner the better."

Scott's mind raced—what had he said last night? The fog of exhaustion and grief clouded his memory. "No, no, no", he said, waving his hands. "I meant your job situation. I can't afford you as my housekeeper anymore. I don't have any more benefits. I don't even have any pay. I thought you'd want to look for better opportunities."

"So ... I don't have to leave?" Megan asked tentatively.

"No", Scott answered. "In fact, I wish you'd stay, but I don't think any of us are going to be able to stay here much longer. I don't know what I'm going to do."

Megan said nothing for a moment but stood staring at him. Then she thrust Grace into his arms and pushed past him into the living room. More mystified than ever, Scott calmed Grace and followed. He found Megan sitting on the couch, face buried in her hands, gasping and sobbing as if her heart was breaking.

"Megan?" Scott asked, now totally befuddled. But Megan just shook her head and waved her hands, clearly unable to speak just yet. Shrugging, he moved a box of tissues within her reach and went to get the coffee going.

Ten minutes later, Megan had calmed a little, the coffee was ready, and a now-awake Grace was gurgling and cooing in her bouncy seat. Scott sat down next to Megan and handed her a steaming mug.

"Scott, Scott," Megan murmured, "I'm sorry. I'm so sorry."

"Sorry for what?" Scott asked. "It was just a misunderstanding. I'm the one who should be apologizing. I should have been clearer."

"But I thought the most terrible things about you", Megan explained. "I lay there all night and cursed you for being so cruel. I even toyed with the idea of slipping away, cleaning out your bank accounts, and vanishing. I have the checkbook and ATM card."

"Well," Scott replied, a bit shocked, "I'm certainly glad you didn't do that."

"So am I", Megan acknowledged, sipping her coffee. "But Scott, what are we going to do?"

Scott blinked, his heart both warmed and weighed by her use of "we". "Well," he stammered hesitantly, "I didn't want to presume, but if you wanted to find a real job ..."

Megan snorted and put down her coffee. "Let's not go around this block again, Scott. I was a music major. If I'd had any marketable skills, we wouldn't have been going through this pretense of your employing me as your housekeeper. But more to the point: unless you want me to go away, we're in this together. You're the only friend I have in the whole world, and you're Grace's father. Who else do we have besides each other? Who else does she have besides us?"

"Nobody, I guess—or nearly nobody", Scott replied. He shook his head. Everything was happening so quickly, with so many unexpected turns and reversals, that he felt like a leaf in a windstorm. "Look, we both had a bad night, and neither of us is thinking clearly. Let's get breakfast and some coffee, and then we can consider this together. I'll cook—I think Grace needs you."

They spent the morning discussing various alternatives, but Scott and Megan were both so scattered from the emotional roller coaster of the past twenty-four hours that they made little progress. After lunch Megan lay down for a nap with Grace while Scott researched using his tablet and considered scenario after scenario. Nothing seemed to be working out no matter how hard he stretched it. Had he been the only party to worry about, there would have been many more options, but having to work in Megan and Grace severely restricted him. He began to consider something that would have otherwise been out of the question. The longer he considered and evaluated, the more it began to look like the only reasonable alternative they had. Of course, Megan would have to agree, and he'd have to make some phone calls. Taking this option would surprise some people, to put it mildly.

"Well, champ," Megan said, coming up behind him and putting a hand on his shoulder, "got it all figured out?"

"Hardly", Scott scoffed. "I didn't hear you get up. Did you sleep well?"

"Well enough to get by for now", Megan answered. "Muffin is still down. I wish I could sleep like her."

"If you had a mommy as good as hers, you probably could", Scott said with a grin.

"Thanks." Megan smiled weakly. "Turn up anything yet?"

"Well, it's pretty grim all around", Scott admitted.

"We knew that", Megan replied.

"I qualify for unemployment, but nothing near enough to let us live here or even in the area. The only places we could afford to live are places we wouldn't want to live, especially with Grace", Scott explained.

"I'm still amazed they didn't give you some kind of severance", Megan mused. "Something to tide you over."

"Yeah, well," Scott said, wincing, "it is what it is. Anyway, nowhere in this state looks any better than San Francisco for either living expenses or job prospects. California's economy is seriously on the skids."

"So you're suggesting ... out of state?" Megan asked.

"It may be our only choice", Scott answered. "If you don't mind."

"I moved here from elsewhere", Megan said, shrugging. "My only ties are to the two other heartbeats in this apartment."

"Okay, then", Scott said, warmed by her response. "I checked it out and it's permissible to draw California unemployment while looking out of state. If it were just you and me, our options would be more open. But with Grace, we'll need more support, since both of us may end up working, and child-care costs are a very swift drain on the budget."

"And I don't want to entrust our baby to some stranger", Megan added.

"That too", Scott acknowledged. "All these factors narrow our field considerably. In fact, as far as I can see, they narrow it down to one option."

"Which is?" Megan goaded.

"My hometown, where my mom still lives", Scott answered reluctantly.

"Oh", Megan said. "That doesn't sound too bad."

"Well, you've never been there", Scott reminded her.

"Where is it?" Megan asked. "You've never talked much about your hometown."

"There's a reason for that", Scott said grimly. "It's a drab little place called Lexington."

"Kentucky?" Megan asked.

"Michigan", Scott answered.

Chapter Twelve

Scott felt a little tense as the phone at the other end rang, but he tried not to show it so as not to alarm Megan, who was watching him from across the table.

"Hello?" came the answer at last.

"Hello, Mom?"

"Joe?" came the response, thrilled but wary. "It's early for Thanksgiving ... is something wrong?"

"Well ... yes, to be honest. We're all okay, health wise and all, but I ... I lost my job. Totally unexpected, so we're caught kind of flat-footed", Scott answered.

"Aw, Joe, that's a terrible shame", his mother answered. "But you keep saying 'we'. Who's 'we'?"

"Well, ah, Mom ..." Scott stammered a bit. This was going to be the tricky part. "There are a few things I need to fill you in on."

"Joe, now you're starting to worry me. What's going on?"

"Mom, there's nothing to worry about", Scott explained patiently. "Everything's good; it's just ... going to be a little much all at once."

"All right. I'm sitting in my living room, by myself, and"—there was a pause—"I've turned off my television. I have all the time in the world, and I'm all ears. Lay it on me."

Scott grinned. This was just like his mom. "Okay. Remember that friend of mine? The one with the baby who's been rooming with me?"

"Megan and little Grace—yes, I remember them both", came the answer.

"Well, Grace isn't just Megan's baby. She's my baby too. I'm her father", Scott explained clumsily. Megan, who was sitting across the table, grinned at him.

There was a long silence at the other end of the line before Scott's mother spoke. "Well, that's ... unexpected. Wonderful, but quite unexpected. I imagine there's a bit of a story behind that?" Scott's mother knew full well of his orientation.

"There is", Scott confirmed. "Someday we'll fill you in. But today there's another detail you need to know."

"What's that?"

"Megan and I are ... legally married."

There was another long silence. "Married?"

"Um ... yeah. For about a year now", Scott confirmed.

"Joe, you sure know how to surprise a mother. Are you telling me that I've had a daughter-in-law for a year now, and a granddaughter for six months, and I haven't known it?"

"Well, yeah", Scott admitted, suddenly feeling very guilty. "I guess that's what I'm saying."

"I'm glad I found out eventually", Scott's mother said. "Did you ... did you get married because of Grace?"

Scott was puzzled briefly but then caught her meaning. "No, not in that sense. It's a technicality, really—just a formality."

"A technicality? How can a marriage be a technicality?"

"If it's necessary to get someone on a benefit plan", Scott explained. "But Mom, I can fill you in on that later. Right now there's more I need to explain."

"More?" Scott's mother asked, incredulous. "I've just learned that I've got a daughter-in-law and a granddaughter, and my son's lost his job, and there's *more*?"

"Yeah", Scott confirmed. "Given the state of things, and the fact that we need help with Grace, I was wondering ... we were hoping we could come back there for a bit until we get our feet back under us."

"Here? To Lexington?"

"Yeah", Scott admitted glumly.

There was another long pause, and when Scott's mother spoke again there was no hiding the excitement in her voice. However, her words were cautious. "I sure don't want to say anything to discourage my son visiting, and I'm anxious to meet my daughter-in-law and granddaughter, but I hope you're aware how hard it is to find a job in Michigan these days."

"I know that, Mom", Scott replied. "Believe it or not, California's even worse just now. But there aren't very many good places anywhere. If it were just me, or just Megan and me, we'd have more options. But with Grace, we need more help. If you're willing, we could come back there for a while, and I'd hunt around for something. I'm not restricted to jobs in Michigan—I can search for out-of-state positions—but we need a place to live and some help with the baby while I do that. I know you don't have any financial resources, and no living space to share, but … but we're about out of options."

"Why, sure, Joe", his mother reassured him. "It'll be a struggle, but at least we can struggle together. In fact, I have a thought or two about living accommodations. Let me make some calls. When would you be looking to be out here?"

"We hope to get going as soon as reasonably possible", Scott explained. "We've got some things to tidy up here but hope to be on the road so as to get there by Thanksgiving."

"By Thanksgiving!" Unbridled excitement now. "Well, goodness—that's wonderful!"

"Yes, yes it is", Scott said with a smile, surprised to find himself agreeing. "The situation is a mess, but at least we'll get to see each other again."

"Well", his mother said, nearly breathless, "I'll have to get right on those calls—"

"Great, Mom", Scott interrupted. "You keep us posted, and we'll keep you posted, and—"

"Wait a minute, Joseph Kyle", his mother came back sharply. "Don't I get to talk to my daughter-in-law? Is she there?"

"Oh, ah, sure, she's here", Scott replied, taken aback. "If you want to talk to her." He raised his eyebrows at Megan, who smiled and nodded.

"If I want to talk to her—listen to the man!" Scott's mother huffed. "Of course I want to talk to my own daughter-in-law!"

"Great, Mom. Here she is. Love you! Bye!" Scott handed off the phone.

"Hi, Mrs. Kyle", Megan said shyly.

"Megan! I've heard so much about you, and today is the best news yet!" Scott's mother said. "Not about Joe's job, of course, but at least I'll get a chance to see him, and you, and that precious baby. How is she, by the way?"

"Lovely", Megan said, beaming. "You couldn't ask for a more sweet-tempered baby."

"Oh, that's wonderful, that's just wonderful", gushed Scott's mother. "I just can't wait to meet you, and her, and we can go out for some girl talk. I have loads of questions—not to pry, of course, and you needn't tell me anything you don't wish to, but I want to get to know you better. Oh, I'm so excited! Sorry for your situation, of course, but so excited! I have another daughter! Why, listen to me run on . . ."

"That's quite all right, Mrs. Kyle", Megan said, smiling.

"Well now, that's quite enough of the 'Mrs. Kyle–ing'. You're my daughter now. Please call me Mom, or Mother—though if that makes you uncomfortable, feel free to call me Angela. But I won't have my own daughter calling me Mrs. Kyle. Understand?"

"Yes, Mrs.—Mom", Megan answered.

"That's better. We're family now. Not a very big family, of course, and kind of scattered, but family just the same. It'll be hard, but we'll be together, because that's what families are for, right?"

"Um . . . right", Megan confirmed, but Mrs. Kyle was off again.

"Oh, I'm so excited—I can't wait. I'd best get on those phone calls. Good-bye, dear! Kiss that baby for me!"

"I will! Bye!" Megan hung up and handed the phone back to Scott.

"Sorry about that", Scott said with an embarrassed smile. "Mom gets a little carried away sometimes."

"That's fine", Megan assured him. "She was very sweet."

"Well, that's taken care of", Scott said briskly, getting up and grabbing his tablet. "Now on to the unemployment website . . ." He bustled out of the room muttering to himself.

Megan sat still for a minute. Then she wiped her eyes with the back of her hand, stood up, and slipped in to where Grace lay napping. She quietly leaned over and placed a gentle kiss on the baby's cheek.

"That's from your grandma, Muffin", she whispered. Then she stood up, but not quickly enough, and two crystal tears fell onto Grace's brown curls.

Scott wanted to be on the road in time to be home well before Thanksgiving, which didn't give them very long. Two adults and a car seat in the Jetta didn't leave much room, so they had to limit their belongings to the bare minimum—which was extremely bare for the adults, considering how much they had to bring for Grace. This was a wrench for Scott, who had outfitted the apartment at considerable expense and knew he'd be lucky to sell the furniture and decor for even a quarter of what he'd paid for it. In fact, time was so short that he was almost despairing of getting even that when he remembered Jake's offer and gave him a call. Jake agreed to undertake posting Scott's household goods and getting them sold off for what he could.

Scott was able to do much of his unemployment filing online, but because he'd be moving out of state, he had to talk to an agency rep. Getting that appointment delayed their departure nearly a week. By the time they were heading east across the San Mateo Bridge, it was three days later than the latest date Scott had wished to depart.

When traveling long distances, Scott was accustomed to packing light and going solo. Megan could work with that, but Grace was another matter. Mellow though she was, she had limited tolerance for her car seat and none for riding in the dark. They were all right getting clear of the Bay Area and made it as far as Reno, but then they decided to stop rather than make it partway across Nevada before the sun set. This was difficult for an already-exasperated Scott, who'd have shot for Salt Lake City that day had he been alone.

The next day they crossed the Nevada desert, where Scott got his real lesson in the difference between traveling alone and traveling as a family. What with stopping to feed Grace and stopping to change Grace and stopping to give Grace time out of her car seat, a trip that could have been done in a fast day stretched into nearly twelve hours. Megan was picking up on Scott's frustration, which made her edgy, which made for more bathroom stops. Everyone was short on temper by the end of the day.

Heading out from Salt Lake City the next morning, they learned that Grace didn't handle abrupt changes in altitude well. Megan speculated that it put pressure on her ears. Nursing helped a little, but mostly they had to drive with a wailing, miserable baby who finally cried herself to sleep. Fortunately the tablelands of Wyoming had no sharp changes in altitude, but there were still plenty of stops. Scott tried not to think about the fact that had he been traveling alone, he would have been well east of North Platte by now. As it was, they had to settle for trying to reach Cheyenne that day.

Megan attributed Scott's tension to his frustration at the delays. It was indeed partly that, though for her and the baby's sake he tried to breathe deeply and take the interruptions as they came. What she didn't know, and he wasn't about to tell her, was how angry he was at himself. He saw now how foolish and proud he'd been to tear up that check Brian had handed him. Sure, fourteen thousand dollars had looked like a pittance in comparison to the hundreds of thousands in stock options he'd been dreaming of. But now, unemployed and running back to a town he'd hoped he'd left forever, carrying all their possessions in one small car, it looked like a fortune. He had a scant unemployment check and was heading into a dismal job market. That check may not have been all he'd hoped for, but it would have made the difference between a little traction in their new situation and grinding poverty—and he'd torn it up in a fit of juvenile pique. When would he grow up?

So they crossed Wyoming, with Scott simmering in self-recrimination, Megan intuiting his distress and trying to figure out how to help, and Grace just being a baby with baby needs. They spent the night in Cheyenne and got started early the next morning. The only indication that they'd passed into Nebraska was a sign by the road—the terrain didn't change for miles. The sky was gray, and they kept passing through patches of rain that were slashing down under a cold north wind.

"How far do you think we can get today?" Megan asked through a yawn.

"At the rate we're going, hopefully Omaha", Scott replied. "Des Moines would be way too much to hope for, even with our early start."

"I'm sorry it's been so frustrating for you, with Grace and all the delays", Megan said.

"It's all right", Scott said, smiling at her. "Traveling as a family is different from driving solo, and I just have to get used to it. Patience is a virtue, as my mom used to say—a lot. I always hated to hear that."

"I think I'm going to like your mother", Megan said.

"I hope you do", Scott said. He was looking forward to seeing his mother as well, and already his thoughts were turning toward their destination and what he'd do when he got there. He'd beaten himself up enough over his folly; it was time to look ahead.

"Ooh, look at that!" Megan pointed ahead. The highway was descending a long slope, and a broad vista was coming into view. The clouds were breaking up, allowing shafts of sunlight to angle down through the misty atmosphere. In places rain was still sheeting down from the slate-gray undersides of clouds. It seemed like the whole prairie, in its vast and vacant glory, was opening out before them.

"That, my dear, is the Platte River valley. This is just the South Platte, which merges with the North Platte further on, but we're clear of the highlands, and the going is mainly flat from here on east. Boring, but at least we won't be troubling Grace with altitude changes. And it's faster." Feeling a little reckless, Scott accelerated a bit.

"What's that other expressway down there?" Megan asked.

"That's I-76. If we were heading for Denver, we'd take that. Nice town, Denver", Scott explained. He was feeling the buffeting of a stronger crosswind now and was glad for the wider tires he'd gotten for the Jetta.

"Scott, aren't you driving a bit fast?" Megan asked nervously. "We're coming up on a merge here."

Scott, who didn't like being nagged any more than the next guy, bit back a sharp response. But maybe Megan was right—the rain had wet the road in spots, the temperature was hovering right at freezing, and they were approaching an overpass with a curve beyond. He let up on the gas a bit right before the merge.

"Thanks", whispered Megan as they cleared the curve and straightened out onto a long merge ramp.

"And ... great", Scott said as he spotted a fast-moving group of trucks coming up on the other expressway. He had to make speed quickly to get ahead of them. He tromped on the accelerator, the tach spiked, and the Jetta shot forward, on a trajectory to merge well in front of the trucks.

"Scott ..." Megan said with an edge to her voice.

It all happened so quickly that Scott barely had time to react. He just heard the whish of water under the tires and felt the buffet of another strong gust of wind, probably disturbed by the wash from the line of trucks he was trying to overtake. But suddenly the Jetta's nose was veering, and the wheels were losing traction, and Megan gave a shriek that startled Grace awake.

Scott's stomach froze, and his senses seemed to lock, but his brain went into high-speed awareness even as his physical reactions responded instinctively to the terrifying sensations he'd known only twice before. He knew that he had lost control of the car; they were going down, and the only question was where. He quickly glanced left as the car veered and skidded. Not in any way toward those trucks—the median was far too narrow. Somehow his arms knew how to work the wheel so as to move toward the far side of the lane. His foot was off the accelerator, but he dared not brake. There—they were going off the road, away from the trucks and other traffic. But too fast, too fast. At this rate they'd nose into the ground and put the engine into the passenger compartment. A flick of the wheel and a tap of the brake pedal turned them sideways, sliding, the steering lost but all four tires bleeding off speed as they tipped down the embankment.

Then in a terrifying jumble of noise and shrieks and thumping metal they were rolling, rolling. Scott felt his seat belt pin him tight and tried to press back into the seat to prevent his head from flopping around. He gripped the wheel until his fingers ached, willing the tumbling to stop.

And it did. They were upside-down in a muddy field, having rolled right through the fence at the edge. Scott shook himself, knowing he was unhurt but that the ordeal wasn't yet over. Megan had a death grip on his arm, and the baby was howling. He had no time to be traumatized.

"Scott, Scott", Megan gasped, her eyes wide.

"Can you reach the baby?" Scott asked, unbuckling his belt and easing himself out of his seat.

"I think so", Megan replied.

"Unbuckle", Scott instructed, throwing the lock and pushing his door open. He stepped out into ankle-deep mud—clearly the field had been recently plowed. He slogged his way around to Megan's door, but it was still locked. He pounded on the window and gestured for her to unlock it, which she did, but it still wouldn't open. Then he noticed that the roof was dented in—that door wouldn't be opening. He worked his way back around to his door.

"Scott, I can't get her out! I can't get her!" Megan cried in frustration, trying to work the car-seat straps while Grace shrieked in terror.

"I'll do it", Scott said, reaching through his door to unlock the back door. "You get out."

"But I can't get her out!" Megan insisted, tugging futilely at the buckle.

"Megan," Scott said sternly, "get out of the car. Now. Your door is stuck, so you'll have to scramble across my seat. I'm getting Grace right now." He pulled open the back door, which thankfully wasn't jammed, and knelt in the mud to look up at the problem. Grace was secure, but her hanging upside down in the straps was pressuring them in ways that made the buckles hard to work. Ignoring her howls, he unsnapped her chest strap, then lifted her up to ease the tension. Then he unbuckled her and worked her free from the straps, cradling her as she fell clear of the seat.

"Is she all right? Have you got her? Is she hurt?" Megan hovered over his shoulder anxiously. Scott lifted Grace clear of the car and handed her to her mother, who hugged her tight and burst into tears.

Scott stepped back. They all seemed to be unhurt. He could feel the unearthly focus wearing off—he was coming back to real time. His hands were starting to tremble, and his insides felt light. He looked around, seeing the embankment down which they'd rolled. There were great gashes in the grass, and some cars had already pulled over onto the shoulder. He could see people on cell phones, and a guy was working his way down toward them.

Scott turned and looked back at the Jetta, his beautiful car, his pride and joy, lying broken on its back and buried in a muddy field in the middle of nowhere. Now what were they going to do? *Now what were they going to do?* A surge of shock and grief and frustration and rage boiled up inside him, and suddenly he found himself railing and screaming, slamming on the car with his fists and kicking it with mud-caked shoes. This latest mishap seemed both to symbolize and to culminate everything that had gone wrong with his life over the past year. From being socially isolated for trying to help Megan, to having his income siphoned away by the endless expenses, to all the stress of work, to losing his job and throwing away his check, to having to leave California and all his dreams, to having to return to his dingy little hometown with no job prospects and a lot of responsibilities—and now this! What else could go wrong? White fury blinded him as he cursed and slammed his fists into the corpse of his car, completely beside himself.

But even that could not last, especially at that intensity. Scott's head started to clear, and he looked over to where Megan was standing, where he saw something that sobered him quickly. Megan was staring at him, wide-eyed in shock and terror, holding Grace tightly and turned so as to shield her completely from him. That cut his heart. Sure, he was frustrated, but he'd never do anything . . .

"Megan, I—" he began, holding out his hand.

"Hey, buddy!" A voice called over the wind. The Good Samaritans who'd worked his way down the embankment and through the mud had gotten within hailing distance. "Everyone okay over there? Anybody hurt?"

Scott waved back and shouted, "We seem to be all right!"

The guy made an "okay" sign and said something into his cell phone. "The law's on the way!" he hollered. "Tow truck too!"

Scott waved acknowledgment and turned back to Megan. "Are you all right? And the baby?" Grace seemed to have calmed down a bit, though she was still fussing and squirming.

"I . . . I think so", Megan answered. "I don't feel more than badly jostled, and she doesn't seem harmed. But . . . oh Scott, I've never been through anything like that! I'm shaking all over!"

"Listen," Scott assured her, remembering the look of fear on her face, "I'm sorry for losing it there. I just . . . lost it. It was just frustration. You know I'd never hurt you or Grace. It's just been one damn thing after another."

"I know, I know", Megan said with understanding. "Oh Scott, what are we going to do?"

"I don't know", Scott said with a shrug, feeling utterly forlorn. He looked at the wrecked car in despair. "God help us."

"Scott," Megan said anxiously, feeling Grace's hands, "she's freezing out here in this wind! Can you get her jacket?"

By this time the helpful traveler had slogged up to them, puffing and red faced. "Holy smokes, buddy, holy smokes!" the fellow gushed, as if rolling the car that far into the field had been an admirable feat. "What a tumble! We saw it all. We were just behind you. You were bouncing and sliding like crazy! You sure nobody's hurt?"

"We seem to be fine", Scott answered, not feeling very patient with enthusiastic rubberneckers, no matter how well intended. "The baby's cold, though, and so are we." They'd taken Grace's jacket off to give her more room in the car seat, which meant it was somewhere in the car tumbled together with all the other loose gear.

Scott didn't want to go back near the car, but he had to, and the guy came with him. Scott squatted in the cold mud beside the open back door and tried to locate Grace's coat. It occurred to him that he ought to locate his phone as well.

"Hoo-eee", the guy whistled. "What a mess! Helluva lotta stuff you got in there, buddy. And look at that! Not even a window cracked! Can't beat that German engineering, can ya?"

"No", Scott said with a thin smile, thinking he was going to have to extricate Grace's car seat before he'd be able to do anything back there. Just then the man's phone rang, and he had a brief conversation with whomever was on the other end.

"Tow truck's just minutes away", the man assured Scott. "Troopers'll be a bit longer, but there may be a sheriff in the area—they're calling to check."

"Thanks", Scott answered, grimly deciding that there was nothing for it but to kneel in the freezing mud to get an angle on the buckle holding the car seat.

"Can I help ya there, buddy?" the man asked.

"Actually, you could take this", Scott grunted, levering the car seat clear and handing it to the man. There—that was better. He thought he could see Grace's jacket in the mess.

"C-could you look for mine too, Scott?" Megan called, her teeth chattering. "I think it was right behind my seat."

"Got 'em", Scott said, crawling into the car and pulling out the garments. He handed them to Megan, thinking they looked terribly thin for these conditions.

"Tow's here", the man announced, pointing at the big flatbed that was pulling up, yellow lights flashing. "Young lady, you look freezing. Why don't you get on over to my truck? It's the black Tahoe. My wife's in there, and she'll have the heater going full blast."

Megan glanced at Scott, who nodded. "That ... that'd be great, thank you."

"Need a hand?" the man asked.

"No, I think I can make it", Megan said with a smile, and began trudging through the mud toward the road. The tow truck had backed halfway down the embankment, and the driver was getting out of the cab wearing knee-high rubber boots.

"Thanks", Scott acknowledged, holding his hand out to the man. "Scott Kyle."

"Steve Prudhomme", said the man, taking Scott's hand in a firm grip. "My wife Ann'll take good care of 'em. Hey, Kenny!" This was to the tow-truck driver who was approaching, shaking his head.

"*This* is what I call a wreck", Kenny said with a low whistle. "This is a good twenty-five, thirty yards here. You sure nobody's hurt?"

"We seem to be all right", Scott said, now shivering in his turn from cold and shock.

"Chalk it up to German engineering and soft mud", Steve added. "And maybe a guardian angel or two."

"That's for sure", Kenny said, leaning over to look into the car. "You got a lot of junk in there, mister."

"Yeah", Scott confirmed dismally. "We're moving. I lost my job back in California, so we're on the way back to my hometown in Michigan."

"You mean to tell me", Kenny asked, "that everything you got is in that car?"

"Pretty much", Scott assured him.

"Damn, fella", Kenny said as he pondered the implications of this. "I'll be able to drag this thing out of the field, but dollars to doughnuts it's not going anywhere but the scrap yard. You're in a bad way."

"Tell me about it", Scott replied, close to tears. "I've no idea what we're going to do."

"I can only think of one thing", Kenny replied, and looked at Steve. "Helge?"

"No question", Steve replied.

"You got her number?" Kenny asked.

"Who doesn't?" Steve said, pulling out his phone.

"Me, for one, because I left my cell back in the cab", Kenny explained. "Give her a call, wouldya? Tell her it's urgent."

"Got it", Steve answered, punching up some numbers.

"Now"—Kenny turned to Scott, who was completely befuddled by this cryptic exchange—"I'll want to flip this thing over before I can tow it onto the bed, and that'll tumble everything around even worse. If you got anything you want to grab—especially anything fragile or electronic—you might want to fetch it out now."

"Oh, good idea", Scott said, thinking of his phone and his tablet.

"And you might want to grab your insurance information and registration", Kenny advised. "The cops'll need 'em, and I'm thinking you'll want to be calling your insurance before you call your mother."

"She's on her way", Steve announced. "She was just up at the stop having a coffee and will be here within five. And here's the sheriff." He pointed to the road, where a cruiser was pulling up with lights flashing. Presently the deputy joined them.

"Word I got was that this was a walkaway, no injuries. We sure about that?" the deputy asked as he surveyed the wreckage.

"Seems to be the case", Steve confirmed. "Two adults and a baby, shaken and stirred but unharmed."

"Thank God for that", the deputy said, peering into the car. "Lotta junk in there."

"And I have to get some of it out", Scott said, remembering Kenny's suggestion. He dropped down and crawled in, poking around until he found his phone, Megan's purse, and his jacket. Fortunately his tablet had been in his briefcase, which was firmly wedged behind his seat. He also gingerly opened the glove compartment and extracted his documents. He could hear the men explaining to the deputy why there was so much gear in the car.

"So," the deputy asked as Scott stood up and handed him the paperwork, "what happened?"

"Don't exactly know", Scott said with a shrug. "We got across the overpass safely and were heading up the merge ramp when we must have hit a slick patch. There was some gusting crosswind, and maybe some turbulence from the trucks, and all of a sudden we were veering and swerving. I tried to steer us toward the shoulder to avoid the line of trucks to our left, and we went down the embankment sideways, which probably was what got us rolling."

"That was good thinking", the deputy confirmed. "Rolling through a field is no fun, but it's better than tussling with semis."

"We were right behind them, officer", Steve chimed in. "We saw it all. They were just accelerating up the ramp, nice and smooth, no funny stuff, when suddenly they're fishtailing all over. Then they went sideways off the road."

"Black ice", the deputy said, nodding. "We're getting reports of it up and down the expressway. We've called out the county trucks, but it's too late for you. Hard luck, this. They tell me you're moving?"

"Headed for Michigan", Scott confirmed.

"And smashed up in a Nebraska field", the deputy said, shaking his head and looking grim. "Hard luck indeed."

"We called Helge", Kenny said. "She said she'd be here shortly."

"Did you?" The deputy's face brightened. "That's good, that's good."

"And here comes the trooper", Steve said, pointing to the patrol car pulling up. Soon they were joined by the state policeman, who, Scott noticed, was walking through the mud in just his shoes, like Scott.

"I gotta get me some of those", the trooper said, pointing to the rubber muck boots the other men were wearing. "Just for such eventualities. So, what have we got?"

"No injuries, thank God", the deputy explained. "But a smashed-up car half buried in mud, a wife and baby in the Tahoe over there, and everything they got thrown around inside the car."

"Moving?" the trooper asked Scott.

"Yeah", Scott confirmed glumly. "Lost my job in California, and heading back to my hometown in Michigan." The situation sounded grimmer with each retelling, depressing Scott even more. The trooper seemed to agree and slapped Scott's shoulder sympathetically.

"As if you'll have any better job prospects back there", the trooper said. "And then this. Tough luck, man."

"Well, here's a little good news", Kenny said, pointing back toward the road. "Helge is here."

Chapter Thirteen

Scott turned to look, hoping to get a glimpse of this mysterious person whom everyone seemed to know and trust. All he saw was a faded green minivan with fake-wood paneling pulling up by the side of the road near the tow truck. Scott scowled in mystification—that rusty van was what everyone had been waiting for? But there was no denying that three of the men seemed markedly more upbeat at the sight. Shortly a figure came stomping around the front of the van, wearing muck boots and carrying a travel mug, and started walking down the embankment.

Now Scott was really puzzled. He didn't know what he had been expecting, but it hadn't been this dumpy-looking woman squelching through the mud. Her dull blonde hair hung out from beneath a brown knit cap, and she wore a dingy green work jacket. "Plain" would have been a polite description of her weathered face, and she walked with a slight bowlegged sway.

"Hey, fellas!" she called cheerily as she approached, waving her mug.

"Helge!" Kenny stepped forward with a grin and shook her hand vigorously. "Thanks for coming!"

"Just up the road a piece, no trouble at all", Helge explained, then turned to Steve. "Thanks for the call, Steve."

"Sure thing", Steve replied, gripping her hand. "The wife and baby are up with Ann staying warm."

"That's good", Helge said with a surprisingly bright smile. Then she turned to the deputy and held out her hand. "Jim! How are ya? How's Peggy coming along?"

"Well, slower than we'd like, but steadily improving", the deputy explained. "She really appreciated the cleaning crew."

"Happy to, happy to", Helge replied. "There's more where that come from, but you have to call me, 'cause she never will." Turning to the trooper, she extended her hand. "And Officer . . . ?"

"DeGroot, Paul DeGroot", the deputy said, introducing himself.

"Officer DeGroot, a pleasure", the woman said, gripping his hand warmly. "Helge Sykes of Big Springs."

"Oh, so just up the road a bit here?" Officer DeGroot asked.

"Just a piece, but I get around. And this is . . . ?" Helge asked, turning at last to Scott.

"Scott Kyle", Steve said, introducing him.

"Scott, pleased to meet you", Helge said, taking his hand in a firm grip and offering him a kind smile with just enough sympathy. "Though I'd have hoped for better circumstances. Helge Sykes of Big Springs. I'm sorry for your misfortune, and we'll do all we can to help."

"Um . . . thank you", Scott mumbled, not knowing what to say.

"No injuries, you say?" Helge asked.

"Apparently not", Deputy Jim confirmed. "Everyone was well strapped in. Walked away."

"Well, you watch things", Helge cautioned, turning to Scott. "Keep an eye out for dizziness, nausea, headaches, blurred vision— sometimes a concussion can take a while to manifest. And the baby—sometimes their heads can flop around even if they're well strapped in. Watch for tenderness around the neck or head bruises."

"Ah . . . sure", Scott answered, a bit surprised.

"Now, let's have a look here", Helge said with brisk authority, turning toward the car and walking around in front of it. Surveying the wreck, she pulled out a cigarette, tapped it down, and lit it with an old-style metal lighter. As she circled the car, muttering to herself and eyeing everything carefully, Scott looked at the other men in amazement. They were just watching her, as if this was normal and expected behavior.

At last Helge came all the way around the car and stood looking at it with a grim expression. Scott noticed that she was careful to keep her cigarette downwind.

"Well, this is a hell of a mess", Helge pronounced. "This car's a total for sure. Kenny, can you get close enough to right this thing?"

"I brought the flatbed, and it has the long cable, so I'm pretty sure I can reach it", Kenny explained.

"Good", Helge said. "If you have trouble, let me know. This is Dan Mason's field, and I can have him here with one of his tractors in fifteen minutes if need be. Scott, have you fetched everything out of the car, including your insurance and registration?"

"Yes", Scott confirmed.

"Okay, because you may want to get on the horn with your insurance company while Kenny drags you out. Do we have a police report number yet?"

"Damn, Helge, we just got here", said Deputy Jim, grinning.

"And you've been standing there with your hands in your pockets the whole time", Helge taunted back. "If I promise a doughnut to the first one to get started, will that generate some action?"

That got a general laugh. "I'll do it", Jim said, waving his clipboard at Trooper DeGroot. "If this kind of stuff is going on, you're probably going to be needed up and down the highway."

"All right, then, if you've got this under control", the trooper said, waving and heading back to his patrol car.

"Steve, can you grab that car seat and bring it back up?" Helge asked. "I've got some calls to make."

For Scott, the next half hour was a tense and frustrating period of watching his car being flipped back over and dragged across the field, as well as trying to get somewhere with his insurance company. Finally the Jetta was ready to be winched onto the truck bed, but Helge stopped Kenny short, reached into the backseat, and pulled out the diaper bag.

"Now we're set", she announced, signaling Kenny to winch away. "Let's see how the wife and baby are doing."

Scott had looked in on them earlier, and they'd seemed to be all right. Megan had nursed Grace to sleep and was sitting quietly, looking shell-shocked. Scott had recognized her expression—a combination of stress and trying to relax against the need for a bathroom. He'd smiled sympathetically and assured her that they'd be going soon.

Now Helge looked in, somewhat surprising Megan. "Hi", Helge said. "You must be Mrs. Kyle. I'm Helge Sykes of Big Springs. Kenny'll have your car winched up in no time, and we can get going. Your choice where we go. Ogallala has more facilities, but it's further up the road and the more costly tow. The next exit is my town, Big Springs. Fewer facilities but enough to get you by—truck stop, hotel, other stuff. Just a few miles up. Your call."

"Please, Scott," Megan pleaded, "the shortest drive possible."
Scott nodded assent.

"All right, then. Big Springs it is, Kenny", Helge announced to the
tow driver, who'd just come up. "Take it to the truck stop."

"Okay, Helge", Kenny said. "But to warn you—I can take one in
my cab, maybe two, but not two and a car seat."

"And Steve was just telling me that he and Ann have to get going",
mused Helge. "I can take 'em in my van"—she turned to speak to
Scott and Megan—"if you don't mind. It's a little scruffy but has
room for you all."

"That'll be fine, thanks", Scott said.

"All right, then", Helge said. "Kenny, head on out." She turned
back to Scott. "Here, Jim gave me this for you." She handed a card
to him. "It's got the report number on it—you'll need that for your
insurance. How'd that go?"

"Terrible", Scott snarled. "They say they won't have anyone available to inspect the car until toward the end of the week." That summary hardly described the teeth-grinding frustration of dealing with
the 800-number customer service agents who were ever so sympathetic but unable or unwilling to do anything actually to help.

"Yeah, well," Helge said, nodding, "I kind of expected that. We'll
see what we can do. C'mon, let's shift to the van so we can get rolling." Grabbing the diaper bag, Helge marched up to her van, leaving
Scott to help Megan. With a practiced hand, Megan eased Grace
onto her shoulder without waking her and made her way after Helge
while Scott thanked Steve and Ann for their help. Then he followed
Megan to the side door of the van, where Helge was busy strapping
in the car seat.

"There", Helge announced, stepping back so Megan could put
Grace in. "We'll get this door shut so as to keep the wind out of her
face—did I see a blanket in that bag?"

"You did", Megan confirmed.

"You may want to tuck it around her—it takes a while for the van
to warm up. Scott, could I see your insurance paperwork for a bit?
Want to make a call or two."

"Ah ... sure", Scott said, handing over the slip of paper. He wasn't
sure what luck Helge would have but was happy to let her try.

"You two settle in; I'll be right along. We'll go someplace warm and get you a good lunch", Helge said, stepping out ahead of the van, lighting up, and flipping open her phone.

"I'd settle for a bathroom and a place to wash up", Megan muttered as they got into the van. "Scott, who is this woman?"

"I've no idea", Scott answered, looking through the windshield at where Helge was talking on her phone with great animation. "She didn't give any title or office, but when she showed up everyone started taking orders from her. Even the cops deferred to her."

"I wonder if she's the mayor or something", Megan mused. "Whoever she is, she has rather . . . simple tastes." She rolled her eyes around the van, which smelled of smoke. The interior was dusty, and the rear seat had been removed. Some boards and a milk crate stuffed with twine and tools rattled around in the back. There was a plastic statue of Jesus stuck on the dash, and a truck-stop travel mug of coffee stuck in the holder between the front seats. Even her cell phone, almost always in her hand, was an older flip model in a camo case that hooked on her belt.

"What, no gun rack?" Megan giggled.

"Guess not", Scott said with a shrug. "She's been quite helpful, though—everyone has."

"I wonder how helpful they'd be if they knew we were gay?" Megan said.

"Don't know", Scott said. "Camouflage can be useful." He gestured toward Grace.

"Oh Scott, Scott, what are we going to do?" Megan's composure melted. "Why did this have to happen now?"

"I don't know", Scott replied, taking her hand. "The insurance company says it'll be three or four days before they can even get someone out here to appraise the damage."

"What?" Megan wailed, causing Grace to stir. "You mean we might be stuck here—"

Just then Helge pulled the door open and got in, handing the insurance papers back to Scott.

"In this neck of the woods, claims adjusters are kind of thin on the ground", Helge started explaining as she started the car and dropped it into gear. "But they all know one another and will cover each other in a pinch. I know Hank Glass, who works up in Ogallala. He knows the guy who adjusts for your company and is going to call him to see what he can do. No promises, but hopefully we'll work something out. Coffee?" She held up a thermos that had been lying in the net between the front seats.

"No thanks", Scott said, waving her off.

"Probably cold anyway", Helge pronounced, dropping the thermos back down. "Excuse me, I have to make a call." She unhitched her phone and thumbed a number. "Just calling the motel up at the exit", she explained with the phone at her ear. "Yeah, hello? Good morning, this is Helge Sykes. Is Judy there? Sure, thanks." There was a pause. "Hey, Judy? Yeah, Helge here. Have you got a room for a family who were just in a wreck up at the junction? Young couple with a little baby." She paused. "No, no injuries, thank the Lord, but they need to wash up and probably get some rest. Kenny's bringing their car into the truck stop." Another pause. "Sure, that'd be great. Friends and family rate, right? Thanks loads, Judy." She flipped the phone closed.

"Judy's the day manager up at the motel—" Helge started to explain, but just then her phone rang again. She glanced at the number. "It's Hank", she said to Scott as she took the call. "Helge Sykes here. Yeah, Hank?" She waited. "Oh ... okay, that's what we thought. Can you scare up anyone else? Sure, anybody but that horse's ass Andy Krueger. After the trouble he gave Lynne Visser over that kitchen fire, I never want to see his face around again. The situation here calls for speed and understanding, not rule quoting and penny-pinching. Sure, whatever you can do. I owe ya, Hank. Bye."

Scott and Megan looked at each other with raised eyebrows. Whatever else they thought about Helge, there was no denying she got things done.

"Hank got hold of your company's adjuster", Helge explained. "Sure enough, he's tied up until Thursday at the earliest. But he's willing to take someone else's write-up and submit it, if we can find anyone free. Hank's looking to see who might be available. Here's our exit."

Helge got off the expressway and turned into a truck stop that looked just like the dozens of other truck stops they'd passed on their travels. Megan was sitting at the edge of her seat, holding the car door, as Helge parked. The moment the van stopped, Megan threw the door open and made a beeline for the restrooms.

"Be right back! You've got her, right?" Megan called over her shoulder as she trotted off. Scott just waved and glanced at the sleeping Grace. Helge had her phone out again and was keying in some number, but Scott couldn't see the tow truck with the Jetta.

"Any idea where Kenny is?" he asked Helge.

"Probably the far side of the stop, over by the motel", Helge said, pointing. "He'd want to drop it off away from where trucks might be moving around."

"Ah", Scott said, nodding. He glanced back at Grace, who was snoozing calmly. He was feeling the urge to be present when his car was dropped off. "You've got her, right?"

Helge just waved as she lifted her phone to her ear, which Scott took as assent. He hopped out and went in search of Kenny's truck.

Megan emerged from the truck stop shortly thereafter, feeling much better, but she froze when she saw the van standing open with nobody nearby, the side door wide open, and Grace's car seat empty.

"Oh my God", Megan whispered, her blood chilling. "Scott, why did—GRACE!" she called, breaking into a dash to the empty van. Only as she approached did she notice that the back hatch was up.

"Grace?" Megan panted, coming around the end of the van to see Grace lying on her changing pad, amid the dirt and sawdust, with Helge wrapping up the diaper she'd just changed.

"Did Scott . . . where did he go?" Megan asked, both relieved and upset.

"He had to go meet up with Kenny", Helge explained, bagging the diaper. "Your little one here—Grace, right?—woke up and was fussing. Turned out all she needed was a change." Helge turned back to the baby. "That's all, wasn't it?" Helge cooed to Grace as she snapped up her outfit.

"Here, I can . . ." Megan offered, not liking the sight of her baby lying on a filthy car floor getting her diaper changed in the Nebraska wind. But Grace didn't seem perturbed—she just looked up at Helge, who was chattering to her as she worked.

"Who's the sweetest baby?" Helge asked as she pulled Grace's jacket back on. "Yes, who's the sweetest baby?"

Megan was amazed at how gently the rough-cut country woman handled the baby. Grace was right at the age when she was leery of strangers—sometimes she'd even turn away from Scott—yet here she was, allowing herself to be bounced and tickled by a strange woman in a work jacket who smelled of cigarette smoke.

"She knows she's loved", Helge assured Megan as she handed Grace over. "I can always tell. All babies are wonderful, but the ones who know they're loved—well, those are the sweetest. She's what? Six, seven months?"

"Six and a half", Megan said, bouncing Grace, who kept turning to look at Helge.

"That'd be about when we lost Jessie", Helge said. Seeing Megan's look of shock, Helge continued. "We had the four, you know, and Jessie was our third. Sweetest little baby but born with a heart condition. She struggled along, poor thing, and the doctors did their best for her. We even took her to out of state, up to Rochester in Minnesota—best doctors in the world. The whole town held a fundraiser to help out. Mike and Connie Wilkins, now, they donated a whole field's worth of grain—a whole field! I'll never forget that.

"Everyone did what they could, but what she needed was a heart transplant, and there weren't any donors. So we lost her. Laid her to rest in the churchyard beside my ma and pa." Helge leaned over to pack up the diaper bag, brushing her eyes with the back of her hand. "I be sure to visit them every week."

"I ... I'm terribly sorry", Megan said quietly. "When ..."

"When did it happen? Decades ago", Helge explained. "I'd guess Jessie would be about your age, had she lived."

"Here," Megan said, thrusting Grace back into Helge's arms, "let me pack that up." She started attending to the diaper bag.

"This jacket here", Helge said, fingering Grace's hooded sweatshirt, "may have done for California, but it's a bit light for Nebraska—and Michigan. We'll have to see what we can do about this."

Scott returned from dealing with Kenny to find Megan and Helge heading toward the restaurant. He was depressed from seeing his car dumped in a truck-stop parking lot, a smashed and mud-smeared hulk, and he was dirty and wet and cold. He would have loved nothing so much as a long, hot shower and a nap, but first they had to extricate their gear from the car and check into the motel. But he and Megan agreed that lunch first was a good idea, despite their condition.

As they were getting ready to go in, Helge's phone rang. She handed Grace back to Megan and answered it.

"Helge Sykes here. Yes, hello, Mark; thanks for calling. Yup, hit some black ice doing seventy, rolled right into a field." She paused. "No, thank God, but the car looks bad. Hold on, he's standing right here." Helge turned to Scott. "Year? Miles?"

"Two thousand four Jetta, about a hundred thirty-two thousand miles", Scott said. "V6."

"Yeah, Mark, it's a 2004 Jetta with about a hundred thirty. Looks very well maintained—or it did." She waited. "Yeah, that's what I'm thinking, but you're the pro. Hold on, let me ask." Again Helge turned to Scott. "Any lienholders?"

"No, all paid off", Scott said.

"Free and clear", Helge relayed. There was a pause, and then Helge broke into a broad smile. "That's very helpful of him, and of you, Mark. Tomorrow morning, then? No, that's great. I'll pass that right along. You've got my number—talk to you then." She snapped her phone closed. "That was Mark Cummings, an adjuster for Nebraska Mutual. He covers this area and was going to be out this way tomorrow. He spoke to your company's adjuster, who's willing to take Mark's write-up and submit it. Mark will come by first thing tomorrow. He agrees that it sounds like a total but needs to eyeball it to verify that. He's hopeful that if everything is cut-and-dried, the claim will be in process by close of work tomorrow."

"That's ... that's good, right?" Megan asked. She had never owned a car and was a bit confused by the nuances.

Scott was stunned. Not an hour before, he had been battering his head against customer service hell, being told it might be a week before his claim would go in. But thanks to this unsophisticated woman and her camo-cased cell phone, they might have resolution by the end of tomorrow. "Yes ... yes, it's very good", he stammered. "I'm ... thank you, Helge."

"Don't thank me", Helge said, waving. "We've got great people around here, and they look after their own—and any who might fall into misfortune. C'mon, let's get some lunch."

The waitress who seated them, whose name tag said "Missy", put them in a booth that happened to overlook the portion of the parking lot where the Jetta had been dropped. Scott almost asked if they could be reseated, not wanting his appetite ruined by the dismal sight, but by then the hostess was bringing a high chair for Grace, so he didn't want to bother.

"She sits up right well, doesn't she?" Helge asked as they strapped in the wiggly Grace. "And look now, two teeth already! Does she eat solids yet?"

"Only little crumbs", Megan admitted. "She's always curious but doesn't always like it."

"What a sweet baby", Missy said with a smile as she handed menus around. "Are you the family who just had the accident up the way?"

"That was us", Scott said flatly, glancing at the Jetta.

"Oh, how terrible", Missy said sympathetically. "A mercy that nobody was hurt, but what trouble! We are so sorry for your misfortune. This is on the house—anything you want."

"Why ... thank you", Megan said.

"Well, it's not much against your difficulties", Missy said with a wave. "But it's a token of our concern."

For his part, Scott was wondering how much of their circumstances were a topic of conversation around Big Springs. He buried his face in the menu.

"Say, Missy, do you have any graham crackers?" Helge asked.

"Why sure, Helge", laughed Missy. "Because of all the demand for graham crackers by our regular clientele." She waved her hand around the room at the truckers in the booths.

"Oyster crackers, then?" Helge asked.

"Those, we got", Missy said. "I'll give you a minute to look those menus over."

"Missy, if you see Raymond back there, could you ask him to step out for a minute?"

"Sure thing, Helge", Missy answered, heading for the kitchen.

"Oyster crackers are just the thing for tiny fingers", Helge explained to Megan. "They can be grabbed but turn to mush when wet, so there's no choking. Babies don't even need teeth to manage them— but it pays to have a damp washcloth handy."

Shortly thereafter a guy in a green cap came out with a couple of packets of oyster crackers.

"Raymond!" Helge hailed him.

"Hey, Helge", Raymond replied, handing her the packets. "Missy gave me these for you and said you wanted to see me."

"Thanks, Raymond", Helge said. "By the way, this is Scott and Megan and their baby, Grace. Favor to ask, Ray—see that mud-covered car out there in the lot?"

"Ah ... yeah", Raymond said, wincing. "What's that? An Audi?"

"VW", Scott said. "Two thousand four Jetta."

"Ouch", Raymond said. "Accident, eh?"

"Yeah", Scott confirmed, wishing there were something else to discuss.

"So I was wondering, Raymond," Helge continued as Grace batted at the oyster crackers now covering her high chair tray, "if you could wheel your power washer out there and spray the mud off that. We're going to need to get in there soon, and it'd be handy not to have to scrape off mud."

Raymond eyed the distance critically. "I dunno, Helge ... I got a long hose, but that looks like a reach even for that. Now, if the motel doesn't mind me tapping their faucets, then no problem."

"I'm sure they won't", Helge said. "I'll call Judy just to be sure, but why don't you do that?"

"It's done, Helge." Raymond touched his hat brim and headed off.

"Normally I wouldn't suggest getting a power washer near that fine finish", Helge explained to Scott. "But I figure it won't make much difference now."

"Yeah", Scott acknowledged glumly.

Scott had a subdued lunch while the women chatted and Grace scattered oyster crackers. He couldn't bear to watch, and couldn't bear not to watch, as Raymond scoured away the mud from the Jetta. When he was finished, if you squinted and cocked your head, it looked just like a parked car. But closer examination even from this distance showed the telltale signs of major damage: the dented pillar, the buckled hood, the slight cant to the frame. His beautiful Jetta.

After lunch they went to the car to gather what gear they needed for checking in at the hotel, leaving the remainder until the next day. Helge introduced them to Judy, who checked them in personally.

"We have one of our premium rooms for you", Judy announced. "A king suite, and we've already wheeled a crib in—"

Scott and Megan glanced quickly at each other, but it was Megan who spoke first. "If it's not too much trouble, could we have a room with two doubles? I ... I take the baby into bed to nurse, and she writhes around and disturbs his sleep. It's just easier."

"Why ... certainly", Judy said. "We have a room with two queens just two doors down. I'll have the crib moved."

"Quick thinking", Scott muttered to Megan as they made their way down the hall. Megan just giggled.

Helge left them with her number, encouraging them to call her with any need and promising to return first thing in the morning. Megan and Grace settled down to their much-needed naps, and though Scott was shaky and exhausted, he was too keyed up to sleep easily. He piled all their dirty clothes in a bag Judy had given him and hung it on the doorknob for pickup. He took a long, hot shower. He toyed with his tablet until the battery drained, and then toyed with his phone. Eventually he dozed off fitfully.

When Scott awoke, Megan was showered and playing with Grace. They found an old movie playing on television, then for dinner went to a steak house that was within walking distance. Scott could tell that Megan was trying to cheer him up, but she knew him well enough not to push. After dinner it was back to the room, having nowhere else to go and no way to get there.

Grace and a still-frazzled Megan were soon ready to go to bed for the night, so Scott acquiesced and turned off the light. But he was still feeling the stress and terror of the day, and he lay staring at the wall. Despite the girls' quiet breathing in the next bed, he felt completely alone. How was he supposed to handle all this? It was outside his experience. When he'd moved from home to Nashville, and then from Nashville to the coast, he'd had friends helping him. In fact, those friends had made all the arrangements—all he'd done was go where he was told and contact certain people. Now it was all on him. He felt completely inadequate and totally alone. What was he supposed to do?

Scott hated this feeling. He was tempted to go looking for some action—that was how he'd always coped with these bouts. But he couldn't do that in the middle of the night in Big Springs, Nebraska, with no wheels. There was no action here past the pot of decaf in the lobby. He was seized with a strong, irrational impulse to head out anyway: to pull on his jeans, grab his light jacket, and head out the door, right into the bitter November wind, to find a country road and walk off into the night. Of course he wouldn't make it far—the cold would get him soon. He'd find a tree in some field, curl up beneath it, and just drift off. At least he'd be free of the weight of all this responsibility. He savored the thought of his life slipping away, sapped little by little in the frigid night. Someone would find him eventually.

This urge was so enticing, so compelling, that Scott even half turned in his bed and started throwing off the covers. But then he heard the girls' quiet breathing in the dark. What would they do? It was his car, and they all were headed for his home. He couldn't just walk off and leave them to face this mess alone. Crushing though the burden was, it wouldn't be right to drop it on them and walk away. Whatever he did, he couldn't do that. He sighed and rolled back over, feeling lonelier than ever and utterly desolate.

"Help", he whispered into the empty darkness, but there was no answer.

Chapter Fourteen

Scott didn't know what "first thing" in a Nebraska morning was, but he suspected it was earlier than first thing in a California morning—and in an earlier time zone. So he pried himself out of bed to shower, then watched Grace while Megan showered. Grace was as happy to see him as always, grinning and chuckling and grabbing at his hands. He was glad that she seemed to have taken no physical or emotional harm from being tumbled around in a rolling car. He wished he could say the same about himself. He was losing the jumpy, jangly feeling that had immediately followed the crash, but there were still a lot of questions about what to do next. It would require many decisions and much effort on his part, for which he felt completely insufficient. He felt like finding a rock to crawl under, but there were none available. And besides—Helge would certainly find him.

At the truck stop Megan ordered the Hungry Trucker's Special while Scott—never a morning eater—got granola and yogurt, which he was surprised to see on the menu. Grace was gleefully decorating the vicinity of her high chair with her newest edible toy, oyster crackers, abetted by the delighted waitresses, who kept feeding her habit with fresh packets. Scott's phone rang as they were finishing up—it was Helge, who was just pulling up. They told her where to find them.

"Good morning, good morning", Helge greeted them cheerfully. "Hello, sweet baby!" She turned to Scott. "Hey, you tried the granola—how do you like it?"

"It's very good", Scott acknowledged. He'd expected something dusty from an old box and had been pleasantly surprised.

"Jeanette Hyde over Brule way makes it herself", Helge explained. "She has such a touch for it that her husband Frank built her a small commercial kitchen. She supplies restaurants and stores from here to North Platte. We can get you a couple of pounds if you'd like.

"Anyway, Mark Cummings just called. He's five minutes out and doesn't have much time, so I told him where the car was and told him we'd meet him there."

"Got it", Scott said. "Megan, can you catch the bill?"

"Why don't I pull my van over so we can unload the car afterward?" Helge suggested. "Mark may want to arrange for it to be towed."

Shortly afterward Mark pulled up beside the Jetta. He was sympathetic but brisk, walking around the broken car with a clipboard and a sharp eye.

"Totaled for sure", Mark said after one walk-around. "And a crying shame, at that. I can see you took good care of her. Did you have a rider covering that paint job?"

"No, I didn't", Scott said with a grimace. He'd had one but had to cancel it to cover the co-pays for Grace's birth.

"Well, those are premium wheels, and the car's overall condition is excellent." Mark made some final notations and flipped his clipboard shut. "I'm terribly sorry for your misfortune, especially since it's clear you loved the car. Jim Oleson's your agent, and I know him personally. He's promised to expedite your claim once I get him this paperwork and the photos. I'm afraid a settlement won't be near what the car was worth to you, but it'll be something."

"Thanks for anything you can do", Scott said, shaking Mark's hand.

Helge echoed, "And thanks for making the effort, Mark—I truly appreciate it. You've got my number. Anything you ever need in these parts, you call me. Anything at all, y'hear?"

Then began the dismal task of emptying the Jetta before it was towed away. There had been a fair amount of loose gear tucked and stuffed and packed around the edges of the passenger compartment, much of which had come loose in the accident. Fortunately, little was broken, but it was a terrible mess.

Helge helped Scott and Megan clean out the car, piling everything in the back of her van. She said something about heading up to her church and the altar guild, and Scott just acquiesced. He had no will to contest anything. It had been sad enough when he'd packed the remnants of his life into the Jetta to leave California. Cleaning up the scattered pieces of that was depressing beyond belief.

The short drive to Helge's church took them right through the center of Big Springs to the northern edge of town, where the trim brick church sat on a corner lot. Handily, it had a walkway that sloped down from the sidewalk to a basement door, which simplified carting their goods inside. They were aided by a bevy of ladies who made much of Megan and especially Grace, passing the baby around to be tickled and fussed over. To Scott's bemusement and slight alarm, a common sentiment expressed was the desire to eat Grace because she was so darling, even to the point of pretending to gnaw on her fingers.

"It's just how women express affection", laughed Megan when Scott mentioned it. "They're complimenting her."

"I hope so", Scott said skeptically. "If I started doing and saying stuff like that, someone would call Child Protective Services."

The ladies laid out all the goods on long tables and began sorting and folding and packing things into boxes that lay about. Meanwhile, Helge pulled Scott into a classroom of some sort.

"I don't want to presume to tell you what to do, Scott", Helge said. "But you're in a fix here, and I want to help all I can."

"Believe me, Helge, all help is appreciated", Scott assured her, wondering what this was leading up to. "I'd rather not have to make any decisions right now, but I know some need to be made."

"I know, it's got to be tough", Helge said sympathetically. "My friend Jack Mills works up at Prairie Lakes Regional Bank, and I called him to explain a bit about your situation. If you'd like, he's willing to drop by and help us sort out options."

"That sounds great, Helge", Scott replied, so within fifteen minutes he and Helge and Jack were seated around a table in the kitchen. Jack looked like everyone's grandfather and listened with just the right look of compassion as Scott updated him on the latest developments.

"Well, son, please accept my sincere sympathy for your troubles", Jack said when Scott had finished. "We here in Big Springs want to do everything we can to help out. It seems your biggest immediate need is transport—getting your family to your destination with no more surprises."

"That's pretty much it", Scott acknowledged.

"I looked up a few things", Jack continued, pulling a file folder out of his briefcase. "Based on current blue book values, you'll be lucky to get a four-thousand-dollar settlement for that car. Now, I could convince my bank to advance you a loan against that settlement, for the purpose of buying a new car, but I'll be honest: I'd advise against it."

"You would?" Scott asked.

"Yes, and here's why", Jack continued. "The only car you could get for that amount would be one I wouldn't trust to take you the thousand miles you have to go to get home. A more reliable car would entail a car loan, which you're not likely to get, being without a job. Loan standards have tightened all around, and the only people who'd even talk to you right now are people I'd recommend you never do business with."

"I understand", Scott said glumly, his thoughts returning to the check he'd torn to shreds. "So ... what options do I have? Take up residence here in Big Springs?"

"We'd love to have you", Jack said, grinning. "But I'm thinking you'd rather go home. Is there anyone back home, any family or friends, who could drive out to get you? I know it's a lot to ask them."

"There's just my mom, and she doesn't even drive", Scott admitted. "She bums rides from her friends when she needs a lift."

"Any siblings, cousins, uncles, or aunts?"

"None", Scott said, shaking his head.

"Hmm", Jack said, knitting his brow. "Thoughts, Helge?"

"There's always a bus line", Helge chipped in. "That's inexpensive and there's a stop in Ogallala."

Scott winced. He'd never taken a bus in his life and envisioned them as dingy, grimy, smelly boxes crowded with dingy, grimy, smelly people. But he was running out of options.

"It might work, just to get you home", Jack acknowledged. "Scott, is there a bus terminal in your town?"

"Lexington? Hardly", Scott replied. "Possibly Port Huron, but I doubt it. Most likely Flint or Detroit."

"Katie Billings used to work in a travel agency", Helge said, bouncing up from her seat. "She still has contacts in the industry. Let me give her a call."

Jack grinned as Helge walked out of the room, flipping open her phone. "She does that."

"I've noticed", Scott said, smiling back.

Scott and Jack talked about car wrecks, used-car dealerships, and other misfortunes of life until Helge returned about fifteen minutes later holding a slip of paper that she laid in front of Scott.

"Katie made some calls for me. We can get you on a bus out of Ogallala tomorrow, which would get you into Detroit at those times, or Flint at those times. Do you have any preference?"

"Flint, if possible", Scott said. "Mom dreads getting near Detroit."

"How far is it? I thought your mother didn't drive", Helge said.

"About an hour and a half to either city", Scott explained. "She has friends who can drive her as far as that."

"Will she be able to pick you up in Flint?" Jack asked.

"I don't know ... I should call and ask", Scott said, pulling out his phone. "For that matter, I should let her know what happened."

"You haven't called your mother since the accident?" Helge asked incredulously.

"Helge, the man wanted to tie down his plans first", Jack interjected. "No purpose worrying his mother until he knows what he's going to do!"

"Well, if it were my son, I'd want to know ..." Helge countered as Scott stepped away to dial his mother. Much as Scott appreciated Jack's charitable interpretation, the truth was that he'd totally forgotten to call her. But he was glad to have a semblance of a plan before he did.

Later Scott realized that there was one sense in which the accident made dealing with his mother easier. Had he just asked to be picked up at the Flint bus station, it would have elicited complaints. Asking her to arrange a pickup because they were arriving by bus having survived a catastrophic auto accident was an easy sell by comparison. Scott had to assure his mother several times that they were fine and even had to walk the phone out to Megan so the women could talk directly. He let his mother know when they'd be arriving, and Mom promised to have someone there to pick them up.

"And I've made arrangements for when you arrive, dear", Mom assured him.

"Oh?" Scott said, instantly skeptical. "What might those be?"

"I've talked to Mrs. Delworth, a friend of mine who runs a bed-and-breakfast", Scott's mother explained. "She has an entire upstairs that she usually closes off-season, but she'd be happy to rent it out at a cut rate just to have tenants."

"Sounds great, Mom", Scott said, thinking that he'd like to examine those upstairs, and have Megan do likewise, before they agreed to any arrangements. "We'll take a look when we get there."

With that settled, there followed the details of reserving the bus tickets and helping box up the goods they'd retrieved from the Jetta. Helge pointed out that trying to bring all those boxes as well as their luggage on a bus journey would be costly and troublesome, so she'd ship them. Then there was lunch and some more delay because Grace was napping. Finally they headed back to the motel with arrangements for Helge to pick them up the next morning and take them to Ogallala.

Back in their room they found their clothes from the day before washed and neatly folded on the bed.

"You know, Scott," mused Megan as they packed away the laundry, "remember when I wondered how these people would treat us if they knew we were gay?"

"Yeah", Scott replied.

"I think they would have treated us just the same", Megan concluded. "Maybe it's just the small-town spirit."

"Megan, I grew up in a small town", Scott reminded her. "I assure you that the small-town spirit isn't always generous and caring."

"Well, maybe your town didn't have a Helge Sykes", Megan replied. "Or maybe you did, but you didn't know who she was."

They turned in early so as to be ready for an early departure. Scott slept well, no longer plagued by the dark despair that had dogged him. When morning came and it was time to settle the hotel bill, Scott was stunned.

"Fifty dollars?" he asked the clerk. "For two nights? There must be some mistake."

The clerk checked the bill. "Nope, no mistake. See that code right there? 'FFR'? That's friends and family rate. Twenty-five a night, inclusive."

"Wow", Scott said. "Well ... thank you."

"You're welcome", the clerk said with a smile. "We hope to see you back under better circumstances."

At the truck stop, Missy was back on shift and insisted on serving them. She loaded them down with handfuls of oyster cracker packets and a pound of Jeanette's homemade granola, as well as sandwiches and water bottles for the bus trip. When Helge pulled in, there were hugs all around, and then their things were tossed in the back of the van and they headed out of Big Springs.

Since they had a bit of time, Helge took them along the Lincoln Highway in the gray dawn light. As they drove she swilled coffee from her travel mug and kept up a steady flow of commentary about the people who lived in the homes and farms they were passing. Scott, who was still trying to wake up, cared little for people and events that didn't concern him, so tuned most of it out. But Megan loved the stories and engaged Helge in delighted conversation the whole way.

Soon they were in Ogallala, another small town, albeit one with a bus station. Scott busied himself with getting the tickets and checking their bags and the car seat. Megan and Helge chatted until boarding time, with Helge playing with a surprisingly placid Grace. Then there were tearful hugs on Megan's part and a rough handshake for Scott.

"Thank you ever so much for all your help", Scott said to Helge with deep sincerity. "You and your friends helped salvage a disaster."

"It's what we do around here", Helge said with a smile. "Now, you have my number, right? Call often, especially when you get home. I want to hear how that sweet baby is doing!"

"We will!" Megan assured her with a wave as she climbed the bus steps. Once inside, she wiped her eyes. "I'm going back someday," she announced, "if only to see Helge. Maybe in summer, but I'm going back."

Scott figured it wasn't a good time to state his candid thoughts about his ever returning to Big Springs. But he couldn't deny that the folks had been generous and helpful, and he could tolerate returning if it meant seeing them again.

To Scott's pleasant surprise, the bus wasn't dingy, dirty, or smelly, but bright, clean, and with a fresh scent. The fellow passengers didn't look any worse than those he might meet on a plane. But there were no recharging facilities, so he'd have to be stingy with the use of the portable devices.

If traveling by bus wasn't the excruciating ordeal Scott had feared, it still called for a lot of patience. He and Megan alternated caring for Grace, who quickly tired of her restricted environment. They dozed and read and walked Grace up and down the aisle as the bus rolled across the seemingly endless prairie. They stopped briefly in North Platte, Lincoln, and Omaha, finally passing into Iowa. There was a slightly longer delay at Des Moines before the route's final leg into Chicago, where they arrived late at night and had to stay in the terminal until their next bus left in the morning.

The Chicago station was more like Scott's worst imaginings of bus travel: large, noisy, crowded, and busy, even in the middle of the night. Poor Grace, already strained by a long day of travel, was restless and fussy. But Megan dealt with her admirably, showing astonishing stamina and resilience.

"Just one more day of this", she reassured Scott. "We can make it."

Yes, but then what? The question was looming ever larger in Scott's mind. He'd spoken to his mother a couple of times while they were crossing Nebraska and Iowa. Mom had everything lined up—a friend had a brother who had an SUV he was willing to let them borrow for the pickup in Flint. The bus station was just off I-69, making the driving easy. Mrs. Delworth had the apartment all ready, including a new crib. Clearly their arrival was the height of excitement for Mom, which Scott could understand. But to him it felt increasingly like a defeat. He'd left his hometown wishing never to return except to broadcast his successes in bigger and better places—and he'd never even done that. Now he was crawling back because he had to, poor and jobless, with a wife and child in tow, without even a car to drive, dependent on his impoverished mother. Hardly the triumphant return he'd envisioned.

They boarded the bus the next morning, and once clear of the exasperating Chicago traffic the roads and towns started to become more familiar to Scott: I-94, which would take them to Detroit; Kalamazoo, where some friends had attended college; Battle Creek; Jackson; Ann Arbor. Despite Scott's disdain for his flyover-state roots, something within him brightened at these familiar places. They arrived in Detroit under gray skies that were pouring rain, and had to wait an hour or so to board the bus that went north to Flint. They called his mother as they boarded, because the timing was such that if she left Lexington when they left Detroit, they'd all arrive in Flint about the same time.

"Feeling excited about being back in your home state?" Megan asked as the bus navigated the freeways out of Detroit.

"Well, I wouldn't say excited, especially under these circumstances", Scott replied. "But it's not as dismal as I feared. With all the tumult we've been through, it's comforting to see familiar roads and cities. It would feel a lot more alien if we were in, say, New Jersey or North Carolina. But then, it's all alien to you. How do you feel?"

"Well, anywhere besides the Phoenix area would be strange to me, and there's no way I'd go back there", said Megan with a shrug. "So I was prepared for alien. As long as you're more comfortable, I'm good—and so is she." Megan indicated the sleeping Grace.

"Just about another hour", Scott said. "But then there's the drive home."

The Flint bus station was a small, rather dismal place, made even less inviting by the gray skies and cold rain. They arrived before Scott's mother did, giving them time to retrieve luggage, visit restrooms, and have Megan feed Grace. At last a white Suburban pulled into the parking lot, and was barely stopped before a door flung open and Scott's mother dashed through the rain to nearly bowl him over in a crushing hug.

"Hi, Mom", Scott said, grinning. It had been years since he'd seen her, and aside from a bit more gray and a few more lines, she looked the same as he'd remembered.

"Joe, Joe, so good to see you!" Mrs. Kyle said. "Oh, this is Tina Eliot, who was kind enough to drive. Now: where are my daughter-in-law and granddaughter?"

"Right here", Megan answered with a smile. "A pleasure to meet you, Mrs.—ah, Mom."

Mrs. Kyle brushed aside the proffered hand and gave Megan a hug, though more gently out of deference to Grace, who was eyeing her askance.

"Megan! What a delight to meet you!" Mrs. Kyle gushed. "And this is Grace! Oh my goodness! The spitting image of Lisa at that age! Except for the forehead, which looks like you, dear—and the beautiful hair."

"Um, Mom?" Scott said with a nudge. "Can I load the luggage so we can get going? We've done a lot of traveling over the past week and are anxious to be finished."

"Certainly, dear", Mrs. Kyle said. "Is that all you have? I thought you were bringing all your gear."

"This is all we brought on the bus", Megan explained. "The rest is being shipped to us by the good citizens of Big Springs—which reminds me, I want to call Helge. She wanted to hear when we arrived."

"Call who?" Mrs. Kyle asked.

"Helge Sykes of Big Springs", said Megan with a grin, punching up the number. "A lady who *really* saved our necks after the accident. Without her and her friends, we'd probably still be—hello, Helge? Hi, it's Megan. We're safely in Michigan. Scott's mom is here to pick us up. Grace? Yes, as sweet as ever. She did okay, but we're all tired of traveling. Oops—there's my battery. Yes, I'll call again. Thanks again for all the help!"

They piled the gear into the Suburban and headed east along the expressway. Now they were in Scott's home territory, roads he had driven often. Megan and his mom sat in the back, and he could hear Megan telling the full tale of their time in Big Springs. Scott was glad he didn't have to contribute much. Tina wasn't very talkative except for a few courteous comments, leaving Scott to gaze out the window at the rain-washed fields. Nothing looked to have changed very much.

After about an hour's drive they reached Port Huron, where Scott pointed out the sweeping arches of the Blue Water Bridge that dominated the skyline.

"And that's Canada on the other side", Mrs. Kyle explained.

"Ooh, Canada! I've never been there—what's it like? Can we go sometime?" Megan asked.

"It's pretty much like the U.S.", Scott said. "Nothing special, really."

"And these days you need a passport to cross", Mrs. Kyle explained. "Not so much to get over as to get back."

At Port Huron, they turned north to follow the lakeshore road. As Scott expected, Megan was astonished by the size of the lake.

"It's like the ocean!" she exclaimed. "You can't see the other side!"

"Big enough for ships to sail on—there's one right now", Scott said, pointing at a lake freighter in the distance.

"Oh … rats, I can't see it. A pity all those houses get in the way", Megan said.

"You'll get plenty of opportunity", Mrs. Kyle explained. "Lexington is right on the water. Not me, of course—I live in a trailer park—but the house you're staying in is only a few blocks from the harbor and has a view of the waterfront. You'll be able to walk down and look out over the lake."

Dusk was falling as they finally reached their destination. To Scott, pulling up to the town's sole stoplight in the gray twilight of a cold, rainy November day seemed the final slap that fate could give. He could hardly imagine a more depressing homecoming.

"Is this it?" Megan asked, looking around.

"I told you it was small", Scott chuckled darkly.

"Why don't we drive down by the harbor, and—" Mrs. Kyle began, but Scott cut her off.

"Mom, we're all tired, and Grace is starting to get fussy. Why don't we head over to our apartment like we agreed? Besides, it's hardly a night for sightseeing."

"All right, all right", Mrs. Kyle conceded, so they drove the couple of blocks to the old house where Mrs. Delworth kept her bed-and-breakfast. It was located in the grandiosely named Historic District, which was actually a few blocks of older homes that had been built by shipping and lumber barons. Many of them were now getting second lives as vacation homes or bed-and-breakfasts, but the establishments always struggled outside tourist season. As they pulled up to the vast white clapboard house with its wraparound porch, corner turret, and gingerbread trim, Megan's eyes grew wide.

"It's *beautiful*", she said in wonder.

"And drafty", Scott muttered, hopping out of the car to grab the luggage while Megan got Grace. There was a dash through the rain to the porch, where Mrs. Delworth came out to greet them. After dumping the suitcases, Scott ran back out to the car to unbuckle the car seat, thank Tina, assure his mother they'd call, and get back under the shelter of the porch before he got totally drenched.

Mrs. Delworth was a kind, quiet lady who seemed instinctively to understand how frayed and tired they were. She didn't press them to visit but let them know that she had some soup and biscuits if they were hungry, and took them directly upstairs so they could settle in. Megan was wide-eyed at the hardwood floors, carved railings, molded plaster ceilings, and beautiful chandeliers. Scott was thinking primarily of how narrow the staircase was and how hard it was to navigate with two suitcases.

The upstairs had plenty of square footage but was carved up into numerous small rooms. Mrs. Delworth explained that she'd tried having two units up there, but that didn't work because the guests had to share the bathroom and there was no good way to divide the rooms. So after the past season she'd had it opened up into one full-floor unit. She'd gotten new—well, period—furniture and was going to try billing the unit as something of a romantic retreat spot. She showed them the kitchenette; the bath; the sitting room in the turret, from which they'd be able to look out over the lake (Megan was charmed); the study, which had been converted into the baby's bedroom; and the rather small living room. At last they came to what was clearly her pride and joy: the master bedroom.

"I've tried to duplicate everything as it would have been", Mrs. Delworth announced as she swept into the room. "Curtains, pictures, chairs, washing stand ... I found that secretary at a yard sale, of all things ..."

Megan and Scott entered the room, stopped, and looked at each other with raised eyebrows. Expectably enough, in the middle of the room stood a king-sized bed covered with a great floral comforter.

"Do you like it?" Mrs. Delworth asked. "It's a classic four-poster, fully restored. Don't worry, that's a modern mattress and box spring under there. I had to have the frame slightly modified to accommodate it, but you can hardly notice. Isn't that bedspread lovely?"

They agreed that everything was wonderful, and Mrs. Delworth left them to settle in. They stood looking at the bed, and each other, with bemused smiles.

"Well," Megan said, "we should have figured on this."

"I can sleep on the couch in the—" Scott began, but Megan cut him off.

"Don't be silly, Scott. First off, that's a loveseat, not a couch. Second, there's no need for you to sleep in cramped discomfort with such a big bed available. There's plenty of room for us both."

"But ... I ..." Scott stammered.

"Don't tell me you're worried about my virtue", Megan said with a knowing grin. "I'm not—I trust you completely. And we are married, remember?"

"It's not that, it's …" Scott started, then stammered into silence while Megan kept grinning at him.

"It's what?" she prodded.

"I tend to pull the covers off", Scott offered.

"I'll pull 'em back", Megan replied.

"I thrash around a lot", Scott countered.

"You never slept with Diane", Megan answered.

"I … I'm used to sleeping nude", Scott said sheepishly.

"That's going to have to stop", Megan said firmly.

Chapter Fifteen

After the stress and tumult of the prior month, and especially of the prior week, Scott felt like holing up to sleep and read for the rest of the month. However much Angela Kyle understood her son's reclusive proclivities, she was going to seize every chance to spend time with her newly met daughter-in-law and granddaughter. So Scott and Megan and Grace spent much of the weekend over at Angela's place in the trailer park that was at the north end of town, in the shadow of the water tower. They walked over to the pickle factory where Angela worked, down the little Main Street with its tourist shops, around the little harbor with its mostly empty slips awaiting the return of the boats the following summer, and out onto the long pier of great limestone blocks that shielded the harbor from the waves.

For his part, Scott felt no nostalgia for the town near which he'd grown up and from which he'd worked so hard to escape. It was the same old streets and landmarks, except that someone had built a big brick mini-mall affair at the east end of Huron Avenue, almost overlooking the harbor. It was Megan who helped him see it somewhat anew—the beauty of blue Lake Huron stretching to the horizon under white clouds floating in a pale sky, the friendliness of the familiar people, the quaintness of the little shops. Seeing his hometown through her eyes helped him realize that many of his memories of Lexington as a dull, dingy little town had been formed over a decade earlier, in the imagination of a sullen high school student. It might not be where he wanted to spend the rest of his life, but it wasn't the end of the world.

Megan also noticed something that Scott had always taken for granted: the stark disparity between the houses that were right along the lakeshore and those even just a little way inland. Of course, things had been that way in California too, with the high-priced homes directly on the water. But in the Bay Area all real estate was in some sense prime, so you didn't see scruffy houses anywhere near the shore. This wasn't true in Michigan, where there could be a waterfront mansion sitting on groomed acres literally across the street from a shack. Megan thought this terribly incongruous, but Scott explained that it was this way all the way up the coast from Algonac to Harbor Beach—nearly every foot of waterfront was occupied by nice, and sometimes opulent, homes, even if they were located in otherwise run-down environs.

When they weren't walking about Lexington, Scott and Megan were either at his mother's place or back at their apartment, where it was becoming clear that Mrs. Delworth was going to be not as much a landlady as an adopted aunt. Megan and Grace charmed both women, and much time was spent in kitchens cooking meals and chatting merrily. The week after their arrival was Thanksgiving, and Mrs. Delworth organized an outing where all the women drove down to the supermarkets north of Port Huron to get the necessaries for the big dinner. Having no desire to accompany them, Scott stayed behind to sit in the turret room, gazing out over the lake and pondering his future.

Scott had a lot of pondering to do. He was back to square one of not only his career but his life and had no idea where he was going to go or what he was going to do. An immediate issue was keeping his paltry unemployment benefits flowing. This meant he had to document his job search, and for that he needed Internet access, which the newly remodeled accommodations didn't provide. Fortunately, it was easy to talk Mrs. Delworth into getting a wireless router, especially when he volunteered to install and configure it, because wireless Internet access was just what every romantic getaway destination needed. This enabled him to check into the California unemployment website, which he was careful to do exactly as prescribed. Though his contact at the unemployment office had assured him that those who lived and sought work out of state were treated no differently from those who stayed in California, Scott suspected that his records would come under a little more scrutiny.

Early in the week after their arrival they received three things that lifted their spirits considerably. One was the remainder of their household goods, which had been shipped by Helge and the good ladies of the Good Shepherd Lutheran Altar Guild. Grace's wardrobe had been augmented by some winter-grade additions, including a sturdy coat, probably from the church's donation box. The mail also brought the settlement check for the totaled Jetta.

The third and most pleasant surprise was a check from Jake for what he'd been able to get for the contents of Scott's apartment. Scott was shocked at how large the amount was and promptly called Jake to ensure there hadn't been a mistake.

"No, no mistake", Jake assured him. "A little ... well, not exactly deceit, but subterfuge. But no mistake."

"This is about three times my most optimistic estimate for what I'd get for all that stuff! What did you do?" Scott asked.

"Well, I knew that if I just posted it all online or somewhere, the vultures would start circling and you'd get pennies on the dollar. So, even before you left, I started making calls to upper-grade boutiques, pretending to be interested in redoing the interior design of my place—which was your place, of course. They were happy to send people to look over my 'space' and draw up plans. When I dropped hints that it would expedite the sale if I could move the old stuff at a good price, they were happy to put me in touch with parties who would take it off my hands. That was made easier by the fact that you had high-quality furnishings in good condition."

"Yeah", Scott said with a grimace, remembering how much those furnishings had originally cost. "But what happened to the salespeople? I'm surprised they're not calling you night and day about your new furniture."

"They probably are", Jake replied, and Scott could hear the grin. "But I got a cheap pay-per-minute phone for dealing with them and threw it away when I was done."

"Jake, you dog", Scott said, grinning back.

"Kind of shady, I know, but it was clear that none of them were hurting, at least not like you are", Jake said. "How was the trip home?"

With a groan Scott filled Jake in on the wreck, and the time in Big Springs, and the bus trip back home. Jake was shocked and sympathetic and even gladder that he'd made the extra effort to get the best deal he could for Scott's furniture. When Scott pressed Jake about having taken a proper percentage as commission, Jake got a little vague, so Scott was sure he hadn't. After hanging up, Scott talked to

Megan, and they agreed that a big bouquet of flowers for Jake's wife and a generous gift card to the local warehouse club was the least they could do to express their gratitude.

The insurance settlement combined with the check Jake sent eased one of Scott's biggest concerns: transportation. His mother might be able to live by walking everywhere she needed in Lexington, but he needed a reliable car even to begin looking for work. He'd known that the settlement for the Jetta wouldn't be sufficient to get a car suitable for regular commuting and big enough for all of them, but the two checks together would be plenty.

Thanksgiving took place at Mrs. Delworth's using her full-sized kitchen, formal dining room, and even her crystal and silver. The three women worked happily together cooking the meal, while Scott was relegated to watching Grace and polishing silver while she napped. When they finally sat down to dinner, there looked to be enough food for half the town. He was glad to see how happy the women were in their work, though he struggled to think what he had to be thankful for, given how much had gone wrong in his life over the past weeks. But he looked at Grace in her high chair, and Megan by his side, and decided that their being alive and unhurt was something right there. He also made a mental note to get Megan a new dress—her nice one was looking a little tired.

The following week was absorbed with setting up bank accounts and visiting dealerships and contacting insurance agencies, but by the end of it there was a late-model midsize SUV parked in the drive. Scott would have preferred a smaller car, but the best balance between price, size, and reliability had been the truck.

Scott had also tapped every resource he could find to post his résumé and search for job openings. What slender pickings he could find were mostly in the Detroit vicinity, one and a half to two hours away, and most of those didn't fit his skill set. But he kept trying and logging his efforts for the sake of the California unemployment office.

One day an opening popped up that was within fifty miles. It was at a small manufacturer in Marysville, just south of Port Huron, about forty-five minutes away. It was for a network administrator position, which wasn't exactly his niche, but he could do the work. Not expecting much, he sent in his résumé and was surprised to receive a response the next day to schedule an interview. Megan was excited, but he didn't want to get his hopes up. He was certain that there were plenty of unemployed techs with decades of network administration experience who'd be piling on that posting. But he scheduled the interview anyway, if only to be able to report progress to California.

The interview was conducted by a friendly but no–nonsense woman named Tamara. She was the information technology director for the site and was refreshingly candid about the position. As with many manufacturers in the area, they were a branch facility of a larger operation. IT decisions were mostly made at the corporate headquarters and handed down to the local staff. This meant there was precious little opportunity for innovation or improvement—they were mostly there to keep the equipment running, put out fires, and implement the sometimes-boneheaded policies dictated by "corporate" and the consultants they brought in. The network administrator post was the only full-time position other than hers and was effectively the job of an assistant IT director, for what it was worth. In actuality it meant getting all the scut work around the site for not very much pay.

Tamara was intrigued by Scott's experience, and they talked for a while about how she'd wanted to implement some virtualization on the site, though as of yet corporate wasn't buying it. She also explained that they'd had dozens of applicants for the position, and she was still sorting through the résumés, so he shouldn't expect to hear anything soon. They parted on cordial terms, and Scott drove away ambivalent about the job. He wanted employment as much as anyone, but the work didn't sound that appealing. But it was an interview, and that should satisfy the unemployment office for a while.

December rolled in with an inordinate amount of snow, even for Michigan, which complicated Scott's task of helping Mrs. Delworth hang her Christmas decorations. One Friday afternoon, after hanging some lights around the second-story windows, he tucked away the ladder and tramped over to his mother's, where Megan and Grace already were. They were playing in the living room when Scott arrived, so he sat at the kitchen table with his mother, sipping coffee.

"I've been meaning to tell you", Angela said, "how great it is to have you around. I know it's hard on you, and I'd never have wanted you to lose your job, but it's been a silver lining to see you again, especially with Megan and Grace along."

"I think so too", Scott agreed sincerely. It had been good to have his mother around and to be able just to drop in on her with the girls.

"I also want to tell you how impressed I am with you as a husband and father", Angela continued. "The whole situation mystifies me, but it's not really my business. There's no doubt you take good care of Megan and Grace both. I'm proud of you for being so responsible."

"Yeah, well, I had a stellar example of how not to do it, didn't I?" Scott said bitterly, sipping his coffee.

Angela glanced over her shoulder to where Megan was gathering up a fussy Grace to take her into the bedroom and nurse her to sleep. She turned back to Scott and said, "You know, Joe, there are some things you should understand about your father and why he left."

Scott looked at her with narrowed eyes. "Mom, don't tell me you're going to try to excuse what he did! I still have nightmares about that day—the day he walked away and wouldn't come back no matter how loudly I called."

"No, no", Angela assured him. "What he did was inexcusable, and you and Lisa bore the brunt of it. But I've seen you bear the pain since then and have known that someday I'd have to tell you the whole truth."

"What truth is that?" Scott asked, his insides suddenly getting cold.

"That I was as much responsible for that day as he was", Angela said dully, staring at her mug.

"What?" Scott scoffed. "Mom, how can you say that? You're the one who stuck by us, who sacrificed so much to raise us. He walked out; you didn't. How can you say you were as responsible as he was?"

Angela sighed and took a sip of coffee. "I met your dad in high school—the same one you went to. He was the son of two doctors who lived in a house on the lake and had a practice down Port Huron way.

"I was from Croswell—the poor section, beyond the river. My mother and I lived in an old house that isn't even standing anymore. My father didn't live with us. He'd visit occasionally, but all I remember about him was how he used to sit around in his underwear and smoke and yell at my mother. I tried to stay out of his way. I'm pretty sure they weren't married—or if they were, Mother never mentioned it. Occasionally other men would come over. I learned either to stay in my room or to slip out of the house when that happened.

"By the time I got to junior high and high school, I was determined not to be like my mother. From magazines and movies I learned how to clean myself up and present an attractive appearance. I quickly learned to mimic the speech and manners of the kind of people I wanted to hang out with, so that I'd blend right in and they wouldn't ask embarrassing questions about where I lived.

"I worked hard in school, and because I was reasonably smart, I did acceptably well. Sports weren't an option, because Mother wasn't going to manage transport for practices. I chose an activity I was good at: quiz bowl.

"Your father was a fellow member with me on the quiz bowl team. He wasn't particularly good-looking, and his simple clothes and awkward mannerisms didn't scream 'son of privilege', so the girls didn't notice him. But he was friendly and courteous. He used to open doors for me and address me as 'Miss'. He and I got along well and became good friends. The other girls started noticing him after his sixteenth birthday, when he started driving his new car to school, but by then it was too late.

"He asked me to junior prom, just as friends, and we had a great time. Afterward we were just ... 'going together'. I'm not sure why. It was partly social expectations, partly loneliness, partly just guy-gal attraction. We kind of went with the flow, and he became my 'boy-friend' and I his 'girlfriend'."

"But wait", Scott interrupted. "Did you love him?"

Angela took a sip of coffee and thought a bit before responding. "We use that phrase so often, but we rarely stop to ask what it means. Did I 'love' him? Were we 'in love'? I certainly loved him dearly as a friend. Were we both starving for attention and affection that we didn't get from our respective homes? Of course. Were we caught up in a cloud of sentiment on occasions like the junior prom? Sure. For all the summer that followed, we seemed to live in a magical glow. We wanted nothing but to be together. We'd take trips north to Port Austin or west to Frankenmuth. He'd take me to movies in Port Huron, and we'd stay up until the small hours at all-night diners just talking and laughing. We'd take long drives through the summer night, with the convertible top down and music playing, holding hands and singing along. Was that 'true love'? If you'd asked me then, I would have said, 'Of course!'

"Our senior year turned out to be the test of that. His path had been long laid out by his parents: he was accepted into premed at Michigan, with a generous scholarship and his parents' support. As the year went on, he was increasingly focused on his future.

"I'd not thought much about my after-graduation plans. I wanted to get out of Croswell but had toyed only with the idea of moving as far as Port Huron and attending the community college. Now I began to dream about a complete escape: marrying a doctor and moving into a house on the lake.

"The problem was that his plans involved a lot of talk about courses of study and medical schools and residencies, and no talk about marriage. I began to get afraid he'd go off to college, meet some other girl, and forget all about me. I started to get touchy and jealous, and we'd argue, which would frighten me even more. Were we falling out of love? What did that imply for our future together—that future I'd imagined but we'd never discussed?

"As graduation approached, I was nearly panicking. In desperation, I decided to try the ultimate appeal: seducing him. Up to that point we hadn't ... you know", Angela chuckled guiltily and sipped her coffee again. "It's embarrassing to talk to my own son about this, but you need to know. Your father had always been a gentleman toward me, never pressing me. Oh, he was a normal young man, and some of our discussions had gotten a bit 'friendly', but he'd always pulled away before things went too far. That was out of respect—for himself, for me as a lady, and for me as a friend. I didn't realize how rare and precious that respect was until after I'd destroyed it.

"In my fear I was willing to tear right through those protective barriers. On the night of our senior prom—I know, how cliché, right?—we went for a drive up to Harbor Beach and found a quiet side road on the way back. That time I didn't give him a chance to pull away. He was apologetic and guilt ridden afterward, but that didn't stop him from showing up the next night to go looking for another side road.

"Now I was sure I had him. We were 'in love' again, no question. He was as eager to see me as he had been the prior summer, and when we were together he wasn't always talking about his college plans. I didn't worry about diseases, because we'd both been virgins, and I didn't worry about pregnancy. I knew lots of girls who were sleeping with their boyfriends and weren't getting pregnant. I had nothing to worry about—I had his heart forever.

"Then I turned up pregnant with you. Even that didn't worry me at first—I didn't think much would change. I have no idea what was going through my head. I think I was imagining him going off to college and coming home from Ann Arbor on weekends to visit me and the baby."

"Oh, man", Scott groaned, burying his face in his hands. He'd had enough experience with babies to know better than that.

"I know", Angela laughed. "How naïve, right? Of course, your father was mortified. He had a far better grasp of the implications. He went home and told his parents and called me later to tell me about it. They were right furious. They took his car away, told him they wouldn't let him ruin his future, and ordered him to 'fix' the situation.

"I didn't understand what that meant—naïve, remember?—until his mother gave me a call. It was the only time I ever spoke to my future mother-in-law. She didn't even use my name. She kept talking about 'this pregnancy' and all the problems it was causing. 'This pregnancy', in a venomous hiss—I can remember it to this day."

Scott, familiar with the code, felt a deep chill as he realized it was him she was talking about.

"Anyway, she started talking about 'taking care' of it and how she was willing to make 'the arrangements' so nobody would have to worry about 'this pregnancy'. I was starting to catch on to what she meant, and I got so flustered that I said I didn't know what she was talking about and hung up.

"Then my mother asked me what the phone call had been about, so I had to tell her, and she blew up. She threw me out of the house immediately, yelling after me from the front porch, calling me a slut and a whore and throwing all my things into the front yard."

"Geez, Mom", Scott said sympathetically, laying his hand on hers as she stopped to catch her breath. "I had no idea—"

"It's okay", Angela said with a wave. "It's been decades now. Would you get me more coffee?"

Scott took her mug to rinse and refill it, giving his mother time to regain her composure. "Listen, Mom, if this is too hard for you, we can—"

"No, I'm fine, I'm fine", Angela assured him. "You need to hear all this. You should have heard it years ago. Is Megan ..."

"She's probably napping with the baby", Scott explained.

"That's good", Angela said, sipping the coffee. "Anyway, my mother threw me out, but a friend I knew through a church youth group let me bunk in her basement. Eventually your father got in touch with me—this was well before cell phones, so it was much more complex. He told me his parents had given him an ultimatum: get me to end the pregnancy; walk away and have nothing more to do with me; or get out of their house."

"Wow", Scott said, the chill settling deeper inside him. "So you both got kicked out of your homes."

"Exactly", Angela confirmed. "And now you know why you never knew any of your grandparents. But I meant it when I said your father was a gentleman—far more than I was a lady. He swore he'd marry me and take responsibility for the baby—you. So we got married at the courthouse over in Sandusky, with a couple of friends as witnesses and no family in attendance. He got seasonal work at the sugar factory in Croswell, and we got a cheap apartment over a store on Main Street. Of course, any talk about going to college went right out the window. Our focus became just making enough to survive.

"We tried to put a good face on things and joked about humble beginnings and needing only each other. But we both knew that we'd acted very foolishly and had trapped ourselves. That didn't excuse how our families treated us, but it was our choices that had put us there. After the job at the sugar factory ended, he found work where he could, while I worked as a waitress at a diner in town. When you came, I couldn't stop working—I had to leave you with whomever I could find to watch you. I used to feel just terrible. When I'd leave you, you'd be howling, and when I came to pick you up, you'd still be howling. But there was nothing I could do.

"Your father eventually found somewhat-steady work at a construction firm, but by then the economy had gone downhill and there was little demand. They kept him on, though—he had a knack for construction. That was a time when a lot of people were leaving the state. We would have left too, had we been able to afford the gas to go anywhere.

"Your father didn't talk much about it, but I suspected that during that time the thought of what he'd given up was never far from his mind. If we hadn't been so foolish, he would have been off to college, preparing for med school. He would have been in touch with his family. He would have had a future. Everything would have been different.

"When I became pregnant with Lisa, that seemed to break him. He started ranting, asking how he could possibly provide for this big family. That was when he started blaming me for trapping him. It was a cruel accusation, but nobody knew better than I how much truth it contained. He began to stay away, which he'd never done before. Supposedly he'd be late on jobs, but he'd come home smelling of beer. He began to resent being home, and I resented his resentment, and we quarreled a lot. Poor child, you spent a lot of time crying. It was not a happy home.

"Then Lisa was born, and I had to devote so much time to her, which he resented all the more. The day he left—the day you say you still have nightmares about—really wasn't all that different from any other day of our life. It just happened to be the day that put him over the edge, and he stormed out.

"That's what you might call the rest of the story. You remember that tragic day and the prominent event, and that was certainly tragic and very, very wrong. But there was a lot of quiet tragedy and wrongdoing that preceded that day, and you need to know it all. It wasn't just your father, it was me too, and for that I pray you can someday forgive me."

Tears were streaming down both their faces now, and they were grasping hands tightly.

"Mom, I don't … I've never …" Scott stammered.

"You asked if I loved him", Angela continued. "I'd say yes, especially when we were best friends, and even when we had the high school romance going. But I stopped truly loving him when I started using him, and I started using him when I listened to my fears. When I made him a means to my ends, my love for him started withering until there was nothing left."

They sat in silence at the table. Scott felt stunned and emotionally stripped. "This ... this is a lot to take in. You seem to have put a lot of thought into this."

"I have", Angela confirmed. "These past few years have been rough, with you and Lisa both leaving. But I've had some good friends who have helped me think and talk through some of these things."

Scott stared at her, struck by her statement that his absence had been hard for her. It had never occurred to him that his departing would matter to anyone.

"It's also been hard for me to be honest with myself", Angela admitted. "It's much easier to put all the blame on him, because his wrong was more glaring. But I've had to acknowledge how I wronged him, and that means I have to deal with—"

Just then Scott's phone rang. Mystified, he pulled it out and saw that it was a number from the area that he didn't recognize. Who could be calling him at 5:15 on a Friday afternoon?

"Excuse me", Scott said with a nod to his mother as he thumbed the call. "Hello? Yes—oh, hello, how are you? Yes, I do. Really? That's ... surprising. That's good to hear. Yes, I'd appreciate that. I'll call you back Monday."

With raised eyebrows he hung up and looked at his mother. "That was Tamara, from that plant in Marysville. They want to offer me the job but are giving me the weekend to think about it."

Chapter Sixteen

Megan was thrilled about the job prospect, but Scott was more cautious. The job was well beneath his skill set, and the pay was barely above what he was receiving in unemployment benefits. He'd been thinking he'd hold out for a more suitable position, even if it was down near metro Detroit or out of state. He could take the local job and still keep his résumé out there, but aggressively hunting for a new position was hard to do while holding down a full-time job.

On the other hand, half a job was better than none, and the position had some benefits. There was no guarantee that the most diligent of job searches would turn up anything better, and there was the fact that Scott had reported the interview to the unemployment office. He couldn't turn down an offer without grave reason, and if the office ever followed up with Tamara and discovered that he'd refused an offer, his unemployment benefits would be cut off. So, though the job was far short of ideal, Scott was bound to accept it. He returned Tamara's call the following Monday and accepted the position.

When Scott began work the following Wednesday, he received a swift lesson in some of the differences between the jobs he'd held to that point and information technology support in the world of small manufacturing. There was no brand-new workstation awaiting him—he got an older laptop handed down from accounting. He had to erase and reinstall all the software before he could use it. He asked for more memory for it but was told there was "no budget" for such an expenditure—a phrase he heard a lot over the following weeks. He didn't have an office but shared a small cubicle with a large printer.

Though Scott's title was network administrator, he was actually technical support for any problems that anyone might encounter, from computer lockups to forgotten passwords to severed network cables. There was nothing rewarding or cutting-edge about the work. It was little of what he liked most about technical work and much of what he liked least. There was no coherent plan for the entire site—everything had been patched and cobbled just to "make do" for years. Furthermore, there was no chance of redoing things properly. Minor expenses were denied because of "no budget", and anything major had to be submitted to corporate, where it would die.

And then there were the people. Scott was dealing with end users all day long: stubborn users and slow users and impatient users and dull users. There was Ellie in receiving, who seemed to have a magical ability to lock up the shipping workstation by walking near it. Ellie couldn't understand why these bothersome computer contraptions were necessary—she could remember when she'd run her whole dock with an array of clipboards and typed documents. The clipboards still hung on their hooks on the far wall of the loading dock, empty and rattling in the wind, while Ellie railed at the workstation and screamed "Tech Support!" when it seized up, which it did at least twice a week, though Ellie could never tell him what she might have done to it.

Though Ellie was Scott's particular bane, there was also Crystal in customer service, who was always finding new viruses; Ken in quality control, who kept downloading "utilities" to try on the lab computer; and John, the chief financial officer, who assumed that Scott could drop whatever he was doing to attend to John's problems. And the list went on. Scott's job satisfaction was almost nonexistent, but he had no alternative. The forty-five-minute drive to and from work every day gave him plenty of time to brood on his situation, when he wasn't fighting heavy snow, of which there was more than usual that winter.

A friend of Mrs. Delworth knew the owner of the pharmacy in Lexington and was able to get Megan a part-time job as a cashier and stock girl. Scott's mother and Mrs. Delworth were delighted to watch Grace during Megan's short shifts, so child care wasn't an issue. Between Scott's salary and Megan's meager hours, they were just able to make ends meet. Scott was even stashing some funds away in hopes of getting Megan and Grace some nice things for Christmas. Unfortunately, all the snow and a near spinout one day forced the issue of new tires to the fore. Just enough money remained for Scott to make a purchase that he'd been contemplating for a while. It wasn't a Christmas present, but it was the best he was going to be able to do.

"Well," Scott sighed when he at last got home that day, "I had to stop along the way and get new tires for the truck. You could nearly see fabric on the old ones."

"I was wondering why you were so late", Megan said as she slipped his sandwich onto his plate. "I was about to text you to see if everything was okay."

"It almost wasn't on the way in this morning", Scott explained. "I hit some slush at an intersection and nearly spun into oncoming traffic—hence the new tires. Pretty much cleared out the fund I'd been building for Christmas presents."

"Aw, Scott", Megan said with a smile. "That's sweet, but you don't have to get us anything."

"Well, there was enough left to get this for you", Scott explained, putting a little box on the table. "I stopped at a tire store in downtown Port Huron, and while they were putting the tires on, I wandered into the little shop next door. The shop is a quaint little family-run place. They have a clock on a post out on the sidewalk. The guy was—"

"Oh Scott!" Megan gasped. She'd been idly unwrapping the box while listening to him but now opened it to see a shiny gold band.

"I hope I got the right size", Scott went on. "Here, let me put it on your finger—that's customary, right?"

Megan said nothing but held out her hand for Scott to slide the band on.

"Ah, perfect", Scott said. "I had to guess at your ring size. The guy at the shop was most helpful. When I explained my situation, he was happy to help me find the least expensive set."

"Set?" Megan asked in a small voice.

"Well, yeah", Scott said. "I figured that back in California we didn't even want these, but here … well, I don't want people giving you the eye when you're out with Grace. At first I thought of just getting you one, but then it hit me that people would give you even more of an eye if you had one and I didn't, so I got one too. Mine's being sized. I'll pick it up tomorrow."

"Scott, you didn't have to, really", Megan said, though she wasn't looking at him. She was gazing at the shiny ring, turning her hand this way and that.

"Understand, now," Scott cautioned, "I'm not considering this as altering our arrangement in any way. This whole marriage is a convenience so long as it works for both of us."

"Of course", Megan agreed, still stealing glances at the band.

"I don't want you to think that I'm trying to bind you, or change you, or put expectations on you, or anything like that", Scott assured her.

"Certainly not", Megan replied.

"Think of this as camouflage", Scott added.

"Good thought", Megan said.

Christmastime was subdued but happy. There weren't a lot of presents, but there were strings of cheap twinkle lights that entranced Grace, and hot chocolate and homemade cookies. Scott's mother had a battered old artificial tree, but Mrs. Delworth insisted on a hand-cut spruce—which, of course, Scott had to haul in and set in the stand. Decorating was an evening-long affair that saw Scott mostly holding Grace while the ladies hung antique glass balls and draped garlands. Megan, Scott, and Grace spent Christmas morning at his mother's trailer, and then they all went over to Mrs. Delworth's for a grand dinner that lasted well into the evening. Scott ran his mother home afterward, and they chatted for a while. They'd grown closer since the dramatic conversation a few weeks before. Finally Scott headed home, where Megan and Grace were almost certainly in bed already. On the way out the door, Scott spotted his mother's purse on the kitchen table, which wasn't where she normally kept it. Looking more closely, he saw that her phone was right on top, instead of in the usual side pocket.

The phone had been silent all day.

After Christmas, life seemed to settle into a dreary monotone. The snow kept falling, heavy even for a Michigan winter. Scott wasn't one of those who detested winter weather, but even when he'd lived there, the drab, sloppy stretch from January through March had been his least favorite time of year. Now he had to rise before dawn and drive forty-five minutes down the coast to a dull, exasperating job that barely paid enough to keep gas in the truck. In the evening, home wasn't much to return to. The apartment seemed smaller than ever and was perpetually chilly because Mrs. Delworth couldn't afford to heat the huge old place properly. The normally healthy and cheerful Grace turned into a bundle of whining misery. Not only was she teething, but she came down with a series of ailments—a fever followed by a rash followed by an ear infection followed by a cough. Only Megan could comfort her during these times, and sometimes not even then. The doctor visits and prescriptions put additional strain on their already-tight budget, and the crying and fussing put a strain on Scott's nerves.

Money was an ever-present concern. Though the drugstore kept Megan on after Christmas, her hours dropped to almost nothing. Between Scott's salary and her trivial earnings, they barely had enough for food and rent and fuel. Being cooped up in the apartment night after night with nothing to do but watch television frayed both their nerves. They found themselves bickering at times, which was something they'd never done in California. Megan began to go out evenings, taking Grace to visit Scott's mother.

One of these evenings by himself, when he'd tired of watching TV and toying with his tablet, Scott was sitting in the turret room, looking out over the lake, pondering how he'd ended up back here. He remembered being back in high school, sitting on the embankment overlooking the harbor and dreaming about getting away. And he had—first to college, then to Nashville, then to California. He comforted himself by reminiscing about those days. College hadn't been much. He'd had a few fun times, but he'd wanted to do well, so between study and jobs he'd never had much time for parties. He'd been known around the gay community, and had had a couple of boyfriends, but hadn't had time for all the rallies and seminars. Besides, the strident tone of it all hadn't been his style.

Nashville, now—that had been great, at least at first. Nashville was where Scott had had his first real job, his first apartment, his first car, his first taste of truly independent life. His work was interesting and had paid decently. He'd met some new friends, and they all quickly became a close circle. They'd hang out for long evenings talking. They'd rent a cabin in the mountains and have parties that would last all weekend. Scott had thought he'd found the life he'd always wanted. But then Ken and Randy had had that falling out, and both had tried to enlist the others to their side, and then everything had fallen apart.

That had been sad, but it had worked out for Scott, since he had started to tire of Nashville. At just about that time he'd connected with Greg through a friend of Ken's, and Greg had put him in touch with Brian, and before he knew it he was moving to the coast. Not just the coast, but the Bay Area, where he'd only dreamed of living.

That had been exciting—visiting bars and clubs and restaurants he'd read about, spending night after night out and never running out of new places to visit, seeing exciting shows and having stimulating conversations. It had been the ideal life. But that too had soured—first with Greg, and then with the job. And, of course, there had been all the complexity with Megan and Grace. Thus Scott had landed back here again.

But this had to be only an interlude. He'd get back on his feet. Scott began to dream about other places. Seattle, perhaps, or maybe somewhere out east. He'd heard there were job opportunities and a vibrant gay community in the D.C. area. Or south Florida. Or maybe—why not?—the Big Apple. He'd visited New York only twice, but he'd liked what he'd seen. Nashville and California were behind him, closed chapters of his life. But who knew what might come next? Surely his current circumstances were only a holding pattern, a temporary setback. Megan would understand—they'd always been open and aboveboard with each other. They both had identities, lives of their own to live. Their marriage had been only to leverage a particular set of circumstances—circumstances that had completely changed. They'd just cut each other loose, like they'd always planned to do. She'd go her way, and he'd move on to other opportunities. Sure, he'd miss her friendship, but there were plenty more friends out there—

Grace. With a crash Scott's fantasies collapsed as he remembered that it wasn't just Megan—there was a baby involved too. Well, wasn't she primarily Megan's concern? And Grace was just a baby; maybe she wouldn't remember ...

No. Scott's father had left them when Lisa was just a baby. Scott couldn't do the same to Grace. It was out of the question.

But where did that leave him? Stuck back in his hometown? Was this the final chapter of his life? All because of Grace? His thoughts strayed back over the past year and a half, and he was amazed at how much trouble that one little person had caused, some of it before she'd been born. Sure, he'd sired her, but as a favor to Megan—and it hadn't even been Megan who'd wanted her but Diane! Then Diane had gotten all jealous and hadn't wanted either the baby or Megan. Scott had been happy to rescue Megan out of that mess, but the imminent birth had meant he'd had to get her on his insurance plan. The immediate consequence of that had not only been the break with Greg but this whole phony marriage that legally bound him to Megan. And he couldn't forget the maternity coverage expenses, the co-pays, and all the other costs that went along with babies!

Then, when Scott had lost his job, it had been Grace's presence that had changed everything. If it hadn't been for her, he and Megan could have just parted ways. He could have just driven off to wherever to live lean while searching for a new job. But because of Grace, that hadn't been an option. He'd had to pack up and drive back to his hometown, a dead-end little place that was good only for getting away from. And he'd wrecked his beloved Jetta along the way!

All because of Grace. Scott knew it wasn't her fault, in the sense that she hadn't done anything but be a baby, but damn! How different everything was because of her. If it hadn't been for Grace, Megan and Diane might still be together. He might have been able to find a job in California, and he'd still be where there was some action. He certainly wouldn't be back here working a dead-end job, driving a hog of a truck, and living on sandwiches and canned soup in a chilly apartment! He was clenching his jaw in frustration at everything that had gone wrong when the thought slipped into his mind, unbidden and almost unnoticed:

She should never have been born.

Scott pushed the thought aside. It was irrelevant, fruitless. Grace had been born; she was here. Nobody could go back to change that.

But still.

Once planted, the thought grew, unobtrusively but always at the edge of Scott's mind. Especially during the long, boring commutes or at a break in a particularly frustrating day, he took solace in reminiscing about better times—those cabin weekends in the Smokies, jaunts to wine country with Greg, that Mardi Gras trip with Randy. There were plenty of good memories to relish. He'd toy with thoughts of

175

where he might be if things were different—perhaps still in the Bay Area, or in Seattle, or maybe down in Scottsdale. He'd heard good things about Scottsdale. How much of that would still be open to him if it weren't for Grace?

She should never have been born.

Adding to Scott's frustration was the fact that he wasn't getting any action, and hadn't in a long time. That didn't look to be changing anytime soon, but he could remember and fantasize. Memories of all his contacts over the years, both long- and short-term, kept thronging back. Jack and Marty and James and Norm—even Greg, despite his other problems, had been good in bed. He ached for the experiences that he'd had but had no more, ached for the life he'd known but was his no longer.

At least for now. At least while . . .

The winter seemed to drag on and on. Every time things looked to be warming up, another blast of cold weather hit and dumped more snow. March passed in gray skies and slush, and April took its time arriving.

A Friday afternoon in mid-April found Scott watching the clock at work while he did one of his least favorite tasks: writing up step-by-step instructions for Ellie, complete with screenshots and arrows. He'd learned that short of standing right at her shoulder, this was the only way to get her to operate the shipping system without bollixing it up. He had his paycheck in his pocket, which meant a stop at the ATM to deposit it and a stop at the drugstore for milk on the way home. He was feeling a little reckless, as he tended to when he felt trammeled. When five o'clock finally came, he saved his work, grabbed his jacket, and hit the road.

Driving up along the river through Port Huron felt so mundane, so drearily ordinary, that Scott just had to mix things up a little. There was a bar downtown where he'd stopped a couple of times. He didn't have much time or money, but he could spare half an hour and a twenty. As he swung out of the car and headed for the bar entrance, he spotted his wedding ring. He'd grown so accustomed to it that he didn't even notice it anymore. Still feeling reckless, he slipped off the band and pocketed it—no need for camouflage in here.

The Friday evening after-work crowd was just getting wound up. Scott sat at the bar and ordered the cheapest draft they had. There was some hockey game on, but few were paying attention because it wasn't the Red Wings. He glanced around the bar and noticed nothing unusual, unless it was those three guys in the booth over there. He looked away and then glanced back, this time catching the eye of one of the guys. They both looked away again.

Scott smiled and sipped his beer. He didn't know what it was. He knew all the colloquial terms for the phenomenon but had no clue how it worked. Maybe it was posture or facial expression or just the lift of an eyebrow, but gays always seemed to be able to find each other—at least that had been his experience. He glanced back again to see one of the guys looking directly at him. Scott held his eyes, and the guy gave an almost undetectable nod.

Scott looked away, gave it another minute, and then picked up his beer and walked over to the booth.

"You guys mind if I join you?" Scott asked. "Getting kind of cold up there."

"Not at all", said the one who had first caught his eye. "Have a seat."

There were introductions all around. The guys were named Jeremy, Thomas, and Steve. They got chatting about where they were from and how often they came to the bar. Nothing was said overtly, but neither was anything hidden. They all knew why they were there. Scott's neck felt a familiar warmth, particularly when Jeremy, who was sitting on his left, looked at him. Jeremy clearly found Scott interesting.

When they asked Scott what he was doing there, he gave the abridged version: he was originally from the area but had gotten a tech job with a firm in the Bay Area, lost the job when the firm was bought out, and was back home working at a local factory as a stopgap before moving on.

Jeremy and Thomas were wide-eyed when they heard where Scott had recently moved from. Scott smiled. There was still a cachet about the place, though it was hardly true anymore—there were plenty of spots with great gay life, some of them better than the Bay Area. Scott called it the "San Francisco mystique" and was happy to leverage it with his new friends.

So Scott began to regale them with tales about trips he'd taken and sights he'd seen. They ate up his tales of the bars and the shows and the night life—especially Jeremy and Thomas. Steve, who had been talking avidly before Scott had joined them, seemed to withdraw, sipping his beer and scowling a bit as Scott continued his stories of wine country and the Castro and all-night revues. For the first time in a long time, Scott was enjoying himself, savoring his beer and playing with his phone and basking in the attention. He'd stayed in places they'd only heard about, and rubbed shoulders with celebrities at exclusive parties. It was heady stuff for guys from a little backwater like this.

"Say," Jeremy said at one point, pushing his thigh against Scott's, "Steve was just telling us about a place he knows in Royal Oak—just an hour's drive from here. We were talking about heading down there."

"Though I doubt it's up to your standards", Steve said dryly, taking a pull at his beer.

"Oh no, I'm sure it's fine", Scott said, his heart pounding. The warmth in his neck returned, and he was keenly conscious of the pressure of Jeremy's leg against his.

"Steve also mentioned a new spot down in Detroit", Thomas chimed in. "In the New Center Area, not far from Wayne State. Maybe we could do that."

"Or", Scott suggested, "maybe we could do both. The night is yet young."

That suggestion was greeted warmly, so they all prepared to leave. Anticipating the long drive, Scott headed for the men's room. He knew Megan was expecting him, but she'd understand. They'd never made any pretenses about their identities or lifestyles or tried to hinder each other. It had been a year and a half since he'd had a chance like this. And he'd just deposited his paycheck. His sense of recklessness redoubled. Megan would understand. They'd figure out the money. He'd text her—damn, he must have left his phone on the table. Anyway, she couldn't object. She just couldn't. He rinsed his hands and headed back.

"So," Scott asked eagerly, looking around at the guys, "where are we headed?" It was only then that he noticed that their demeanor had changed. Jeremy gave him a look of scornful disgust and started walking away. Steve looked at Thomas and gave a sneering laugh.

"*We're* heading off", Steve said caustically. "*You* have an errand to run—Daddy." He pointed at Scott's phone on the table, then turned and walked off with Thomas.

Stunned and mystified, Scott looked down at the screen. There, prominently displayed, was a text from Megan.

"Please get infant ibuprofen for Grace. Fever again."

Scott's excitement and anticipation collapsed. He looked at the door through which he'd hoped to be walking, back into his old familiar world, if only for one night. The opportunity was gone, and he was left behind.

Trapped.

Chapter Seventeen

"How about going for a drive?" Megan asked.

"Drive where?" Scott responded sullenly. The day had dawned gray with a heavy overcast. It was a bit warmer and wasn't raining, but all the past rain and snowmelt made the outside so soggy that there was no walking about. Scott had stayed inside, nursing his disappointment over the debacle in the bar the night before and his resentment over his circumstances. Megan had perceived his distress and had been avoiding him as much as she could in the little apartment. But they were all getting restless, so Megan had ventured the suggestion.

"Oh, I don't know", Megan responded. "Anywhere to get out. Isn't there some town just west of here?"

"Yeah, Croswell", Scott confirmed. "There's nothing there."

"Isn't there some sort of bridge? Your mother said something—"

"Sure, there's the swinging bridge", Scott said with a shrug. "A footbridge across a river. Goes from nowhere to nowhere."

"Can you walk on it?" Megan asked.

"Sure, you can walk on it."

"Well ... could we go see?" Megan asked.

"All right", Scott agreed. Megan clearly wanted to go, and wanted him to come, and he didn't have it in him to resist. He was feeling utterly defeated. May as well drive to Croswell as stay here.

The drive west on Peck Road was quiet, with Grace laughing and kicking in the backseat.

"Thanks for picking up that ibuprofen last night", Megan said. "It really helped with her fever, and she's much more cheerful."

"Sure", Scott replied abruptly. Megan had no idea how painful that topic was. Discerning that he wasn't feeling communicative, Megan fell silent and watched the brown fields pass by.

The five miles to Croswell passed quickly, and as they came into town they drove past the high school Scott had attended. That triggered memories. He'd been a geeky kid, painfully shy, longing to talk to girls but never able to muster the courage. His few stumbling attempts to interact with them had been cruelly rebuffed, so he'd ceased trying. He'd been able to deal with girls in classroom settings, and hadn't minded fixing their band instruments or helping them solve math problems, but he had felt inept at even the most casual social interaction. So he'd holed up in the band room or computer lab while the other guys had done sports and gotten their girlfriends.

Then, the summer between his junior and senior years, his friend Dustin had helped Scott discover his identity. It had been at a band camp that was held at a college, and they were staying in dorms. The schedule had been full, but they'd had some downtime, and one afternoon Dustin had taken him into an empty room. Dustin had noticed how uncomfortable Scott was around girls and suggested it might be because Scott was gay. Scott was a little shocked at the suggestion but was good enough friends with Dustin to hear him out. Then Dustin had suggested some, ah, experimenting, and Scott discovered a whole new world.

It wasn't just the excitement of the sex. It was also the tang of the forbidden, the thrill of the secret, and the comfort of belonging. Scott learned that there was a small gay subculture at the school, necessarily underground because the area wasn't that tolerant yet. In this subculture he found acceptance that he'd never known before. Among his gay friends he wasn't just a poor, clumsy bastard in ill-fitting clothes from Saint Vincent DePaul—he was accepted. He knew what he was and where he belonged.

But now, Scott mused, that world seemed closed to him. He shook his head and sighed, his heart heavy in his chest. The ever-perceptive Megan looked over and seemed poised to ask him something.

"Hmm", Scott said, mostly to head her off. "I don't recall that burger joint being there. Are you hungry?"

"A little", Megan admitted. "Could we stop? That is ... if we ... if there's enough ..."

"We can cover it", Scott said, remembering the change from the twenty still in his wallet. He turned into the parking lot, moodily reflecting on how this was another indicator of how far they'd fallen: a cheap lunch at a fast-food restaurant was a rare treat.

Scott got the food while Megan settled Grace into a high chair. They ate in silence for a bit while the baby gummed some french fries.

"She's not contagious, you know", Megan finally ventured quietly.

"What?" Scott asked. His mind had been elsewhere.

"Grace. She's not contagious. These are just childhood fevers, rarely transmitted to adults because we've usually had them already", Megan explained.

"I know", Scott replied, mystified. "Why do you think I'd be concerned about that?"

"Well," Megan said tentatively, "it's just that you seem ... reluctant, I guess. Reluctant to deal with her."

"Reluctant?" Scott asked irritably. "What do you mean?"

"Maybe it's just me", Megan replied. "But you seem to be avoiding her. You used to pick her up and play with her and change her. Now you rarely touch her—in fact, you hardly even look at her."

"Psh", Scott scoffed, his temper rising. "That's ridiculous."

"It's true", Megan pressed, looking at him frankly with her penetrating blue eyes. "Especially over the past few weeks. You don't even want to be in the same room with her. I've watched. If I bring her into a room where you are, no matter what you're doing, you'll get up and leave within ten minutes. It's her, I know. You don't do that with me."

"I ... that's just stupid", Scott blustered. "I'm just fine with her. I'm sitting next to her right now!" He looked down at Grace mangling her fries, and the thought again flashed unbidden into his mind.

She should never have been born.

"She misses you, Scott", Megan continued, watching him as if she could read his mind. "That's one reason she's been so fussy recently. Sure, there are fevers and teething, but her daddy has gone away and she misses him."

Megan's words were hitting home, though Scott was stubbornly fighting them. He looked at Grace, trying to find the affection he'd once known for her. All he could feel was seething resentment.

"I ... I haven't gone anywhere", Scott protested lamely.

"If there's something I've done," Megan said, "I'm sorry. If there's anything—"

"Megan, stop trying to analyze me!" Scott barked. It was a long-standing irritation between them. Megan sometimes wanted to discuss what was going on inside Scott, and he had little patience for it.

Megan fell abruptly silent, and Scott immediately felt remorseful. He wanted to apologize, but the words seemed to stick in his mouth. They finished their meal in silence.

"So ... where is this bridge?" Megan asked once they were back in the car.

"Not far", Scott explained. "Just up ahead on the left." Overhead the clouds were beginning to break up, and patches of blue could be seen amid the gray. Scott turned left at the only stoplight in town and drove across the river—to the "poor side", his mother had called it. She'd grown up over here, though she'd said the house was no longer standing. He turned and drove down the residential street that led to the park by the bridge.

"Wow", Scott said as they came to the top of the driveway that led down to the park. The park gates were locked across the drive, and it was easy to see why. The river was so swollen that it had overflowed its banks. The little park, which lay down on the floodplain, was covered by at least a foot of cold, brown water.

"We'll have to come back in summer", Scott said. "I've never seen the river so high. Must be the melt from all the snow, and the rain runoff. But there's the bridge—see?"

"It's cute", Megan said. "A shame we can't get there."

"Not unless you want really wet feet", Scott replied.

"Wait—could we go around to the other end? Where does it go? That end looks higher", Megan asked.

"It's on a street behind the Main Street stores", Scott explained. "Sure, we could go there if you want. Not much point in trying to cross, but you could at least walk out on the bridge."

They drove around through town to the east end of the bridge, which was anchored on the rise overlooking the river. In part to show Megan he wasn't slighting Grace, Scott unbuckled her from the car seat and carried her to the bridge.

" 'Be good to your mother-in-law' ", Megan said, reading the sign over the end of the bridge. "What does that mean?"

"Croswell's idea of humor", Scott said. "Families come here, and it's a cable bridge, so one or two people bouncing on it can get the whole bridge wobbling. There's no danger, because the railings are too high, but it's plenty scary. We used to do it in high school to get the girls shrieking."

"You charmer, you", Megan replied. "So, if I bring your mother here, I promise I won't wobble the bridge." She started reading the historical plaque mounted on a stone by the bridge. "Hey, it says here that the railings were a later addition—the first bridge was just planks on cables."

"Yeah", Scott replied absently. He walked out onto the bridge, which was steady enough if you didn't run or bounce. It had been over a decade since he'd last walked here. He went further out, looking down at the swollen river churning beneath. Truly, he had never seen it this flooded. He'd mostly come here in the summer, when the river was slow, brown, warm, and a bit smelly. Now it was swift, turbid, and at least six feet deeper than its usual level. Scott stared with grim fascination at the rushing water. By the standards of rivers and lakes in the area, this river was a small one, but it was plenty dangerous now. Anything that fell in would be pulled under and swept away instantly, drowned in the icy water.

Anything that fell in.

Scott looked down at Grace's head, covered by the red ladybug hat that Mrs. Delworth had knitted for her.

She should never have been born.

Scott gazed back at the surging torrent. It would take only a moment. One quick flip, the work of three seconds, and his problems would vanish. Things could be like they were before. He'd be free. He pictured the red hat being swallowed up by the current, carried away without a sound. No chance of rescue. The current would sweep her away too quickly. Gone. Erased. All the trouble, all the expenses, no more. She should never have been born anyway.

Somewhere inside, a part of Scott was dazed with horror at the thoughts flooding his mind. Even more horrifying was the fact that he seemed trapped, paralyzed, unable to do anything. He was helplessly observing himself gazing in hypnotic fascination at the flood while toying with the idea of hurling his own daughter in.

Then Scott's hand began to rise slowly, reaching up under Grace's arm to get a good grip on her torso. Out of the corner of his eye he could see her turning to look at him, as if she sensed something wrong. He didn't look back at her. He kept looking at the surging water, which seemed to hungrily await his offering. He could feel himself turning a little, his right arm starting to lift her so his left hand could get a better grip.

The horrified Scott, the paralyzed and helpless Scott, raged and fought. *No! No! This can't be! Stop it! Help! HELP!* But still his arms moved, as if on their own, while his gaze stayed fixed on the river.

"Scott?" Megan's voice came as if from far away or being heard down a long tunnel.

Megan! cried the inner Scott. His arms stopped moving.

"Scott? Is everything all right?" Megan's voice was nearer, heavy with concern. Footsteps on the bridge now, hurried footsteps pounding hard, shaking the cables. His eyes broke away from the river and slowly turned to see Megan rushing toward him, anxiety etched on her face.

The fit was broken. Scott's vision cleared. The sun was shining, the wind was blowing, and he was Scott Kyle, free to choose. He shook his head and blinked as Megan came up to him, breathless.

"Scott, what's going on?" she asked.

"Take her", Scott said brusquely, thrusting the baby into her mother's arms. "Get her away from me, away from this place." He shoved past the mystified Megan and started walking quickly off the bridge.

"Scott? What—" Megan began, but he interrupted her, calling over his shoulder.

"Get her somewhere safe! Take her home! Don't worry about me. Get her out of here!" He was off the bridge now and broke into a run, heading north, leaving a dumbfounded Megan standing on the bridge staring after him.

Scott didn't know where he was going or what he planned to do. He was literally reeling in horror—he was actually having difficulty keeping his balance—over what had just happened. Could he really have done that? Murder his own daughter in cold blood? The images of the rushing river returned, of a small body falling, a little red hat being quickly pulled under—but now the images slashed and stabbed at him. How close he had come! He'd been just about to do it—if Megan hadn't called. His own little Grace! Different images crowded in now, memories of her smiling, or cackling with glee as he played with her, or sleeping swaddled on the couch while Megan read beside her. Torn with anguish, he stopped and leaned against a tree, crouching down and grabbing his hair while he rocked on his feet. What kind of monster was he?

Scott realized that he needed to keep moving. Megan would probably come looking for him, and he couldn't face her now. She'd come this way, so he trotted down a side street and turned up another. Whatever he did, he had to stay away from Peck Road, because that would be the route she'd take home. He couldn't have her spotting him. He turned again, back north, toward the edge of the village. After a few blocks he hit an east-west road. Neither knowing what to do nor caring, he headed east, toward the lake. Just outside of town the pavement ended.

The wind had fully shifted now and was blowing from the northeast, scattering the overcast until only a few puffy billows remained. The sun was bright and warm, but the wind was off the lake. In high summer this was pleasantly cooling, but this time of year it was bitter. There were still patches of ice floating, and the wind blowing across that frigid water was brutally cold. It cut Scott to the quick as he tramped along the road, but he barely noticed it. His attention was turned inward, reliving those terrible minutes on the bridge, imagining what might have happened, wondering what kind of person would even consider that.

One thing Scott knew: he could never go back. Given what he had almost done, he could never be trusted near Grace again. He had to leave—immediately. Except now it didn't feel like the liberation about which he'd been fantasizing for the past several weeks. Now it felt like exile. He'd never see her, or hold her, or smell her curls again. His last meal with her had been mushy french fries, and he'd ignored her throughout. But at least someone would get to enjoy meals with her, which wouldn't have happened if he'd succeeded—ah, he fell back into a torturous cycle of imaginings.

But, Scott considered, if he couldn't be trusted near his own daughter, whom could he be trusted near? If he came so close to doing that to the apple of his eye, what wouldn't he do to anyone? The old fantasy returned of wandering off into the woods, sitting down beneath a tree, and dying there. Maybe it would be best. It wouldn't take long under these conditions either—he was already shivering in his light jacket. He gazed at the strips of woods visible from the road. They edged fields here and there, a few acres of untended growth, windbreaks to prevent erosion. He'd played in woods like that as a boy. One of those patches would be a good place. He even tried a couple of times to turn toward likely looking ones, but his way was always blocked by flooded ditches or sodden fields.

So Scott continued eastward into the teeth of the wind, not knowing where he was going or what he would do when he got there. Maybe he should throw himself into the lake. His mind was filled with turmoil and his heart with darkness. His body, however, had its own opinions. He might fantasize about succumbing to the cold while seated on a log in the woods, but the hard reality of hypothermia was starting to grip him, and his body was fighting fiercely. He blew on his numb hands and tucked them under his arms to keep them warm. He began to look for roadside structures, or even a large tree, to break the cutting wind. His shivering was becoming uncontrollable, and his jaw ached from clenching. His physical distress was starting to shout down his emotional agony, but still he stomped on.

Suddenly a rusty blue pickup stopped and the passenger door flew open just beside him. An unshaven farmer in a dirty cap was sitting back up from having leaned over to open it. He glared at Scott.

"Get in, buddy!" the farmer barked.

"I ... I'm fine", chattered Scott. "I don't need—"

"The hell", the farmer replied bluntly. "I don't know how you ended up on this road under these conditions dressed like that, but you'll freeze before another mile. Get in, I tell ya."

Scott started to offer another excuse, but the farmer and his own frigid body were glowering at him, so he scrambled into the cab. The farmer flipped the heat on full blast.

"So," the farmer asked as he accelerated, "have a breakdown?"

"Ah ... yeah, in a way", Scott replied.

"I'm surprised you didn't call for help", the farmer said. "Most people these days have cell phones."

"I, ah, left mine at home. Charging", Scott said. In fact his phone was in his pocket, but he'd turned it off.

"Damn batteries", the farmer grumbled. "Always go out when you need 'em. Where can I drop ya?"

"Lexington", Scott blurted out without thinking, then instantly regretted it.

"All right—I'm going by there", the farmer said. He chatted the rest of the short drive about the effect of the snowmelt on the water table. Scott just sat with his hands in front of the vents and wondered what he'd do when he got to Lexington. He certainly couldn't go home, and he didn't know where else to go.

"So," asked the farmer as they came into town from the north, "where can I drop ya?"

"This corner here is fine", Scott said, pointing.

The farmer looked suspiciously at Scott. "I'll take you to your door", he said. "Lexington's not that large."

"Seriously, this is fine", Scott insisted. "It's only a short walk from here."

"All right", the farmer acceded. "You stay warm."

"I will", Scott replied as he got out of the truck. "Thanks."

The corner was right where Saint Agatha Church was located, which Scott knew of but had never been inside. Not wanting to stay on the main road lest Megan happen along, Scott walked around behind the church. A door was propped open, and a janitor was tinkering with a vacuum cleaner just outside it. The janitor looked up and saw Scott.

"Man, you look cold", the man said.

Scott shrugged and nodded.

"You got anywhere to go?"

Scott shook his head.

The janitor looked about, then nodded conspiratorially, gesturing through the open door with his head. Scott took the hint and went past him into the church. It was warm and lit only by ambient light through the windows. The walls were stone up to about chest height, then white to the top of the arched ceiling overhead. The interior was divided into halls or wings—Scott was at the end of one and he could see another, and as he walked forward there was yet another on his right merging with this one. The halls were filled with rows of long benches that were pointed toward an ornately carved wooden table on a raised platform in the center of the wings. There was a cross hanging above the table, and to the right of the platform was a foyer or vestibule of some type.

None of that interested Scott as much as a small alcove to his left, which looked secluded and warm—just the conditions for his current temperament. In the alcove there was a statue of a woman holding a baby, which Scott guessed was a Madonna, and a couple of iron frames holding large candles, most of which were lit. Scott wasn't sure of the religious significance of the candles and hoped he wasn't offending anyone by warming his hands over them. Then he sat down on the floor of the alcove, his back against one wall, and just stared at the floor.

Presently the janitor, having completed his work on the vacuum, came back through the wing. He nodded discreetly to Scott as he passed, and went into the vestibule on the far side of the platform with the wooden table. Shortly thereafter a different man, with wire-rimmed glasses and a white goatee, looked around the corner of the vestibule at Scott. Scott wasn't sure if he was in trouble for being there, but the fellow just smiled and waved, then went away. Scott took that as implicit permission to stay.

The emotional shock of the incident on the bridge was ebbing, but Scott was still tortured by the question of where that murderous impulse had come from. Never in his wildest imaginings had he ever contemplated violence against even Megan, much less Grace. He hadn't known he had it in him, yet there it had been at the critical moment: not simply the will to murder his own daughter but the near execution of the act. He still shuddered to imagine what would have happened had not Megan called to him when she did.

Scott searched his memory for any hints of violent tendencies or inclinations. With the shock and horror still so near, all illusions and pretenses had been blasted away. He had looked into his own heart and seen the maw of hell. He knew now that there was nothing he was incapable of. In this light, his attitudes and actions looked very different than he had ever seen them.

Scott's thoughts strayed back to the incident in the bar the prior evening, when the three locals had scorned and humiliated him. Painful, but what of his own actions? He saw now that his tone and demeanor had been haughty and condescending, that of the well-heeled traveler deigning to speak with the hayseeds from fly-over country. He remembered back in college, or even in Nashville, when visitors from New York or LA would put on airs about the gay communities they belonged to. How he had hated that—yet here he'd been doing the same thing. He'd become what he hated! All the while living an impoverished life in a town even smaller and more rustic than theirs! Small wonder they'd scorned him as a phony—he was, and a worse one than they knew!

Suddenly Scott was conscious of someone standing nearby. He looked up to see the goatee guy there holding a cup of coffee.

"Am I ... should I leave?" Scott asked.

"No, no, you're fine", the guy said. "I don't want to disturb you but thought you looked cold and might want this." He held the cup out to Scott. "It's black; if you want stuff in it, the pot is just through the door at the back of the vestibule, to the right."

"This'll be fine, thanks", Scott said.

"The bathrooms are to the left, as is my office, if you need anything", the man said, backing away as he spoke. "I'll leave you to yourself, then."

Scott sipped the coffee, which was no worse than most office coffee, and plunged back into his memories. He thought about how he dealt with people at work, and saw how curt he was with them, how scornful of their technical ineptitude. He thought back to how he'd treated Brian—how cruel and unfair he'd been! He recalled how he'd dealt with Greg, particularly in the final months. He remembered how he'd treated the assistants who had been assigned to him, and his coworkers, and so many others.

Sitting in that quiet alcove, Scott was inundated with recollections from his past. Illuminated by this harsh light of self-realization, he saw that how he'd treated others had been much less harmless and innocent than he'd supposed. Scott had always thought himself a decent guy—not perfect, to be sure, but not a pure jackass like so many in the world. He didn't consider himself a bad person. But with that illusion stripped away, and faced with the brutal reality of just how bad a person he actually was, he saw that he could be just as big a jackass as anyone he knew.

Waves of anguish and remorse washed over Scott as memories rushed back to him. How he wished he could call back words or actions! How he wished he could bring people up from his past to apologize for his treatment of them—real, heartfelt apologies, not flimsy excuses or lame rationalizations. He even wondered if he

190

could hunt down Jeremy, Steve, and Thomas to repent of being so arrogant. Scott felt that he was getting a glimpse of himself as he truly was—and it wasn't a pretty sight.

Scott didn't know how long he sat there, immersed in his thoughts, but there came a time when he was aware of the goatee guy again standing nearby.

"I hate to disturb your privacy", the guy said when Scott looked up. "But I thought it only fair to warn you that, in about an hour, people are going to start showing up to get ready for Mass."

"Oh", Scott said. "What time is it? And when is Mass?"

"It's just three o'clock. Mass is at five, but musicians and others start arriving just after four, and there's a Rosary at 4:30."

Scott had no idea what a Rosary might be, but it sounded somewhat official. "So ... should I leave?"

"No need", the guy said with a wave. "You're welcome to stay right through Mass if you wish. I just wanted to warn you that you'll be losing the quiet and solitude before long."

"Ah", Scott replied, pondering this. "Thanks."

"I also wanted you to know that if there's any way I can help, I'm available. I don't want to intrude on your personal affairs, but I couldn't help but notice that you came in here looking a little ... battered."

"Well, I ..." Scott stammered. His instinct for privacy and withdrawal was warring with a shredded psyche that was desperate for reassurance from anyone that he wasn't completely horrid. "It has been a rough day."

Sensing Scott's turmoil, the guy sat down on the end of one of the benches. "I'm Francis", he said, holding out his hand. "I work here at Saint Agatha."

"I'm Scott", Scott replied, shaking his hand. "Are you a minister?"

"Not really. I'm a sacristan, but I do other things too."

"A sacristan?" Scott asked quizzically.

"I set up for Mass and take things down afterward", Francis replied. "But never mind about me. Want to talk about what's been so rough about today?"

"Well, I ..." Scott again hesitated, his throat constricting around the words. Francis just looked at him calmly through his wire rims, and before Scott knew it the whole terrible story was tumbling out.

Tears streamed down his face as he recounted the day's events, sparing nothing, omitting nothing, laying bare to this sympathetic stranger the darkest corners of his heart, corners he hadn't even known were there. He cast aside all restraint, spilling everything, hoping that even a small shred of it would be understood.

Francis sat quietly through it all, gazing at Scott without expression, listening. Even when Scott finished, Francis said nothing but held up a finger asking for a minute, then went quickly back into the vestibule area. Dark fear rose in Scott—was he going to call the police, or Child Protective Services? But Francis reappeared momentarily bearing two bottles of water and a box of tissues.

"Thanks", Scott said, grabbing some tissues and taking a swig of water. "What do you think? Am I some kind of homicidal maniac? Am I insane?"

"Well," Francis said slowly, "I'm no professional, but based on what you've told me, I'd say not. I'd say you're human."

"But ... but ..." Scott gasped. "Just 'human'? When I came that close to drowning my own daughter?"

"There's an old saying", Francis replied. "'There are things within each of us that would shame hell'. I've been married for forty-one years, and I've raised five children and nine grandchildren. If I were to tell you some of the things I've been tempted to do to them over the years, it would curl your hair. You wouldn't believe it."

"But ... even violence?" asked the astonished Scott.

"Of the worst kind", Francis assured him. "The important thing is that I never did any of it. Neither did you."

"Well, maybe not", Scott said. "But you have no idea how close I came."

"No, I don't", Francis admitted. "But the point is that you didn't do it, no matter how sorely you were pressured and tempted."

"Only because of Megan", Scott said. "If she hadn't intervened, Grace would be dead."

"You don't know that", Francis cautioned. "All you know is that help came in time. That help happened to be Megan, but had she not been there, who knows what else might have come to your aid?"

"Well," Scott replied doubtfully, "it certainly tells me what I'm capable of. I'd no idea I could consider something like that!"

"I wouldn't be too hard on yourself there", Francis said. "Like I mentioned, I've had bouts like that too. They're usually not so much internal as external. I call them fire arrows."

"You call them what?" Scott asked.

"Fire arrows. Like in the movies", Francis explained. "When the settlers were safely inside the stockade, and the Indians had them surrounded, sometimes the Indians would shoot arrows with burning pitch over the stockade walls. They'd try to get the barns or hay piles burning—don't you remember?"

"Not really ..." a mystified Scott replied.

"Before your time", Francis said with a wave. "Anyway, the point was that the folk inside the stockade had to extinguish those fire arrows quickly. One arrow by itself didn't do much damage, but if you didn't attend to it, it could get a whole building burning."

"I see that", Scott said, wondering where this digression was going. "But what does that have to do ..."

"Just this", Francis explained. "We all get these horrible, perverse suggestions shooting into our minds from time to time. I do, you do, we all do. It's part of being human. When they come, we have to extinguish them immediately by paying them no attention and putting them out of our minds. If we entertain them, they catch and spread. In your case, it wouldn't surprise me if there was some vile thought that entered your mind a while back, maybe even something about Grace. You didn't extinguish it, that is, put it behind you and ignore it. You tolerated it, maybe even entertained it. Mind you, I don't know this—I'm just speculating—but it wouldn't surprise me. Do you know what I mean?"

"Yes, I do", Scott confirmed, a little unnerved by the accuracy of Francis' speculation.

"If something like that had taken place, it wouldn't have helped at the moment of crisis", Francis went on. "The moral here: Put out such things the moment they appear."

"But ... wait", Scott said, intrigued and disturbed. "Where do these 'arrows' come from? You said they were more external than internal—is someone 'shooting' them?"

Francis said nothing for a minute, looking at his hands as if thinking. "Let's talk about that some other time", he said at last. "For now, it's enough to know not to tolerate them. But that's only one aspect of what happened to you today, and not the most important. There was another thing that was much more vital."

"What other thing?" Scott asked.

"The one you've been telling me about since we started talking", Francis explained. "You got a message today, a message with many parts. You learned that you were capable of horrendous things. The fact that all people are capable of such things doesn't—and shouldn't—lessen the shock. You also learned that you aren't as great a guy as you thought you were. That's a lesson we all need, early and often. It's always bitter medicine, but it's medicine, and we need it to stay healthy."

Francis was talking like nobody Scott had ever heard, but in his chastened state Scott was in no condition to argue. In the church beyond, a doorway opened and some people walked in. It was 4:15.

"But", Scott pleaded, a little panicked, "what should I *do*? I can't go home."

Again Francis didn't reply for a bit but just gazed at his hands. Then he looked up at Scott with a keen light in his eyes.

"Actually, I think home is precisely where you need to go", he said.

"What?" Scott asked, stunned.

"Of course, I can't order you", Francis continued. "It's your call. But something tells me that the messages aren't finished for the day."

"Messages?"

"Yes. You got the hard ones, the ones that brought you here. But I think there is at least one more message, and it's at home", Francis explained. "Make of that what you will."

Scott was dumbfounded. Home was the last place he'd considered going right now. The door opened again, and a few more people walked in. Some went to a large wooden thing that looked like an organ, not far from where he and Francis were sitting.

"I'm sorry", Francis said, looking about at the people trickling in. "I wish we had all day. You can use my office if you wish some more time alone, because I have duties to attend to. But after Mass—about two hours from now—I'll have to lock up."

"That's okay", Scott said. "I ... I think I'll go home."

194

"Good idea", Francis confirmed. He pulled a card out of his pocket. "Here's my contact information. Give me a call if you'd like, and we can talk under better circumstances."

"Thanks", Scott said, pocketing the card.

"One last thing", Francis said as he stood. "What we've talked about stays between us. It's not the seal of the confessional, but I don't discuss private conversations with anyone else—not even my wife."

"Sure", Scott replied, not understanding all of that but grateful for the confidentiality.

Chapter Eighteen

Since nothing was very far from anything else in Lexington, it took Scott less than ten minutes to walk to the apartment. He didn't hurry, but neither did he dawdle—the cold wind was still coming off the lake. He wasn't entertaining any more self destructive fantasies. He had no initiative left. He felt completely drained. He had no idea what awaited him back at the apartment, but he hoped it wouldn't ask too much of him.

The truck was parked in the drive, so Megan was home. Scott went up the steps as quietly as possible, still hesitant about facing Megan and her inevitable questions. He didn't know what he'd say. He wondered about Francis' intuition that there was another "message" awaiting him. He didn't know what to make of that, whether it was just nonsense or whether there was something behind it.

Scott closed the apartment door quietly and listened. He could just hear the sound of another door closing—it sounded like the door to Grace's room. There was movement, then a pause.

"Scott?" came Megan's voice, quiet and tentative.

"Yeah", Scott replied, just as quietly. Megan stepped around the corner and stood looking at him. Her eyes were red, and her posture was cautious. They both sensed how fragile the moment was.

"Grace?" Scott asked.

"Just down for her nap", Megan said, stepping closer to Scott, her eyes fixed on his. They looked at each other for a long minute.

"Megan ... I ..." Scott began to stammer, but she lifted a finger to his lips.

"We need to talk", Megan said gently, taking his hand. "But not here. We don't want to disturb the baby." She led him into the bedroom and closed the door behind them.

"I'm not going to ask what happened at the bridge", Megan assured him. "It's clear that it involved Grace, and it was something horrible, but she's safe now. It's also clear that we've both had a long, tough afternoon. I've had hours of fear—worrying about her, worrying about you, worrying about her and you. At times I felt like grabbing her and our clothes and running. But I got to thinking, and remembering, and—well, I realized there are some things I need to say to you."

"Megan," Scott interrupted weakly, "you don't need to—"

"Yes, I do", Megan insisted quietly. "Your turn will come. Right now I need to talk and you need to listen." For emphasis she pushed him back until he sat down on the bed. She stood just beyond his knees, her hands on his shoulders, her eyes locked on his.

"I haven't thought all this out very well, so I hope you'll understand if it's a little scrambled", Megan began. "I don't know what demons you were wrestling with on that bridge, but I know you've been struggling a lot over the past few months—and I haven't been helping as much as I should have been.

"I never knew who my father was. I was raised by my mother in a slum in Phoenix. My only experience with men was the guys who'd come around after her. To them, I was just an obstacle between them and her bed, and they treated me accordingly.

"Until I met you, I never knew what a real man was. Men were the enemy. Men were predators. Men were to be avoided as much as possible. The only reason I befriended you was that you were gay and therefore had to be different—and you were. I just didn't appreciate how different, and I mean that in the best sense.

"I've lived with you for over a year now, Scott Kyle, and I know you", Megan continued with unusual vehemence. "You see yourself as a clumsy, geeky faggot bumbling through life. But that's not how I see you. I see you as a champion. I see you as a hero. I see you as a strong man. You saved our lives. Understand me? *You saved our lives*, both Grace's and mine. You think I'm exaggerating? Think again. If you hadn't stepped in to rescue us, if you hadn't extended your arms to shelter us, she would have been aborted and I would have disappeared into some bondage farm to be the plaything of whichever client could pay the entrance fee. And that means I'd certainly be dead by now, or wishing I were, because some of those clients play rough. Don't pretend it doesn't happen, because it does—you know that as well as I."

Scott stared back, horror-struck, wanting to deny what she was saying but knowing he couldn't. He'd heard whispers, dark rumors, of secret chambers where nothing—literally nothing—was forbidden to anyone, gay or straight, willing to pay the price. He had always walked away from such conversations, but he'd known those who wouldn't. With shock he realized that his disdain had always been grounded in aesthetics. He'd never given thought to the victims in those horrid dungeons: who they were or how they had gotten there.

Megan interpreted the look in his eyes as skepticism so pressed on. "You don't think that kind of thing goes on? You should have seen some of the people Diane used to hang around with. They were beyond scary. They used to come over some evenings, and Diane would dress me up in one of those frilly outfits and make me play cocktail waitress. They'd sit around drinking and staring at me with flat, dead eyes. The message was clear: As long as I was Diane's, they couldn't touch me.

"Why do you think I was so terrified that day Diane repudiated me? Why do you think I called you in panic? I had no idea what would be waiting for me if I went home alone. You may think this just hysteria, but it happens a lot more than people think—it just isn't discussed. You have no idea how mean those streets can be to an unprotected lesbian girl whom nobody cares about. I would have just ... vanished.

"It was you—you, Scott Kyle—who rescued us both. The only reason Grace and I aren't dead right now is because of you. But saving our lives wasn't enough. You sheltered us and fed us and made sure we had medical care. Don't think I don't know how much it cost or what you gave up to take care of us! You even contrived that facade of hiring me just to mollify my qualms about accepting your generosity. And I know about the other costs too—how you were ostracized by your friends and cut off from your social circles. You could have decided the price was too high and sent us packing, but you never did. You didn't even hint at it, and believe me, I was listening.

"Then you stuck with me through the pregnancy and the childbirth. I could see how uncomfortable you were in that delivery room, how you wanted to be anywhere but there, but you stayed for my sake and hers. And then—and then you brought Grace home and took her in as your own."

"Well," Scott offered, "she was."

"I know, but you never signed up for that. You were just trying to help me and Diane. You had no idea Diane was going to back out and turn on me. When she did, you would have been perfectly justified in washing your hands of the whole matter and walking away. But you didn't.

"And again, when you lost your job, you could have just thrown your gear in your car, waved good-bye, and driven away. But you didn't! You didn't!" Megan was now kneeling astride his legs, her hands holding the sides of his head to force him to look into her face, her eyes blazing with passion. "You could have dumped us on a curb and kited off, but instead you sold most of your stuff and packed up what little remained to drive cross-country—losing your beloved car along the way—to return to this little town you thought you'd left behind, and live in a cramped, chilly apartment and work at a frustrating job that pays well below what you're worth. Why? *Why?* So Grace and I don't have to be separated. So Grace and I have a roof over our heads and food on the table and beds to sleep in.

"Don't think I don't see all those sacrifices. I haven't said this nearly enough—hell, I haven't said it at all, but I'm saying it now: You're our hero, Scott Kyle. You saved her life, you saved my life, you've given and given and given and never asked for a thing in return." Her eyes were inches from his now, as if by the intensity of her gaze she could force him to understand. "I don't know what darkness you were fighting on that bridge, but you need to know that you're not all darkness. You're good and noble and kind and generous and sacrificing and courageous. I haven't thanked you enough, but I'm thanking you now."

Scott was stunned. This message wasn't as harsh as the other ones, but in its way it was just as intense. He'd never looked at any of this in that light. He wanted to protest, to point out all she'd done for him, but he was too drained. All he could do was gape. Still gazing at him intensely, Megan seemed to arrive at a decision.

"I know what you need", she said, pulling her sweatshirt over her head. "You need comfort. And I know just how to give it to you."

Scott stared as she pulled off her T-shirt and yanked his jacket off.
"But ... Megan ... I ..."

"What?" Megan stopped briefly to look at him with a quiet smile.
"We are married, remember?"

He was urgent, almost violent, in his passion, but she did not fear.
She held him tight, drawing him closer, giving herself to him. When
he finally collapsed, she still cradled him. His pants became gasps, and
the gasps became sobs, and then his whole frame was shaking, but she
held him close, calming him with her touch and soothing him with
her whispers, trying to fill the dark emptiness and to quiet the beast
that raged and howled within him.

Eventually he rolled away and lay still, gazing at the ceiling. "Thank
you", he whispered. "You didn't need—"

"Shh", Megan interrupted, laying her fingers on his lips. "Don't
deny me the chance to be generous too. Oops—there's Muffin."

Scott lay still while Megan slipped away, returning a minute later.
She sat quietly, nursing the baby. This was the closest Scott had been
to Grace since the bridge, and he was a little surprised that he didn't
feel jumpy. But everything seemed so natural that he was completely
at ease.

"She isn't nursing very much these days, is she?" Scott asked idly.

"No", Megan replied. "This is mostly comfort nursing. She likes
it when she just wakes up but doesn't do it for long. Your mom and
Mrs. Delworth have her almost completely on solids. Good thing
too—my supply is drying up. There, she's done." Megan turned with
the sluggish Grace and handed her to Scott.

"Megan, I ..." Scott sat back a bit, still fearful of touching the
baby.

"Go ahead, take her", Megan urged, pushing her into his arms.
"You're her father. She's safe with you. Off to the bathroom—be
right back."

Scott cradled the dozing baby tenderly. Holding her was so familiar, so normal. He leaned over to kiss her curls. Megan was right:
Grace was safe with him.

In the weeks that followed, many things changed. The wind blew
more from the south and west, bringing welcome warmth. The land
shed its grubby coat of tired and dirty snow and robed itself in pale

green leaves and gay daffodils. Megan, who had arrived in the middle of gray November, now regularly exclaimed in delight at the beauty all around.

For his part, Scott felt utterly shattered by the events of that tumultuous day. Had it been an option, he would have retired to a cabin in the woods to meditate and reconstruct his life. But he had to go to work the following Monday nonetheless. He was more subdued and tried to be more patient and understanding with even the most annoying users. The daily commute was an opportune time to think, because random memories and realizations were still flashing into his head, and it was good to be alone when that happened. He'd find himself shaking the wheel in rage, usually at himself, or weeping in remorse, or hanging his head in shame—sometimes all on the same trip. He felt as if entire sections of his mind and heart were being sliced open and laid bare for examination. Sometimes these were dark, long-closed sections where he would rather not look. It was demanding but cleansing.

One thing Scott did early in the first week was to compose an e-mail. Some weeks earlier, Brian had sent Scott a tersely worded request for Scott's current street address for mailing tax documents. Scott had replied with the data. He pulled Brian's new e-mail address up and wrote a very humbling message.

Brian—

I want to apologize for how I treated you at our final meeting last November. I see now that the situation was at least as hard for you as it was for me. I could have expressed my frustration without ripping into you. I'm sorry that our professional association and personal friendship had to end on such a sour note. The fault was all mine. You made every attempt to be helpful. I hope you can find it in your heart to forgive me.

Sincerely,
Scott

"Hopefully he doesn't have a filter set up to delete anything I send", Scott muttered to himself as he transmitted the message.

Megan was also grappling with her own questions and struggles. As a result, Scott and Megan's home life was a little like walking on eggshells, but in a good way. They went out of their way not to intrude on or pressure one another, and at the same time were gentler and more considerate when they did interact. They took turns watching Grace to give each other time alone to think and reflect.

About two weeks after the fateful weekend, Tamara called Scott into her office and closed the door behind him. Not knowing how to interpret that, he sat down with some trepidation.

"Well, Scott," Tamara asked, "how have you liked the five months you've been here?"

"It has called for some patience", Scott answered slowly.

Tamara laughed warmly at that. "I can just imagine. I especially want to thank you for working so hard with Ellie. Those step-by-step instructions with the screenshots have been just what she's needed. She calls them her 'Scott sheets' and has them clipped to those clipboards she used to use for manifests and bills of lading."

"Does she really?" Scott smiled at the thought of those rattling boards being pressed into service once more.

"Yes, she was showing me just the other day. She knows where every Scott sheet is, so she always knows where to go for every situation. That was no small service. Ellie is only a couple of years from retirement. She was trying hard to master the new shipping system but just couldn't get the hang of it. She's run that dock forever and didn't have any other skills. Corporate was telling us either to get her up to speed or to get rid of her. Those sheets probably saved her job", Tamara explained.

"I'm glad to hear it", Scott said, surprised.

"That's just one example", Tamara continued. "Everyone tells me how helpful and capable you are and how they can always count on you to solve their problems."

This surprised Scott even more—he'd thought he'd been much less friendly.

"But we both know that the work is well beneath your skill set. I'd like to pay you far more, but—"

"There's no budget for it", Scott interrupted with a grin, and Tamara chuckled.

"Exactly. That's why I thought of you during a conversation I had earlier this week. I have a friend who is an IT director at a firm in Port Huron. Big outfit, complex environment. He's retiring and didn't think he'd be able to find anyone in the area with the requisite skills and experience. You immediately came to mind. I told him how well you'd done here, and recommended he consider you favorably."

Scott's vision seemed to be narrowing, and his head felt light. What was he hearing?

"The environment is challenging, but I think you'd be up to it: virtualization, cloud apps, service-oriented architecture—the works. Plus, it pays about twice your current salary, with better benefits", Tamara said, smiling. She picked up a note from her desk and handed it to Scott. "Here's his contact information—he's expecting your call."

"Thank you very much", was all Scott could manage.

"It'll be difficult to lose you", Tamara admitted. "But I couldn't in good conscience keep you when I knew about an opportunity like that. I told Alan I'd let him hire you on the condition that he'd let you moonlight if I had a crash project I needed help with."

"Certainly", Scott replied.

"Give him a call", Tamara said, standing and shaking Scott's hand. "You'll have to go through the interviews, but I doubt you'll have much competition."

Scott wandered back to his cube in a daze. Twice what he was currently earning? It would still be well shy of what he'd been making in California, but given how they'd been living ... He'd best not mention this to Megan. It sounded promising, but he didn't want to get her hopes up. He grabbed the phone, punched up the number on the slip, and soon had an appointment for an interview with Alan early the following week.

It was hard to keep it quiet from Megan, but Scott managed. She seemed to notice that he was more cheerful over the weekend, and subtly pried for the reason, but he kept mum. The interview went well enough; toward the end it devolved into a discussion of the pros and cons of various technical strategies. Scott left feeling cautiously optimistic but wasn't going to say anything to Megan yet.

When he got home that day, Scott found an envelope waiting. It was hand lettered with no return address. Scott tore it open to find a handwritten note on copier paper.

Scott—

Got your e-mail. Apology accepted. Yes, all those interviews were rough, and yours was one of the worst. I need to apologize too. You guys deserved better than to have that sprung on you. I should have told you about the buyout and that there'd be no IPO. But VXN Group wanted it kept quiet, and the VCs agreed, so I caved. It was unfair to you guys, and I'm sorry.

Things here at VXN are so-so. It's work, which is something, but a lot of promises made haven't been kept. They say it's the economy, but they take care of their own, while we who got hired in get the leftovers. A lot of our guys have left already; some are still hanging on.

You can thank Julie for the enclosed. When you left I was so hot that I wanted to spread this out among the other guys, but she said wait. She said you were just hurt and to give you time. I said I'd give you a year, so here you are.

Best of luck,
Brian

Enclosed with the letter was a new check for the amount of the check he'd thrown back in Brian's face.

Scott's vision swam a little, but he braced himself against the table. He looked over to where Megan was preoccupied with fixing dinner. He slipped out to sit in the turret room, look out over the lake, and think. This was another thing he wouldn't tell Megan about just yet; first he would consult with Francis.

Since their meeting on that fateful afternoon, Scott had been in regular touch with the gray-bearded man with the quiet smile. They regularly exchanged e-mails—long, pensive e-mails—and met for coffee at least twice a week. Francis didn't talk much—he mostly listened as Scott poured out what was transpiring within him, his triumphs and setbacks. Francis rarely gave advice on what Scott should do, but his insights were keen, and he had a way of pointing out things that were plainly obvious but that Scott wasn't recognizing. Scott told Francis everything: what he'd learned from his mother about his father, his own trials as a gay man, the complexities of his relationship with Megan. Nothing was held back. Through it all Francis listened and nodded, offering the occasional word of insight or encouragement. Scott felt like he'd found a wise and concerned uncle.

Scott's buoyant hopes were brought back to earth the next day, when Ellie managed to both scramble some shipping data and freeze her workstation, throwing her into a complete panic. It took almost an entire day of patient hand-holding to settle her down, and then Scott had to draw up the lengthiest and most detailed instruction sheet yet. But even that couldn't discourage him. Fortunately, there was enough time in the day to do some web research and fire off an e-mail to Francis.

A few days later there was a package awaiting Scott when he got home. "Something came for you", Megan said, pointing to the bag with some curiosity.

"Actually, it's for you", Scott said as he swept Grace onto his lap.

"For me?" Megan asked, turning the package in her hands. "I didn't order anything."

"I did", Scott explained. "I ordered you a dress."

"A . . . dress?" Megan asked, her eyes narrowing a bit.

"Yeah." Scott caught the concern in her voice. "I noticed that yours were getting a little worn. Don't worry, though—I checked your size and did some research before I ordered it."

"Research?" Megan's eyebrows lifted.

"Um . . . yeah", Scott said. "Lots of advice was available. From the clothes you like to wear, I'm pretty sure you're a sporty-natural with winter coloration. Based on that and your personality, I ordered you that."

Megan's eyes widened a bit, then narrowed again. "Scott, can we afford this?"

There Scott felt much more confident. "Yes", he assured her with a smile. "We can afford it."

Still skeptical, Megan headed off to the bedroom to try on the dress. Scott played with Grace and grinned. It was so hard to keep quiet about all this, but he had to wait for a few more things to fall into place.

"Oh Scott", Megan breathed as she returned to the kitchen. "It's perfect!"

The dress did look extraordinary on her. It was a light taupe affair with simple lines and a smooth sweep. The skirt fell to her knees, and she twirled this way and that just to watch the fabric swish around her legs.

Scott was surprised to find himself blinking back tears. He felt he was seeing Megan for the first time, in the perfection of her feminine beauty, her familiar face glowing and her eyes sparkling with delight. He wanted to preserve this image of her forever. The thought passed through his mind: This is the mother of my child.

"I ... I'm glad you like it", Scott finally stammered. "It looks good. You look like you should be strolling through a meadow full of wild flowers or heading off to a dance."

"Well, a country dance, perhaps", Megan replied, still swinging the skirt. "It's not suitable for a ball." She laughed at Scott's pained expression. "That's not a criticism! It's beautiful, and the fact that it is so casual means I can wear it more places. And the fit is perfect."

"Well, you could wear it now", Scott suggested, thinking that the dress was a major improvement on her usual sweats and T-shirts.

"Oh, I wouldn't wear it for cooking dinner", Megan assured him. "And I'll want to wash it first anyway. But thank you so much, Scott. Nobody's ever gotten me anything this pretty."

Scott, who thought the dress paled in comparison to its wearer, made a mental note to bookmark the site from which he ordered the dress.

Two days later Alan called to schedule a second interview.

Chapter Nineteen

On a lovely day in the last week of May, Scott's phone rang while he was preparing for work. Noticing who was calling, he stepped into the turret room to take the call. The conversation wasn't long. Afterward he thought for a bit, then called Tamara to tell her he wouldn't be in that day. He stepped into the kitchen just in time to see Megan coming out of the bathroom.

"Hey, Megan", Scott said. "I have an idea. Today let's be fudgies."

"Be what?" Megan asked.

"Fudgies", Scott repeated. "It's what we call tourists here in Michigan. Fudge shops are a staple of Michigan tourist towns. You should see Mackinac Island."

"So . . . we're going to buy fudge?" Megan was clearly still mystified.

"Not necessarily, though we could", Scott said. "There's a shop in town that sells it. What I mean is, let's be tourists, walk around, enjoy the sights."

"Don't you have to go to work?" Megan asked suspiciously.

"Not today. I called Tamara and told her I wouldn't be in."

"Why did you do that?" Megan persisted.

"So I could spend the day with you and Grace", Scott laughed. "Come on—you can wear your dress."

"Dress?" Megan asked with a puzzled look.

"You know—the new dress I just got you", Scott said, puzzled in turn.

"Oh, that", Megan said, looking down at the sweats she'd already put on.

"Please?" Scott pleaded.

Shortly thereafter they were walking Grace in her stroller down to Main Street with its little shops. It was too early for most of the shops to be open, but the diner offered a cheap breakfast sandwich,

so they got a couple of those with some coffee to take down to a pic-
nic table in the little park by the harbor. It was a gorgeous morning,
with the sun sparkling on the blue lake and the warm breeze ruffling
the leaves. Megan was lovely in her dress, but her expression was the
slightest bit troubled.

"You look nervous this morning", Scott commented as he balled
up the sandwich wrappers.

"Nervous?" Megan asked.

"Well ... agitated. Edgy. Preoccupied. All of the above. Anything
going on?"

"Um ... maybe. I may need to tell you something", Megan said.

"May?" Scott emphasized. "That's okay, because I have something
to tell you. A couple of things, in fact."

"Like what?" Megan asked, braced.

"Why don't you tell me first?" Scott asked.

"No—you first", Megan insisted. Scott, who was nearly bursting
anyway, told her first about the check from Brian and then about the
new job he'd just gotten.

"Oh Scott!" Megan said, clasping his hands and then rummaging
through her purse for her tissues. "That's ... that's fantastic news!
Twice the pay! This means—oh Scott!"

Scott gave her a moment to regain her composure, then asked,
"Okay, what about what you wanted to tell me?"

Megan looked at her hands for a minute, then looked up at him
with a curious smile.

"Guess what?"

Scott gazed back in puzzlement for a minute, then his eyes widened as it dawned on him. "No!" he exclaimed.

"Yes", Megan said, nodding. "Pretty certain. I was starting to
wonder, so I picked up a test at work. Last night's results were incon-
clusive, so I tested again this morning. It was clear."

Scott was reeling from the news, which was the last thing he'd
expected. "But", he asked, puzzled, "weren't you like—you know—
on the Pill or something?"

"Scott Kyle!" Megan exclaimed with indignation that was only
half feigned, throwing one of the crumpled sandwich wrappers at
him. "What possible reason would I have to be contracepting?"

"I ... well ... none, I guess," Scott admitted, "now that I think about it. Sorry. I guess I just thought all women were on the Pill as a matter of course these days."

"If I did have any reason to contracept, I certainly wouldn't do it by pumping my body full of artificial hormones", Megan went on. "Do you have any idea how bad that is for a woman's metabolism, not to mention the environment?"

"No, I guess I don't", Scott said. "Honestly, I'm sorry if I offended you—I just wasn't thinking."

"It's all right", Megan assured him. "It's an easy mistake to make these days."

"So," Scott asked, trying to recover from his faux pas, "how far along are you?"

Megan snorted and playfully pitched the other sandwich wrapper at him. "About six weeks, ninny. You can count as well as I can. Though that's about eight weeks as the doctors count things."

Scott slapped his forehead. "Gee, I can't win for losing today, can I? This is ... wow ... this is great."

"Is it?" Megan asked.

"Why, sure it is!" Scott answered firmly. "Unexpected, but great. I mean, you think so, don't you?"

"Yes", Megan said, her face relaxing as if she'd only just realized that for certain. "Yes, I do. And you're two for two. In certain cultures that would earn you quite the reputation, you stud."

"Please," Scott said, wincing, "not that word."

"Um ... okay", Megan replied.

"Nothing to do with you", Scott explained hastily. "So, this means we'll have two kids under two?"

"Yup", Megan confirmed. "Pretty good pace for a couple of gay folk."

Scott rubbed his jaw pensively. This was a lot to absorb, especially after the tumult of the past few months. "Come on", he said to Megan. "Let's walk out on the pier."

The day was warming nicely, but out on the long pier that sheltered the harbor the breeze across the lake surface made the air considerably cooler. As they walked out, pushing Grace's stroller, Scott noticed a couple of guys on the deck of a sailboat down in the harbor.

They were readying the boat for the season, tugging and folding the sails all over the deck.

"Hmm", Scott said after watching them at their work. "I never thought about that."

"Thought about what?" Megan asked.

"How heavy the sails must be", Scott answered. Seeing she was puzzled, he went on. "I used to come down and sit on these rocks, or up on that hill, and look out over the lake to watch the sailboats tacking to and fro. Their sails looked like gossamer wings, catching the lightest wind to sweep the boat across the water. From miles away they seemed almost ethereal, as light as a feather. It wasn't until I saw those guys lugging them around that I realized how heavy all that much fabric must be."

"Well," mused Megan, "I guess you have to work with something to understand it fully."

"True, but I was thinking of it the other way", Scott said. "If all you ever saw of sails was the sweaty work of laying them out and rigging them up, you might miss how beautiful and useful they are."

"That's certainly true", Megan admitted.

They arrived at the end of the pier and sat on a big block of lime-stone under the post that held the light marking the entrance to the harbor. They looked at the white clouds wafting over the crystal-blue water. There were a lot of things turning over in Scott's head, things he wanted to share with Megan, but he didn't know how to begin.

"So," Scott ventured, "tumultuous few weeks, eh?"

"That's for sure", Megan confirmed.

"You know, you said something back there that got me thinking", Scott said. "Actually, I've been doing a lot of thinking lately, about this and other things."

"What did I say?"

"When you said that two kids under two is pretty good for a cou-ple of gays", Scott explained. "Truth is—and this is just me, mind you, not anyone else—I don't know what that term means anymore. I thought I did, but now I'm not sure at all."

"Isn't it clear?" asked Megan. "Attracted to people of the same sex."

"Well, that's what I would have said", Scott said. "But when I think back to how I first got involved with my gay friends ... I was

a geeky kid, a social outcast, and some of my band buddies introduced me to the gay lifestyle. I became involved in sort of a gay
underground at my school. I was thrilled to be accepted, to belong
to a group, and of course there were all those orgasms without having to worry about things like pregnancies—plus I didn't have to
worry about dealing with those mysterious and troublesome girls.
What lonely adolescent boy isn't going to go for more orgasms rather
than fewer, especially with social acceptance thrown in? I jumped in
with both feet, embracing my gay identity.

"But lately I've been pondering: for the past thirteen years or so,
I've been defining myself by where I prefer to get my orgasms. Isn't
there more to me than that? I mean, what about friendship? What
about real caring?"

"Didn't your friends accept and care for you?" Megan asked.

"Yes, they did", Scott acknowledged. "At first. But here's what
got me thinking: the more our friendships included sex, the more
manipulative they became. This was especially true of me, I can see
that now. As long as a friend could give me more and better orgasms,
I'd want to be with him. But if I got tired of him, or if he got tired of
being used for my pleasure, I'd move on. And I was just as sensitive
to when others were only using me for their pleasure.

"At first, I thought that pattern was just because I was dealing
with immature high school kids, and things would change once I got
beyond that. Well, they didn't—not when I got to college, and not
when I got out into the 'real' gay world down in Nashville. Relationships would start out friendly, but they'd always devolve into
the couple using one another as a biological sex toy—at least in my
experience."

"Gays can be friends", Megan said somewhat defensively.

"Of course they can", Scott agreed. "You and I are. But I remember something an older gay guy said to me once: If you want to ruin
a good friendship, get sex involved. I found that to be true from high
school on. Once sex got involved, a relationship quickly deteriorated
into using and being used."

"Straights do that too", Megan pointed out.

"I know they do", Scott replied. "And that's what really got
me thinking. It doesn't seem to matter whether it was Greg and
me cruising the Castro for some action or a couple of Saturday

night cowboys working the honky-tonks along Broadway for easy cowgirls—it's still people looking for other people to use for their pleasure."

Megan was silent, so Scott continued.

"It seems like we put up with all this mutual manipulation in hopes of somehow 'finding love' in the midst of it. But I'm starting to wonder if it doesn't go the other way."

"What do you mean?" Megan asked.

"My mother said something interesting when she was explaining what happened between herself and my dad", Scott replied. "She said, 'I stopped truly loving him when I started using him.' I don't doubt that my mom and dad loved each other, at least as much as a couple of high school kids can. They were certainly good friends before they were romantically involved. Apparently he worked hard to be honorable toward her. But she decided to use him as her ticket to a better life and ended up getting pregnant with me. Of course, he was happy to use her for as many orgasms as possible—so what real love they had was gutted, and he eventually walked out.

"So that got me wondering. Maybe starting with manipulation and hoping love will grow out of it is the wrong tack. We have a perfect example right here—our relationship. We've been friends since the start, thrown together by circumstances. There's even been sex involved. But, unusually, the sex was never for my good. I was truly trying to help you and Diane. Honestly, it was kind of uncomfortable, and not because you're a woman."

"I know", Megan said with an embarrassed chuckle. "I remember. It was weird."

"As circumstances changed, we had to adapt. First we had to care for each other, and then make sure she was cared for", Scott said, pointing to where Grace was sleeping in her stroller. "Our relationship never fit that manipulative pattern, so it's stayed strong."

"But we've had sex", Megan pointed out.

"Yes, we have", Scott admitted. "For that matter, so has Francis. He and his wife have been married forty-one years and have five kids, so clearly there's been some sex."

"Wait—who's Francis?" Megan asked.

"He's a guy I met at Saint Agatha's that afternoon when we were on the bridge", Scott explained.

212

"He's ... Catholic?" Megan replied. "I thought Catholics hated gays."

"Well, this one doesn't", Scott said. "He works there and helped me that day."

"Is he a priest?"

"No, he's a sacristan", Scott answered.

"Sacristan? What's that?" Megan asked.

"It has to do with setting up and taking things down—he doesn't go in to detail. I've been talking to him about ... life and stuff. Don't worry", Scott said, seeing Megan's concerned expression. "He doesn't repeat any of what we discuss to anyone. I've told him everything about me, about us. Want to know the weird part?"

"What's that?" Megan asked, still unsure how comfortable she was with some stranger knowing so much about her life.

"He says it sounds like we have an exemplary marriage."

"Really?" Megan said with a scowl. "Exemplary? How can that ... he does know that our marriage is a formality, doesn't he? That we're not in love?"

Scott paused a bit, looking at her, before responding. "Yes, he knows all that. He doesn't seem to think it matters much. He points out that we support and help each other, and we provide Grace a good home. He says that that right there is better than many couples, including Catholic ones.

"Maybe that's the key. Sure, I'm attracted to guys. But what am I really attracted to? The guy, or the potential for a sexual thrill? I suppose if I were straight, I'd be saying the same thing about a woman. Once or twice I thought I really had it—with Randy in Nashville and with Greg in California. I thought I'd found real, lasting love. Greg and I even talked about marriage. But in the end, we couldn't rise above that pattern of manipulation. I was happy to use Greg's contacts to advance my career, and then I turned around and resented how he used my apartment as a crash pad and short-order restaurant. But he was just using me like I had used him.

"So ... am I gay? I sure plugged into the whole 'gay lifestyle' and 'gay brotherhood', if that's what it means. But then I found out that the brotherhood can turn on you savagely if you violate its protocols. You found out the same thing."

"I sure did", Megan acknowledged.

"So, I'm wondering about this whole gay-straight way of think-ing", Scott went on. "What does that mean? Which gender I exploit to get my orgasms? Is that the most fundamental thing about me? The basis for my identity? I'm tired of exploiting and being exploited. There has to be more to life than that. There has to be more to love than that. What if it's more about caring for others, taking care of them when they need it? My former coworker Jake is straight, and he put a lot of effort into helping me just when my gay 'brothers' were closing ranks to ensure I couldn't get a job in the Bay Area. Francis just wants to help me and is spending a lot of effort doing it."

"And don't forget Helge Sykes of Big Springs!" Megan said with a grin.

"And Helge Sykes of Big Springs!" Scott confirmed. "Another sterling example of someone who just helps others out of pure, dis-interested love.

"So here I am, thirty years old, and I don't know how to love worth a damn. I thought I did. I thought I was all about love before I was about anything else. I loved Dustin, I loved Alex, I loved Randy, I loved Greg. But looking back, I wonder if I ever knew what it meant to love someone. Things would start off with an emotional rush, and I'd think: Here it is, this is it, I've found the one who completes me. It certainly added a kick to the orgasms, but it had no root. Whatever relationship we tried to build only dried up and crumbled and blew away, leaving us with bitterness and resentment and old hurts."

"That happens to straights too", Megan observed.

"Damn right it does", Scott agreed. "All the time. Remember, I lived in Nashville, home of country music. So it gets me wondering, does anyone know anything about love? Or are we doomed to these passing, flash-in-the-pan relationships?"

"I don't know", Megan responded. "Your care for Grace and me seems pretty loving."

"Maybe so", Scott acknowledged. "But does that mean that real love has to involve babies?"

"It might be better to say it involves giving", Megan said after pon-dering for a minute. "If someone were to ask me how I knew you loved us, I'd point to how much you gave up for us."

Scott nodded. "Maybe that's a clue. I'm still trying to sort it out. I'm thinking that I know so little about terms like 'love' and 'gay' and 'straight' that I want to put them off to the side and not use them, so I can focus on what I do know."

"So," Megan asked, "what do you know?"

"I know that you're the most important person in my life", Scott replied. "Followed by her, followed by ..." He waved toward her abdomen.

"Him", Megan said.

"Him", Scott echoed, then furrowed his brow. "You know that already?"

"Just a hunch", Megan replied.

"Okay", Scott replied. "You and I have never had any kind of romantic relationship in the typical sense—how could we?—but even the thought of living without you opens this big void in my insides. I know, because there were a couple of times in California when you almost left, and even the prospect was devastating."

"Is that why you were so eager to hire me as your household manager?" Megan asked.

"Precisely", Scott confirmed. "The thought of you leaving made my life seem dusty and flat and empty."

"I didn't want to go", Megan admitted. "I was torn. I felt like we'd made a home, you and I, where I was protected. But I didn't feel like I should accept all that money."

Scott smiled and shook his head. "And I couldn't have cared less about the money. Sure, it crimped my single gay lifestyle, but the truth is, all those outings and weekend trips and binges were just my trying to fill the hours. Coming home to you was far more fulfilling, even if all we did was watch a movie. Oh, the fresh linens and clean bathroom and stocked kitchen were all great, but you were the real reason I looked forward to coming home. Just your ... being there, I guess. And then Grace on top of that."

Megan bowed her head for a bit and seemed to be having trouble speaking. "I ... I've never had anyone value me for me before", she finally whispered. "It was always for something. My mother valued me as a household servant. Diane valued me as a cook, a household decoration, a pet, and—how did you put it?—a biological sex toy."

"Well, I value you for you", Scott assured her. "And so does Grace—so I guess we've got a fan club going."

They both fell silent for a while, listening to the waves lapping against the rock and the gulls crying as they soared overhead.

"You've been doing a lot of thinking lately", Megan finally said. "Does this mean ... that is, do you plan on making any changes?"

"What kind of changes?" Scott asked.

"I don't know ... moves, or ... well, whatever", Megan stammered clumsily.

"No, not in that sense", Scott said. "I've tried that. I tried leaving here because I thought the problem was this place, but the same problems followed me to college. So I thought that once I got out on my own and moved out of state, that would solve them. It didn't. So then I thought that if I just moved to my dream location out on the coast, that would take care of things. It didn't. So, in a twist of irony, I'm back here where I started. This time I'm going to try a different tack than just changing geography and relationships. I'm going to try becoming that person who loves others for themselves, not for what they can do for me. I may not succeed, but I'm going to try."

"You seem to be doing pretty well so far", Megan said quietly.

"I'm doing crappy so far", Scott said bluntly. "Mediocre at best. If you could see it from my perspective, you'd see how much more I could be doing."

"I suppose we could all say that", Megan pointed out.

"Anyway, that's what's been going through my head recently", Scott said. "There's actually been more, but I've talked long enough. Is there anything you'd like to say?"

Again Megan was quiet for a bit. "It's been a turbulent time. I've been concerned about you, especially since ... that day. I've been worried for her. But I've had someone I've been talking to as well."

"Who's that?" Now it was Scott's turn to be concerned. The only people Scott could think of whom Megan could talk to were his mother and Mrs. Delworth, neither of whom he wanted in on the most intimate details of his life.

"Really want to know?" Megan asked, then held up her phone. "Helge. We have each other's phone numbers, and she called to ensure the shipment arrived, and one thing led to another, and I've been calling her all winter. Two or three times a week over the past few weeks."

"Helge", Scott said with relief. "That's great."

"It is", Megan confirmed. "It's been quite a lesson for me. When I first met her, I looked down on her for being a coarse, rustic hayseed—as if I was such a cosmopolitan sophisticate. But beneath that Nebraska exterior she's got a heart of gold. She's patient and kind and very insightful. She's calmed me down at times when I was near panic. She's also full of helpful baby tips. She knows all about our marriage too. She encourages me to stick by you. She says you're a good man—that you've got some growing up to do, but you're a good man."

"She's right about the growing up", Scott admitted, thought it grated a little to hear it.

"So she's been helping me", Megan continued. "Also, there's been something I've been wanting to tell you, but I haven't found the right opportunity. This seems like a good one."

"What's that?" Scott asked.

"It's about that morning ... at the bridge", Megan began. Seeing Scott wince a little, she reassured him. "I don't know what was going on for you, and I don't want to know unless you want to tell me. But you need to know what was going on with me.

"You remember how I was hanging back, reading those brass plaques? You hadn't been gone very long—a minute or so—when I heard a voice. It was uncanny. It spoke as clearly as you've been speaking, but there was nobody there."

"What did the voice say?" Scott asked, chilled.

"'Help Joseph. He needs you.' Just that. I looked for the speaker, and there was only air. Then I looked at you and Grace.

"It was the weirdest thing I've ever experienced. The whole landscape looked different. The bridge, the river, the sky, the little valley, the woods on the far side, had all changed to look like something out of an impressionist painting. You know, kind of blurry and distorted. No bright colors or pastels, though. Everything was grays and blacks and drab browns and dirty whites.

"You and Grace were the only things in focus. But around your head and shoulders were swarming a bunch of bright dots."

"Bright dots?" Scott asked, his mouth dry.

"Yes. To look at them, you'd have sworn they were a cluster of gnats. You know how they hang in the summer air? But they were bright, like sparks from a sparkler on the Fourth of July. And they weren't around Grace, only around you.

217

"I didn't know what they were, but I didn't like the look of them, and I didn't want them near my baby—or my husband. I called your name, but you didn't respond, though I saw you moving. So I started toward you.

"The moment I set my foot on the bridge, my vision—or whatever it was—straightened out. The landscape returned to normal, the swirling dots disappeared, and there you both were. I ran to you, calling, and you turned slowly. You looked like you were just coming out of some kind of trance. Then you shoved Grace into my arms and ran off.

"The whole thing was spooky, especially the voice. But since I could tell that something weird had happened to you, your behavior didn't surprise me as much as it otherwise would have. Of course, I was frightened and confused and worried about you, but I couldn't indulge that too much, or Grace would have picked up on it."

They both fell silent. Grace was starting to wake up.

"That's ... wow ... how strange", was all Scott could say. "I'll have to tell that to Francis and see what he thinks."

They were quiet again, alone together with their thoughts. When Grace began stirring in earnest, Scott lifted her from her stroller so she could look around at the lake.

"Well," Scott asked, "shall we head back?" As they strolled along the walkway back toward the shore, Megan said coyly:

"There's one more thing I wanted to say. You know that, ah, comfort I gave you about six weeks ago?"

"The comfort that has had such profound consequences?" Scott said with a smile. "Yes, I remember it well."

"I didn't find that the least bit objectionable", Megan continued.

Scott looked at her in genuine surprise. "No?" he asked. He'd thought ...

"Not in the least", Megan said, smiling back. "Not to put any expectations on you, but I wouldn't protest if you were to get any, um, ideas."

Well. Well now, thought Scott. He hadn't expected that. He looked at her, so fresh and graceful in her new dress, and grinned. "Does this mean I can start sleeping nude again?"

Megan chuckled. "Sure, if you want to. I may even do so myself."

Scott actually stopped and rocked back, as much as he could while holding a baby, and stared at Megan. She looked back with an innocent expression.

"We are married, remember?"

That got a laugh.

"So," Megan asked, "what's next? All these positive changes, so much happening—do we have a plan?"

"Well, I wanted to talk to you before doing anything definite, but I did get a jump on one thing", Scott replied. "Between my new pay rate and the check from Brian, we could start looking for a house. There are a lot of foreclosures and vacancies in the area, especially down north of Port Huron. I called a real-estate agent to have him start working up some properties for us to look over."

"A house! Oh Scott!" Megan said. "Whatever we do, let's try to stay as close as possible to your mother. Mrs. Delworth too. She's very nearly adopted Grace by now, and she has no children of her own."

"Well, sure", Scott said. "If you like it here, we can look around here first. I just thought you'd want to live closer to a city."

"If possible, I'd prefer to live closer to family", Megan assured him. "Speaking of which, why don't we drop in on your mother? We have a lot of good news to relay."

"Sure. We could take her to a celebratory burger and root beer", Scott said.

So they strolled through town and up along the highway to the trailer park. They gave a perfunctory knock at the door to Angela's trailer and walked in.

To their amazement, Scott's mother was sitting at the kitchen table, clutching something in her hand, tears streaming down her face. They rushed to her immediately.

"Mom, Mom, what's wrong?" Megan asked. To their surprise, Angela just shook her head and smiled through her tears, though she kept weeping.

"Nothing, nothing", she gasped at last, holding up the object, which was her phone. "That was Lisa. She's coming home again, maybe to stay."